Angela J. Ford

Song of the Dawn

A Tower Knights Tale

Editing & Proofreading: Lyss Em

Cover Art: Juliet Bxromance

Naked Hardcover: Cover Dungeon Rabbit

EZRA

"I want it back!" Unable to restrain my shimmering rage, I smashed my fist into the stone table.

My knuckles cracked, sending a sprout of crimson gushing down my fingers. The burst of pain that shot up my arm made me feel alive, as though I had some control over my fate. Although, losing my temper in front of the sorceress was futile; she was all-powerful, and I was delicious prey for her insidious games.

Crossing her bare legs, she tapped her clawlike nails on the white bone of her throne and stared at me with somber black eyes. "Ezra," she scolded, lips pursed, her manner beguiling. "Anger does not become you. Besides, you'll have it back once you've completed my terms."

The problem with getting angry with the sorceress was that it didn't bother her at all. She waved her hand as if I was a mere nuisance instead of a knight who'd fallen out of favor. Except our relationship went much deeper than that. I'd broken a sacred vow, and she was well within her rights to punish me for eternity.

Grinding my teeth, I took a deep breath to keep from exploding again. The scents of incense and myrrh stung my nostrils. "I've done everything you've asked, yet each time I return, you change the requirements—"

Her cruel, disdainful laugh cut me off midsentence, making a muscle in my cheek spasm. I hated interruptions, and she knew it. Another wave of resentment surged, but instead of punching stone, I clenched my fists so hard my nails dug into the skin of my palm. My gaze shifted past her bare legs to the pyramid of skulls surrounding the throne. Why didn't she take my head and add it to her collection? I suspected we'd both be happier.

"You have a lesson to learn, Ezra," the sorceress cooed in her superior tone. "Everything isn't about you, nor have the terms changed. You simply perceive them differently. If you bring me enough magic to bind the King of Hearts, I will discharge you from my services. Only then, and not a moment before, will I return it to you. Now go, play your violin and summon a foul servant for me."

"How do I know you will keep your word this time?"

"Because you are the one who has failed before, not I."

The sorceress stood, her sheer white gown rippling like water over her body as she bent to lift a skull, tapping it in warning. "You have twelve cycles of the moon to complete your mission, because I'm tired of waiting. If you delay, I will take another one of your loyalists and destroy them."

She dropped the skull, which landed with a sickening crack that echoed through the cavern. "You may lose your temper, dear Ezra, but I am the sorceress because I perceive the hearts and minds of people. I know what they crave and how to manipulate them until they swear utter fealty. I should have cast you away a long time ago. Anyone else might have, but I see one final use for you. You aren't as far gone as my other knights who sinned and fell from grace. But you'll never dwell under the protection of my name again. The faster you do this, the sooner we'll never see each other thereafter."

The swimming madness in her soulless eyes was the only thing that kept me from protesting even though fury clogged my throat, threatening to choke me. But she was right. I'd sealed my fate the moment I'd broken my vow. Freedom was within reach once I completed this last task. Although, part of me feared she'd lock me up or kill me once I was no longer useful to her. Evidently banishment was not enough. I promised myself if, by some miracle, I gained a second chance, I'd never use magic again, for I had opened the door to demons and paid dearly for it.

"You'll give it back," I demanded hoarsely, "the moment I send that foul beast through the portal to you."

"The very moment," she purred, placing her foot on a skull. "Now go, Sorcerer of Portals, and do your worst. I will accept nothing less."

Turning from that somber chamber, a cave of conquered bone, I strode with purpose to the portal. The vortex of light, deep purple and soulless black, flickered, encouraging me to slip through and return to the realm of mortals. It did not matter what I wanted when I'd broken my vow to the sorceress and she'd caught me.

Punishment was severe, and anyone else would have been grateful to still draw breath, but the reminder of what I'd done was mentally agonizing. Even though she'd banished me from her realm, she kept me tethered to her, like a child suckling on its mother's milk. To tighten the metaphorical noose around my neck, she'd taken something precious from me, and I desperately needed it back.

The portal flashed, a million silvery stars

reflecting the heavens. I moved through it, ignoring the intense cold until I stumbled out of the depths of starlight into the pale glimmer of dawn. Leaning against the rough wall of the cave, I gasped for breath, waiting for my energy to return. The wounds on my knuckles healed themselves, the skin knitting together as if I'd never broken it. I scowled, for it only served as a remnant of her court, a reminder of what she could do to me, even beyond the portal.

The thunder of the cascading waterfall pulled me out of my morose thoughts. Straightening my blue waistcoat, I walked across the dew-damp ground. It would take less than an hour to return to the inn I now called home, but after my audience with the sorceress, my mind wouldn't calm itself enough to sleep.

I hoped the stagecoach to the city would be ready, for I needed a diversion to take my mind off the endless days I served, hoping for freedom. Upon my return, I'd focus on summoning the monster the sorceress demanded. But if it escaped, if I could not control it with my song, I would damn myself and the Dawn to the grave.

MILA

Tawny candlelight flickered in the hollows of the wide hall, casting malevolent shadows on the walls. I watched the frightful shapes they created and swallowed hard, a bead of sweat trickling down my neck. No monsters hid within those shadows. It was just my nerves making my eyes play tricks on me. Standing in the shallow entryway beside the black curtain that covered the stage, I shifted from foot to foot as I waited for the signal to enter and perform.

The symphony was new, the pungent stink of paint and drying mortar still too fresh and potent to be comfortable, but I waited for my chance. This was it.

Straightening my shoulders, I urged words of encouragement through my mind and tried to relax the death grip I had on my violin, painfully aware it needed new strings. If I gained one of the prestigious positions at the symphony hall, there would be plenty of money to replace the strings and even save up to buy a new violin. Instruments were expensive, and I should treasure mine more, especially since it had come from my grandfather, but it was old.

Every little noise increased my agitation. The scratch of the conductor's pen, the pacing of his assistant, the steady tap of Lady Hawthorne's high-heeled shoes against the carpeted floor. A recent tragedy at a remote castle called High Tower had caused an influx of musicians to enter the city of Solynn, searching for work at the symphony. Aside from the opera, the hall recommended musicians for the private balls and galas hosted by influential lords and ladies. Occasionally a wealthy lord would sponsor a musician to play at all their parties, and the sum was better than what I could make as a lady's maid. Tonight's audition would determine if I possessed enough skill to secure a position. I had my doubts, for the woman who had gone before me was magnificent. Listening to the way she played—drawing emotions from the strings of her instrument—reminded me of my lack of skill. But I was confident given the opportunity to practice, I'd soon be as good as her.

The conductor cleared his throat. "Mila Hadria, you may perform."

Licking my lips, I shook back my purple hair and strode out onto the stage. My long skirts rustled, adding to the faint sounds in the room. The spotlight was bright, blinding, but I blinked quickly as I took a seat. Tucking the violin under my chin, I sucked in a deep breath and slowly let it out, counting each heartbeat. When I closed my eyes, I felt everything, the stillness of my body, the pounding of my pulse, the lump of anticipation swelling in my throat. This was a pivotal moment. My one and only chance to become a musician and provide for myself and Mother.

I decided not to think about the dingy flat we lived in or Mother's recent injury, which had quickly drained our savings. I would not think of how late the rent was, nor the threats from the landlord if we did not pay in full. The only thing that mattered was music.

When my fingers touched the strings, the shadowy hall, the scratch of the pen, and the odor of paint melted away. It was just the music and me. Lifting my bow, I drew it across the strings, sending a sonorous melody through the hall. It vibrated and echoed, filling the air with life.

Drawing strength from those first few strands, I pressed my calloused fingertips against the strings and played. With each note, my confidence grew, and the music swelled. I played slow, then fast, to show off the breadth of my skills. Tapping my foot against the floor to keep the rhythm, I increased the tempo, my fingers dancing over the neck of the violin, the bow vibrating in my fingers. This was what I loved.

The song crescendoed, but suddenly an ugly, jarring sound popped me out of my musical high. A flash of pain whipped across my fingers as the notes turned sour. I opened my eyes, heart dropping as I stared at the broken string. The quick playing had strained the old strings, causing one to snap. My heart sank to my toes, and I bit my bottom lip hard to keep tears from falling. An apology rose, but the tightness in my throat made it impossible to speak. New strings. How much would that cost?

Shoulders sagging, I stood and bowed. The silence was deafening, but my eyes had grown used to the spotlight. The cool gaze of the conductor—quill poised just above paper—appraised me. Even his assistant had paused midstride to gawk at my misfortune.

Lady Hawthorne sighed and waved her hand. "Dismissed," she called, her tone cold. "After replacing your strings, I recommend more practice. You have promise, but your skills are too rudimentary for the symphony. Come back in three to six months when you've improved and we'll give you another chance to audition."

It took a moment for the words to sink in. Practice. Three months. Improve. Audition again. I couldn't. It would be too late by then. Nodding, I stumbled away and glimpsed golden hair and a blue waistcoat in the back of the concert hall. Someone else was there, sitting in the shadows, watching. Likely a lord listening in on auditions so he could choose a musician to sponsor. It was not uncommon, but without the endorsement of Lady Hawthorne, I would not gain sponsorship.

Disappointment squeezed my chest like a weight as I moved backstage and placed my violin back in its case. I held the broken string for a few moments, knowing I wouldn't be able to replace it soon, which meant I could not practice, and my dream of becoming a musician grew further from reach.

Leaving the hall, I stepped out into the evening air. It was late spring, and soon the dense humidity of summer would descend, hot and relentless. I strode down the street, mulling over the two choices I had. I could either take a job as a maid or go live with my sister in the countryside. Both options made my stomach clench, for they were dream killers.

If I took a job as a maid, at least I could stay in the city and save for a new violin. But working would leave me little time to practice, and I doubted a lady would tolerate my practicing in her home. The countryside was less attractive because I was unaware of the opportunities available for a single young woman, aside from marriage. My spirits sunk lower at the thought.

Something moved behind me, and I whipped my head around. A masculine presence wearing gold and blue walked behind me, at a distance, so I was unsure whether he was following me. It wasn't quite nightfall, but it was close enough. I quickened my steps. It was best to get home, where I'd be safe behind a locked door.

Tonight I'd wallow in grief and in the morning make a plan. But even my hopefulness could not dispel the sinking sensation in my gut. No matter how much I loved music, it wasn't enough. I had to give up and settle for less.

MILA

Early the next morning, before the surge of heat, I went to market to buy food for the week. Fresh air lifted my spirits, distracting me from the unwanted choices looming ahead. At market, one of the vendors had a sale, and I left with more food than I'd originally intended to buy.

The brown paper sacks were heavy in my arms as I climbed the stairs up to the flat Mother and I shared. By the time I reached the third flight, I regretted deciding to carry them all at once. But I hadn't wanted to do the four flights up the landing twice.

A jar of fig jam teetered dangerously with each step. But when I tried to stabilize it, my arms trembled from the exertion, sending it closer and closer to doom.

The thud, thud of footsteps warned me someone was approaching from above, which was odd considering my mother and I were the only ones who lived at the top. Perhaps it was the doctor come to check on Mother's injury. Although, we also owed him money, and our funds were quickly dwindling, reminding me I needed to make a decision fast.

Taking another step, I lost my balance. The fig jam seized the opportunity and rolled off the top of the bag. I caught myself against the wall as it hit the wooden stairs with a thump, then rolled down the steps behind me, gaining speed until it shattered with a jarring thud on the landing to the second floor. I stared, miffed at myself, while flies buzzed, eager to drown themselves in the sweet, sticky jam. Mother loved figs, and the jam was a rare treat that would have brightened her day.

When I turned back around, a tall man dressed in a blue suit and waistcoat stood at the top of the stairs. My mind flashed back to the evening before, the gold and blue I'd seen outside the symphony hall. But there was nothing menacing about the man that stood above me. Thick golden hair framed his elegant face. He raised an eyebrow, his vibrant green eyes going from my full arms to the shattered jar.

"Going up?" He spoke with a slight accent I could not place.

"Yes." My response came tentatively as I glanced

from the jar, back at him. "Apparently I picked up more than I could carry."

"Apparently," he repeated, a faint smile coming to his lips. "Allow me."

An odd aura settled about him, something I couldn't quite put my finger on. Whether it was due to his height; the way he moved skillfully, quickly; his deep-set eyes; or the curve of his mouth, my apprehensions about the stranger faded. Closing the distance between us, he took one bag. His fingers grazed my arm, but instead of flinching away, I stood still, captivated by how my skin warmed at the accidental touch. He smelled like fresh citrus, and my mind went to oranges, a rare treat Mother and I had during the holidays, the only time they were in season. That delightful smell made me wistful for the carefree days of my youth.

"Thank you," I told the golden-haired man, my shoulders sagging with relief.

"It would be rude of me to deny help to a lovely lady." His smile was small, shy as he pivoted to the side. "I'll follow you up."

"It's just one more flight," I explained. "I simply didn't want to walk up and down twice."

"Nor should you have to. It is quite a march, but I suppose you're used to it, since you live at the top?"

His amicable conversation set me further at ease,

and the fact he'd called me lovely. The citizens of Solynn came in all shapes and sizes, but my rich brown skin and expressive purple hair drew looks and whispers that weren't entirely welcome. Although, the color of my hair was my own doing, dyed by the pigment from the roots of Maiden's Blush.

"Yes," I confirmed. "I'm quite used to it, but Mother fell and sprained her leg. There's no going up and down the stairs for her."

"Oh, I'm sorry to hear that." The man's eyes darkened.

"She scared me," I admitted, finding it easy to talk to him. "Her injury means she can't work for months, and so we are leaving the city for the countryside."

There, I'd said the words, and they felt true. All along, the choice I'd needed to make had been waiting for me to speak it out loud.

"Ah." He hummed, making me realize I was babbling while he was merely being polite.

"I'm sorry," I blurted out. "That was more than you wanted…er…needed to know."

"Not at all," he said as we reached the fourth floor.

There was a landing space and then a cramped square of four doors. The other flats had been empty for a while because of the negligence of the owner. I fumbled for keys, my face warm from the heat of the day and the attentive gaze of the man.

"I assume you look forward to leaving for the country?" he asked, his tone sincere.

Shaking my head, I lowered my voice in case Mother was listening on the other side of the door instead of napping. Honesty rose on my tongue, for confiding in the friendly stranger was easier than going to the cathedral to confess to a priest. "My sister lives in a charming estate with her husband and son. I should be grateful to go there with Mother, but..." I took a deep breath, unable to keep the disappointment out of my tone. "I want to be a musician, and as soon as I leave here, that opportunity is gone. In the country there's no value in music, and nothing interesting happens there like it does here in the city. I want the opportunity to play, experience passion, excitement, change..." I trailed off, my heart pounding as the words rushed out of my mouth. It was more than I should have said, and yet a lightness came over me after venting to him.

The golden man nodded, his perfectly pink lips curling into a smile. "You like the excitement of change and the ability to chase your passion."

"Yes," I breathed, wondering why he wasn't running away or scolding me for talking too much.

"I hope you find what you are searching for."

"And you as well." I furrowed my brow as I put the key in the lock. "What were you doing up here?"

He cocked his head, his deep gaze holding mine. "I thought I took a misstep. Turns out I was wrong, since I could assist you with your groceries."

The moment felt intimate, stretched as he moved closer. The lock twisted, and the door clicked as it swung open. My heart kicked as the man's arms brushed mine and he passed me the other bag of groceries.

I inhaled another whiff of orange, and my belly flipped. It was dangerous, the way the man looked at me, and his proximity. But nothing within me wanted to move away even though Mother warned me about handsome men with sinister secrets carefully concealed behind beautiful eyes. She'd taught me to guard my heart, withdraw from their advances, but I was curious.

"What's your name?" he asked, a low purr in his tone.

"Mila," I whispered. When his cheek brushed mine, a hint of stubble grazed my skin. Involuntarily, my eyes closed, and my heart pulsed so loudly I was sure he could hear it.

When he pulled away, I keenly felt the loss of his presence. I held still, relishing that moment in my mind as his footsteps thumped down the stairs. A few seconds later, his voice floated up them. "Until we meet again, Mila."

And then he was gone.

I allowed myself to smile at the encounter with the handsome stranger even though a slight warning twisted through me. But I'd never see him again. What happened to Mother wouldn't happen to me. Once, a gallant man had tricked her, leading her on with a pull of attraction she could not resist, until he'd left her homeless with two young children.

Long ago I'd made a promise to myself I wouldn't be like my mother and fall for a handsome face. But the golden-haired man had been kind and attentive; plus, the scent of orange lingered in the air. Gingerly placing the sacks on the table, I locked the door and tiptoed down the hall in search of Mother.

Our tiny flat was built in what we called the arrow style. One could open the door and shoot an arrow straight to the back door, which led out to a tiny porch. Sometimes I'd open the back door to air out the rooms, which often were hot and stuffy, with the faint scent of mold, especially in the summer.

On walking in, the table was to the left and the kitchen to the right. The kitchen held the woodstove and was the warmest room in the winter but almost unbearable during the summer, hence my reason for buying food that didn't have to be cooked.

Down the hall were only two rooms, Mother's

room on the left, since it butted up against the neighboring flat, which was now empty. When I was younger, we could hear our neighbors snoring and making other unpleasant sounds. My room was on the right, and I'd used to share it with my older sister, Aveline, until three years ago, when she'd gotten married. I planned to vacate the room for Aveline when she arrived tomorrow.

Mother's door was cracked. When I peeked inside, she lay on her back, foot propped up on a pillow, eyes closed. Her slow and steady breathing told me she was sleeping, so I slipped away to make lunch and something soothing for her to drink.

A movement by the door caught my eye. A piece of cream paper lay just under the door, my name written on the paper in swirling black handwriting: *Mila Hadria of Solynn*.

What could it be?

Forgetting about the tea, I picked up the envelope, noting the richness of it, the gloss of gold on the edges. With shaking fingers, I flipped it over, and on the other side were two words: *The Dawn*.

The words were embossed, almost glittering. Curious. Why would I receive a letter from a remote inn? Lifting the flap, I pulled out the letter and read.

MILA

Dear Mila,

We had the honor of listening to your audition with the symphony in Solynn. Although they turned you down, we believe you are talented enough to join the staff of the Dawn. We are in need of a musician for the summer to play three nights a week for guests and on special occasions as needed. We will provide a new violin along with room, board, and food. Your monthly salary will be 300. Should these terms be agreeable to you, we expect your arrival the first week of June. Travel expenses will be reimbursed. We look forward to a positive response.

—Management

MY LEGS GAVE OUT, and I dropped to the chair behind me. Lifting the letter, I read the words again and again until my throat ached and my nose tingled as a sort of euphoria came over me. I squeezed my hands together, wanting to laugh and cry at the same time. I was leaving the city to pursue my dream.

And then it happened. A whiff of citrus came to my nostrils, and I inhaled, sharply reminded of the golden-haired man. Blue. Gold. Was he a messenger from the Dawn? Had he watched my performance last night? A devilish whisper tickled my ear, and my heart skipped at the thought of meeting him again. Folding the letter, I decided to wait until Aveline arrived to break the news to her and Mother.

SHE CAME THE NEXT MORNING, a breezy May day, before the warmth of the sunlight would become unbearable. I eagerly watched from the balcony as the stagecoach pulled up, then I rushed down the four flights of stairs to meet her. By the time I arrived, the horses were stamping in the street, eager to be off again, and Aveline's bags were stacked in front of the building.

A grin lit up the features of her oval face, rounder than when I'd seen her last. Glossy black hair was braided around the crown of her head, and she wore a simple blue gown, her traveling dress. She held out her free arm, the other holding her six-month-old son, Luc. Warmth filled me, along with a familiar pang. I'd missed her.

"Aveline," I breathed, hugging her tight while Luc stared at me, his dark eyes round with curiosity.

"Mila." She squeezed me in return, my older, protective sister. She smelled like lavender.

When she pulled away, her dark-brown eyes were misty. "Look at you"—she touched my hair—"still wild and beautiful, sister. The purple looks good on you."

"Being a mother looks good on you," I laughed, lifting a finger to stroke Luc's arm. For a moment, he simply stared before his chubby cheeks curved up in a smile.

"Oh, he likes you. Little flirt," Aveline teased.

"I'm sorry Mother and I weren't there for his birth," I said, a tinge of regret pinching my heart. He was so precious it made me ache to hold him. When I was around children, I yearned to squeeze them tight and kiss them, to have someone to love and protect. It was the mothering nature within me, and it tugged at me until, unable to resist, I took Luc in my arms. His eyes widened in alarm before he settled, sensing his mother trusted me and would stay close by.

"Don't be sorry," Aveline scolded as she lifted the bags. "I had plenty of help. Come on, I'm eager to see Mother."

Mother was waiting for us at the table, her foot propped up on a chair.

The lines of pain on her face disappeared as Aveline strode toward her, arms wide open, and held her for a long time. I looked away, tears brimming while I bounced Luc on my hip. We were together again, the three of us, like it had been for so long when I was young. Aveline had invited us many times to move in with her, but Mother said Aveline and Tomas were newlyweds and family shouldn't intrude. I, too, hadn't been ready to leave Solynn, but in the blink of a moment, everything had changed.

"Oh, my sweet girl," Mother murmured even though Aveline wasn't a little girl anymore. "Come, let me see my grandson. And where is Tomas?"

"Tomas has business." Aveline waved her hand. "Always has business. He'll be here tomorrow, but I told him I wanted a day alone with the both of you."

I wondered if she'd guessed I wouldn't be going back with them.

Luc, who had been so happy so far, wailed, his perfect face wrinkling, his tiny lower lip sticking out in a pout.

"Oh, come here, little man," Aveline cooed. "You've been so patient. Time to eat."

Sitting across from Mother, she opened the top of her dress and pulled out her breasts, her nipples engorged and long. "I'll never get used to feeding my son with my body," she said once Luc was happily sucking away. "It makes me feel powerful and protective. I'm in awe of you, Mother, all you've done, with little help. Right now I can't handle the thought of letting Luc out of my sight."

"Bah." Mother wagged her head to brush the compliment away, although she smiled. "He'll grow, and then you'll want your space. It won't be so hard when the time comes."

After retreating to the kitchen, I poured three glasses of water flavored with mint leaves, and added tomato sandwiches to a tray. "It's teatime." I grinned. "Minus the tea."

Ever since yesterday, my spirits had been lighter, anxiety gone. My secret burned inside, waiting for the right moment to be revealed.

"Oh, my favorite refreshing drink." Aveline took a sip and let out a happy sigh. "Thanks for that, Mila. Now tell me everything."

By "everything," I knew, she meant the gossip from Solynn, but first Mother explained her injury, claiming it wasn't as serious as it sounded. By the time she finished, Luc was yawning, and Aveline excused herself to lay him down for a nap.

Mother and I waited quietly, swaying to Aveline's soothing lullaby. An ache inside me grew, a longing to have someone to take care of, somewhere to belong. I blamed it on the cusp of change, making me want things I couldn't have. Aveline, tall and lovely, had been lucky enough to catch the eye of Tomas, a businessman from the country. They were neither rich nor poor, but Aveline claimed she was content, and from her letters, it sounded as though she had everything she needed.

Tomas was kind, and I liked him, although he wasn't the sort of man Aveline was usually attracted to. Had she settled for him because she'd been ready to escape the city, the oppressing heat, and the tiny flat? She'd always wanted a home full of children and plenty of space to run wild in open meadows. Was she sincerely happy with her choice? I'd seen the pride on her face when she'd fed Luc, but the way she'd waved her hand at the mention of Tomas suggested he was nothing more than background.

Mother always said love was different for everyone. Her affairs had been wild, violent, and passionate. And they'd all ended. When I was younger, I'd used to catch her crying while she mended our clothes. I'd assumed love was too much because it took and took and took until it left a shell.

I wasn't sure if I wanted love, but I didn't want to settle like my sister, and I didn't want to give until it broke me like my mother.

Aveline returned, all proud and put together. Stopping by the kitchen, she refilled her glass of peppermint water, making herself at home with all the familiar places.

When she sat, she touched my arm, studying me for a few seconds. “Mila, spill. You’ve been quiet, which is unlike you.”

Reaching into my pocket, I pulled out the letter and spread it on the table, looking from Mother to Aveline. “Yes, it’s because I have an announcement. I’m going to work at the Dawn.”

MILA

Mother and Aveline both stared at me, shock written across their faces. Aveline was the first to recover, slapping a hand on the table, her mouth agape. "*The* Dawn?" she stressed. "It's a magnificent old inn, quite remote, but a few of the businessmen Tomas works with have been there. Apparently it's a paradise, set in the foothills of the Lagoda mountains. I believe there's a popular horse breeder in the vicinity, which encourages people to make the journey. I can't believe you're going to work there!"

"Yes." I passed the folded paper to her. "Here's the official letter."

Mother snatched it before Aveline could, her dark eyes hastily scanning the words, and then her eyes filled. Pressing a hand to her lips, she stared across the table at me. I held my breath, unsure what she'd say. "I'm proud of you, Mila," she said at last. "I've always told you to follow your heart, your dreams, fight for them." Her fists tightened at the word *fight*. "I'll miss you, but I'm sure you'll come visit during your time off."

"I will," I promised.

"Let me see." Aveline took the letter and breathed in. "It smells like oranges, heavenly. Remember when we were young? Mother, you'd bring us oranges for Christmas. What a treat. This reminds me of those times."

Her smile was wistful, and it took me back to Christmas mornings when we were children. We'd creep out of bed, dressed in our long wool nightgowns, our braids bouncing on our shoulders. Barefoot, we'd cross the cold floor to find the three-feet-tall tree, snug in a corner, with oranges and chocolates and toys hanging off its branches. We'd squeal as we unwrapped gifts, trying not to wake Mother, but she knew. She'd march out of her room, pretending we'd woken her, then stoke the fire and make sticky buns. We'd cuddle around the fire, faces glowing, bellies full of sweets, and I could not think of a happier time.

Aveline's mouth fell open. "They are quite generous with pay, and I'm impressed. Most jobs for women involve cleaning, cooking, or childcare. This is highly unusual."

"I know," I agreed. "I'm grateful for this opportunity to follow my passion for music."

Aveline rubbed her hands together, her excitement mirroring mine. "Promise you'll write and tell us about the curious people you see come and go."

"Of course." I reached across the table to squeeze her hand. "And I expect both of you to do the same. I'm only sorry I won't be there to help you settle in, Mother."

"Don't be sorry." Mother held my gaze with her dark eyes. "This is an excellent opportunity, but if you don't like it, you always have a place with us."

Nodding, I smiled even though I disagreed. This would be the start of a new life. I'd forge a fresh path for myself with music, and when I returned to Solynn after summer's end, the symphony would accept me.

"You know, it's odd." Aveline dropped her voice. "But the inn makes me think of that nasty business that happened with High Tower Castle."

Crossing my arms, I poked Aveline with my foot, wishing she hadn't brought it up. Turning my attention back to Mother, I spoke quickly to assuage her concerns. "The Dawn is nothing like High Tower. That was a place for performers and pleasure...this is simply a place for people to stay. Nothing more."

Wincing at her mistake, Aveline passed the letter back to me. "You're right. High Tower Castle had a theater. I'm sure the Dawn will boast reputable entertainment."

"I recall reading of High Tower Castle in the papers." Mother frowned. "Mila, I do trust you to make wise choices. If you ever find yourself in a situation that is overwhelming, I know you'll ask for help."

"I will." Reaching across the table, I squeezed her hand, looking her in the eye to confirm I'd be fine.

Aveline cleared her throat and stood. "Luc will probably sleep for another hour, and I want to see Solynn in the daylight. Mila, I'll walk you to the stagecoach to book your trip, and you can tell me everything I've missed. Only, Mother, if you promise not to lift a finger."

Mother laughed. "Go, girls. I need a nap myself."

"TELL ME PLAINLY, what is your financial situation?" Aveline asked as she looped her arm in mine.

We walked the crowded streets, conscious we had little time to discuss. My heart lurched, and my lips twitched. Whenever we discussed money, resentment and shame came over me because Mother and I relied on Aveline's generosity.

Shrugging, I tried to make my words light. "It's just the rent for the flat and Mother's medical bills. They were unexpected..."

"Debtors have no remorse." Aveline snorted in disgust. "What about your job at the market?"

I'd assisted the herbalist with deliveries and grinding herbs. She was getting older, and the work made her joints ache. "Her daughter moved to the city to take over the family business. I've been searching for employment since then and considered it worthwhile to pursue music."

"Oh," Aveline breathed. "That is disappointing. I didn't know you wanted to play the violin so badly."

"I assumed I'd have to stay here in the city because there aren't any opportunities where you live, are there?"

"No. I'm sorry the symphony did not accept you, but this offer to play at the Dawn is quite generous. I don't want you to worry about the money for rent or the doctor's fee. I'll pay for those debts and for your trip to the Dawn, but I'll eventually need the money back."

"Of course," I blurted out. "I'll send the money as soon as I receive my first month's salary, and I'm sorry I'm not coming with you to help with Mother."

"Don't be," Aveline scolded. "We all deserve the opportunity to pursue what we want. Besides, I'm excited about the idea of you working at the Dawn.

According to the papers, the owner is eccentric. Apparently he snubbed the gentlemen's club here in Solynn by refusing to join even though he owns a significant amount of trade goods. But aside from gossip, I know little about the inn."

I latched onto her words. "Curious. Of course I've heard of the Dawn, but I was unaware inns hired musicians to amuse their guests. When I envision an inn, I think of it as a place to rest and eat before moving to the next location."

"This one is unusual," Aveline agreed. "It's luxurious, a place for the affluent to rest, almost like a resort. I'm sure it's ever changing, and I'm sorry I brought up High Tower in front of Mother."

I frowned. "Yes, High Tower was a theater where lords and ladies went for entertainment and debauchery. The Dawn is nothing like it."

Aveline nudged me. "Maybe you'll find a lover there, or even better, a wealthy husband."

My thoughts went to the golden-haired man in blue who smelled of citrus. If he worked there as a messenger, he'd be no wealthy man, but I'd enjoy getting to know him all the same. "I don't need a husband," I protested. "Or lover. Look what happened to Mother."

We stopped just outside the stagecoach building. The bustle of people coming and going was loud. Horses tossed their heads, snorting and stamping as they waited for passengers to embark. Aveline let go of my arm and faced me. Her expression was fierce, and her dark eyes drilled into mine. "Never base your life on Mother or her past lovers who left. That was her lot in life. You never know where you'll find love. It is indescribable, life-changing, better had for a little while than not at all."

A beat passed as her words sank in, and I cocked my head. "Is that how you feel about Tomas?"

There. Her eyes flashed with just the briefest hint of hurt and regret. "No. Tomas is my husband, my safety net, the right choice for me. Go, Mila, have an adventure at the Dawn. Like Mother said, you'll always have us to come home to, should you choose."

A chord of sadness struck me, like the mournful melody of a funeral tune played on a flute. Aveline had loved someone once, but she'd settled for safety instead. I didn't blame her for her decision, but I wouldn't have to make a choice between love and need. Because I didn't intend to fall in love.

MILA

Within the week, it was time for me to go. I hugged Mother and Aveline goodbye, kissed Luc's head, and shook Tomas's hand. Later, after the flat was empty, the four of them would take a private carriage back home.

I'd forgone packing a trunk of clothes and only carried a satchel and my violin. The expense to add a trunk to the stagecoach was too high, and the job required new clothes anyway. I wore a simple blue traveling dress and a duster Mother had mended for me. The duster could only do so much to prevent my skirts from getting grimy, but at least I wouldn't be completely dirty when I arrived at the Dawn.

The trip was long even though I was adept at amusing myself. By the third day, my bottom was sore from sitting, my stomach was queasy from the constant rocking back and forth, and my shoulders hurt from hunching to make room for the other passengers. I understood why lords and ladies paid for a private carriage. Although deeply uncomfortable, I focused on the view of green meadows, lush forests, sparkling rivers, and bright flowers. Soon I'd arrive. Soon it would be over.

As we neared the Dawn, the passengers became scant, more and more leaving at each stop. The scenery changed as the horses maneuvered a steep track. The view from the window made my heart flip-flop. In the distance, a range of blue mountains rose, pointed peaks white with snow or fog, which one I did not know. Pine forests dotted the landscape with shades of evergreen, and open meadows with honey-dew-colored grasses, bright flowers, or rows of orchards covered the land.

When my eyes filled with tears because of the beauty, I blamed it on my ragged emotions, for leaving home and traveling so long had left me feeling out of place. I couldn't wait for a hot bath and a comfortable bed to sleep in. I wondered about the stagecoach driver and the trips he made. Did he often long for home? Or was the change of scenery enough to keep him amused?

Eventually it started to rain, and my fingers shook as I twisted my plum hair around my slender fingers. I kept my eyes focused on the window even though droplets of water covered it. The only other person in the stagecoach snored on the bench opposite me, breath smelling like mushrooms and sour eggs. He'd ignored me the entire journey, and I'd done the same, although, as our travel lengthened, I realized we were both going to the same place. When I'd received the letter inviting me to work at the Dawn, I'd assumed it would be off the beaten track but not this remote, so near the mist-covered mountains of Lagoda. How did anyone stumble upon it out here, so far away from civilization?

Not for the first time, my stomach lurched at the thought of being a seven-day journey away from my mother and sister. In Solynn it had been easy to feel bold and brave about my new job, but out here, moments before my arrival, gloom and rain lowered my spirits further.

The stagecoach came to a halt with a jerk, sending me sliding. My snoring companion sat up with a curse. "What was that?"

"Final stop at the Dawn," the driver bellowed.

Seizing my satchel and violin, I reached for the door handle, eager to escape the claustrophobic compartment. Without waiting for help, I jumped down onto the sand-colored ground, rain dampening my head. My lips parted at the sight.

The Dawn rose, a weathered castle, old and intimidating, with ivy and vines trailing about the windows. White flowers held their heads stiffly up despite the rain, as if their tenacity would be rewarded by golden rays of sun. If it ever came out.

A grove of trees rose on my left, and on the right, a path snaked through a meadow, leading downhill toward the glimmer of what might be a lake. Even though mist was gathering, I made out a range of blue mountains in the distance.

Picking up my heavy skirts, I strode through the light mist to the entrance. As I went, a tantalizing sound drifted to my ears, long and low, almost mournful. Pausing midstep, I leaned toward it. Was that music? Yet it didn't sound as though it came from within, which was where I'd expect music to come from. Instead, it sounded as though it was out in the moors, somewhere leading to the blue mountains. Shaking my head to dismiss it, I continued my trajectory when it came again, louder and forceful. Demanding.

The music was clear, commanding, insistent, and for a moment, my foot hovered, turning toward it as though answering its call. My heart beat in my chest, fluttering as if under a spell, and as the sweet noise swelled, a desire flared up, sudden and strong. A wave of dizziness washed over me along with a certainty. I had to find that song, that sweet note, and drown myself in its pleasure. All my hopes and dreams of becoming a musician would come to pass, if only I listened long enough to learn.

"Make a decision, missy," the snoring man said, mildly annoyed as I hesitated in our path.

Whatever grip the music had on me faded, like I was coming out of a dream. I opened the double doors, carved with intricate patterns of vines and mythical creatures, and crossed the threshold into the Dawn. The richness of the velvet carpet, the silver drapes, and the stone decorations edged with gold made me conscious of the dirt on my skirts, sprinkling the entry with ash-like dust.

Sounds and scents washed over me: constant chatter, roasted meat, sweet mead, and an undercurrent of citrus.

The entryway was a wide hall with low-lying couches on one side and bay windows that overlooked the rotunda. Someone had done their best to make it appear elegant and welcoming. Clutching my violin tighter, I walked down the hall, noting the doors on either side and a staircase directly in front of me that led up, presumably to the guest rooms.

To the left was an opening, and I walked into the dining hall, where all the noise took place. A bar was right next to the entrance, but beyond it were tables full of chattering guests. In a back corner, a man perched on a stool, playing a lively jaunt on his banjo. Eventually I'd sit there, playing my violin. The atmosphere was lively, and my nerves sang as I faced the bar.

Two women stood behind it, one young with a black braid over her shoulder. She poured mugs of frothy ale and slid them to a man waiting on the other side of the counter. He winked at her and slapped down a few coins, which she deftly tucked into her pocket.

The older woman spoke to the man who'd entered behind me. She was unusually tall and willowy, with large brown eyes and short black hair cropped just above her sharp jawline. Her skin was pale, but it was her red lips and nails that caught my eye. Paints were often used to enhance a women's features, and rouge used on the lips, but I hadn't seen paint applied to nails. It was both scandalous and brave.

The man moved to take a drink from the girl with the black braid, and the tall one's eyes landed on me. Her eyebrows lifted, swiftly taking in my appearance. If she thought ill or well of me, it was impossible to tell, for her face gave away nothing. "Are you Mila?"

"Yes."

"Good, we've been expecting you. I'm Ginger. Welcome to the Dawn."

MILA

"Rachelle?" Ginger called to the young lady with the black braid. "This is Mila. I'm going to step out for a few moments to show her to her room."

Rachelle grinned at me. "It's not so busy now. I will take care of whatever comes up."

"Come." Ginger moved from behind the bar and led me back out to the hall. "I don't want you to assume you're here under the wrong impression, but one of our hostesses ran away, and we are short-staffed during the summer rush. I'm aware you were hired to play three nights a week in the dining hall, and that agreement still stands, but we will pay you an additional salary if you'd be willing to work behind the bar with Rachelle, just until it slows down."

I weighed her words as she opened the door into another room, which held a lounge with sofas and chairs, a fireplace large enough for me to stand in, and a staircase leading up to the second floor.

"You don't have to decide tonight," Ginger went on, pausing to eye my hair. "Think on it and let me know in the morning. Before you decide, I'll have you know the Dawn is a prestigious inn. We pride ourselves on offering concierge services to our guests, who usually stay a few weeks at a time. Our clientele includes lords and ladies who come here on business, or need to rest before returning to their demanding lives. As staff here, you represent the values of the Dawn, and in turn, you are treated with respect. As a staff member, you are not a servant, nor are you expected to work yourself to the bone. I encourage each member to take breaks, especially during the slower times, which are afternoons and the winter months. Summer is the height of the season, which is why you are here."

I blinked, her words resonating in my fatigued mind. I was here for the summer to play, but three nights a week left me plenty of time to do…what? I wasn't sure, and I didn't need all day to practice. "I'll do it," I told her breathlessly. The money would help me pay back my sister, buy my own violin, and save for my return to Solynn.

"Good," Ginger said, her expression unchanging.

"I'll change your salary, and all tips you earn at the bar are yours to keep. Rachelle will train you in the morning. For now, rest. I'll have a tray of food sent up unless you prefer to eat in the dining hall."

Even though she was difficult to read, I appreciated her thoughtfulness. "Thank you, a tray in my room would be preferred."

Shaking back her short hair, Ginger pivoted and spread her arms. "This is the staff lounge. Aside from myself and Rachelle, we share these quarters with Moses, who is our cook, and his assistant, Marley. You'll meet them tomorrow. Dusty and Giselle live beside the lake and manage the gardens and vineyards. Ezra, owner of the Dawn, has chambers on the top floor but spends most of his time in his tower. There's a door to outside here"—she pointed—"but we keep it locked, since the guests are not allowed in our wing of the inn. I'll provide you a key so you can come and go as you please."

I nodded, trying to keep up with the amount of information she rapidly shared with me. Without giving me a moment to respond, Ginger marched up the staircase. I followed her down the carpeted hall until she pulled a brass key off a chain and unlocked a door. "This is your room. It's adjoining to Rachelle's, and you'll both share the washroom."

Light filled my vision as I stepped inside, my feet sinking into the carpet. I stilled, heart in my throat as a note hovered in the air, long and low, enchanting as if calling, summoning, whispering secrets. Sucking in a deep breath, I made my way to the window, the largeness of the room lost as the music came again. What was it?

The drapes had been pulled back to let in the light. Below my window were orange flowers, a view of the rotunda and the drive that led back out to the world. Dark-green trees arched over the road, and tiny green fruits hung from their branches.

Nothing else appeared in the courtyard, aside from the invisible evening breeze that made the branches sway. The chord died away like the echo of a tender memory. Puzzled, I pivoted to take in my enchanting room. Ginger watched me closely.

"We have a dress code here at the Dawn," she went on as if those moments of silence had been to allow me to take in my surroundings. "We wear black and white so it is clear who works here and also to blend in. I had a few gowns made for you, but you are welcome to go into town and meet with the dressmaker to have them altered to fit. You'll have a stipend for clothing. And here"—she pointed to a case beside the wardrobe—"is the violin you'll play, although I see you brought your own."

"Only as a keepsake," I told her, swallowing hard. "The strings broke, but it was my grandfather's…"

"I see." She stepped back. "I must return to the dining hall. Any questions before I go?"

"No." I shook my head, sure a dozen questions would come to mind as soon as she stepped away.

"Good, I'll have a tray sent up shortly."

She brushed away without closing the door, and I stood still for a moment, breathing in the rose-scented air. A surge of relief went through me at my arrival, the unexpected shift in my position at the inn, and the violin.

Picking up the case, I laid it on the bed and opened it. There lay the most exquisite violin I'd ever seen, the wood of its body shiny, ornate, the strings taut as though begging me to pick it up and play it. I stroked my fingers admiringly over the wood. Soon enough. I'd practice. I'd play and become more than Mila Hadria. I'd become Mila the violinist, and soon I'd be back in the city, in high demand, and I would want for nothing.

Sunlight went soft under the anticipation of evening as I opened the wardrobe, examining the simple yet luxurious dresses hanging there. A lump swelled in my throat at my good fortune. I'd write Mother and Aveline with the good news, and the knowledge that soon there would be money to pay off the debtors and help Mother's recovery made me want to weep. My fingers went to the buttons of my dress. Slowly I undid them, preparing for a relaxing bath after such a long journey. As I discarded my dress, the air in the room shifted.

Standing in the washroom, I sniffed. It smelled damp in there, although it was neat, with towels stacked on a shelf, soap sitting by the tub, and a rug to put my wet feet on. The flat Mother and I lived in did not have a washroom, so for an immersive bath, we had to go to the steam houses in the city, which lacked privacy. The ability to wash in peace made me feel rich, and yet goose bumps prickled on my bare skin as a hint of icy breath hissed around me. A faint sound came, as though something was sucking, slurping. Crossing my hands over my bare breasts, I listened while I waited for the tub to fill. It was uncanny, slightly spooky. What was that?

A shudder went down my spine. I was in a remote location with strangers, far, far away from everything I knew. The sound increased, and my heart kicked until it faded. When I climbed into the tub, I let out the breath I'd been holding. As the warm water covered me, I blamed that moment on exhaustion. My mind was merely playing tricks on me. Besides, old homes made strange noises. Once I got used to the Dawn, everything would be fine.

MILA

Rachelle nudged me awake. "Your turn to collect the eggs," she announced.

"Eggs?" I asked, rolling out of bed.

Slowly I was settling in to the rhythm of the Dawn, and two days had passed in a blur. Rachelle was friendly, talkative, and more than willing to train me.

"Every Tuesday," Rachelle confirmed. "Follow the path down toward the gardens. There's an old barn there, painted red on one side. Giselle is peculiar, but she'll have a basket of eggs waiting for you."

The sky was still a pale pink as I dressed. "This early?"

"Yes, so Moses can use them for breakfast. I'll go see who wants breakfast in bed, and hurry."

"I'm going," I told her, hopping on one foot as I put on my shoes.

The morning air was refreshing, slightly damp with a promise of heat as the sun fully rose. Light streamed about me as I took the path that led downhill to the gardens. Still, my eyes were drawn to the tower that perched on the rise just above the inn. It didn't look habitable but more like a ruin covered in vines. Part of the top was crumbling away, and I found it hard to believe anyone lived there, especially the owner of the inn. Wouldn't he be happier in the inn itself?

But then I recalled the chatter of the guests, the creaking of the floors, and the constant sounds of merriment. Even in my room, I heard faint bumps and muted voices, indistinguishable but there. I was used to it, for it reminded me of the flat I'd grown up in. It was an inn, not home, nor a grand estate, although once it might have been.

Wild grass grew alongside the footpath, coming as tall as my waist, bowing before me as though I was a queen. I imagined, for a moment, that I was a sun queen, at home among the plants and the faint scent of lilacs. The path dipped, and the kingdom spread out before me in all its brilliance. The vegetable garden lay on my right, enclosed by a fence, but on the swell of a hill was the vineyard, winding back toward the road.

To the left was the barn and, in the distance, a tiny log cottage with smoke curling out of its chimney. My heart twisted at the enchantment of it, as if I was walking into an illustration from a storybook. The bleating of animals drifted to my ears before I saw them. An assortment of sheep and goats trotted up the hill, carrying the scent of wool and animal musk. A man holding a staff herded them, and a black dog dashed behind, barking as it drove them uphill to trim the unruly grass alongside the path.

"Morning!" the man called, touching a hand to his gray cap.

"Morning." I waved back.

"Are you looking for my wife?"

"If she has the eggs, then yes."

"You'll find her in the barn," he said cheerfully.

"Thank you."

"My name's Dusty."

"Mila."

"Good morning, then!"

When I reached the bottom of the hill, a sense of awe stole over me. A lake lay to my left, a glistening body of blue-green shimmering in the early light. In the distance was a blur of green. Maybe an island? Light cut over the water, sending the arc of a rainbow across the cornflower sky. Clasping my hands to my heart, I inhaled, moved by the majesty of nature. Nothing like this could be seen in Solynn, not with the buildings, which blocked out all greenery. I felt as though a wish had been granted to me, a promise that something life-changing would happen during my sojourn in the foothills of Lagoda.

"Lovely, isn't it?" a voice called, low and smooth and slow like honey.

Pivoting, I acknowledged the women walking toward me. She carried a basket in her arms, and the sunlight highlighted her golden-brown skin. A yellow scarf held back her bouncy red curls. She had a flat nose, big brown eyes, and a mouth that looked like mischief.

"It's gorgeous," I agreed, my eyes going to the little house with smoke coming from the chimney. "Do you live here?"

"That I do," the woman confirmed, "and I count myself lucky every day to walk out with this loveliness on my doorstep."

"I've seen nothing like it," I admitted.

"You must be the new girl," the woman said. "I'm Giselle."

"Mila."

"Where are you from, Mila?"

"Solynn."

"Ah, that explains it." She rested the basket in the grass and put her hands on her hips, shaking her head mournfully. "Cities will be the death of people, but they are too blind to see."

"What do you mean?" I asked cautiously, surprised by her bluntness.

"Those poor children, growing up without a place to run and play. They don't have adventures or plant gardens and harvest from the soil. Or get dirty playing in the mud or learn how to swim like the fishes. In the city, they stay inside, growing fat and lazy, forgetting about the land, arguing over money and politics, instead of enjoying this. Life is simple, but the whims of society make it complex."

I almost laughed until I realized she was serious. Covering my mouth with my hand to hide my amusement, I asked, "Are you from here?"

"Lagoda? Naw. Dusty and I came up this way years back when Ezra visited our farm and made us a deal. We were falling behind, couldn't keep up with the land or make enough money to sustain ourselves. He welcomed us to this paradise, and we've been here ever since. He has a good heart, he does."

Ezra. Owner of the Dawn. Shielding my eyes against the sun, I glanced back at the tower, which appeared taller and even more forbidding from down in the gardens. I opened my mouth to ask her what he was like, since I'd yet to meet him, but Giselle went on.

"I admit, I was curious when he made the offer,

because according to legend, mysterious things happen here."

Her words caught my attention. "Like what?"

Giselle's eyes sparkled as she lowered her voice. "Not long ago, something strange happened on the island out yonder." She pointed at the lake. "Since then, rumors have spread that we are not alone. Beings of myth commune with nature, although they hide from human eyes. Some call them fey, woodland folk. Others calls them spirits, but the tales are the same. A maiden from the village got lost in the woods for days and came back with no memory. A pair of horses disappeared from a farm, a widow found a sack of coins on her doorstep, and a couple, barren for years, suddenly had twins. The spirits are mischievous, blessing some and punishing others. Legend is, if you visit the island on a night when the barrier between worlds is thin, you can dance with the spirits and they won't harm you. Although, you won't remember a thing the next morning."

I stared in astonishment, unsure what to say, especially because Giselle looked serious. Did she believe in the supernatural? "Have you gone to the island on such a night?"

"If I have, I don't remember it." Giselle suddenly snorted. "Tell you what, come with me one night, and we'll see if the legends are true."

My skin itched with the desire to escape from her

outlandish tales, and suddenly I remembered my duties. I snatched up the basket, which was heavier than I'd expected, and grunted. "If I don't have to work," I told her, the guileless words slipping from my lips because I had no intention of joining her.

"Well, I'll let you get back to work." Turning, she waved. "Until next time, Mila."

"Bye, Giselle," I called after her retreating form.

Taking the eggs, I made my slow way back to the inn, but the wonder of the morning stayed with me, as though the sight of the rainbow had given me a blessing.

Back inside, the rush of the day pumped through my veins. I walked behind the bar, to the kitchen. Walls that did not quite reach the ceiling divided the kitchen into three parts. The first had a round table where the staff ate and where trays to go up to the guest rooms were placed.

Beside it was the mechanical lift, a device that carried one to the next floor. It was a clever way to alleviate the need to constantly run up and down the stairs, and Rachelle had showed me how to turn the crank to select a floor. Beyond it was a short hall with a door leading to the cellar. On the other side of the wall was a space for cutting, cooking, and preparing and another room where the meat was stored.

As I set the heavy basket on the kitchen table,

Moses, the cook, came over to look. "Oh, that's unique," he said, picking up the eggs one by one.

Moses was a slight man, a little shorter than me, with tight gray curls covering his head. His skin was dark and leathery, but he had blue eyes that twinkled, and tended to hum when he wasn't talking. He was easy to like, a bit absentminded but an excellent cook. "Look at this. A little blue egg. Now, that's unusual. I'm going to save this one for something special. Maybe a cake." He winked at me.

"It is pretty special," I agreed.

He tapped his head. "You're Mila. Correct?"

"Yes, this is only my third day here. I'm still learning."

Moses winked again. "Ah, you're the one who will play during the dinner hour. Now, I look forward to that."

"Thank you," I beamed, only slightly nervous. Tomorrow night would be my first night to perform, and aside from practicing, I'd never played for a lengthy amount of time.

"I bet you haven't eaten yet." Moses picked up the basket. "Don't move. I'll make you a plate. Breakfast is the best meal. If you eat a good one, it'll keep you going all day."

"Thank you." I perched on the edge of a chair, determined to eat as quickly as possible before helping Rachelle.

My stomach growled as Moses returned not five minutes later with a plate of eggs, mushrooms, biscuits, tomatoes, and cheese. At first glance, it looked like too much food, but when I started eating, delicious flavors burst on my tongue, making it impossible to stop.

Halfway through my meal, a shadow darkened the doorway. A reminder of the discomfort I'd experienced when bathing my first evening made me shiver. I jerked my head up and almost choked as I caught sight of the golden-haired man.

MILA

He walked into the room, and his presence was like sunshine breaking through stormy clouds. My unease morphed into pure anticipation. Slowly I returned the fork to my plate of half-eaten food, relishing my second meeting with the handsome man.

His hair was damp as if he'd walked the lush fields to capture the morning dew, and as he neared, tiredness lingered behind his vivid green eyes. His smile was faint, almost shy, and so endearing it made my heart twist.

Under the power of his magnetic gaze, a yearning made me crave his attention. Hope bloomed in my heart like a flower unfolding under the warmth of spring. I was in his court, and he was the sun god, gracing me with his splendor.

"It's you," I blurted out, cheeks warm.

"It is, and so we meet again," he said, voice low and hoarse, as if he hadn't had enough sleep.

He held something in his hands, and my eyes darted to it as I cleared my throat uncomfortably. "I guessed you might work here after I received the letter…"

His smiled widened. "You guessed right." Setting the object on the table, he slid it toward me. "I brought you a gift."

It was a jar of jam. No, not just any jam but fig jam. I sat back in the chair, dazed. Our meeting had been brief, inconsequential, but the fact that he recalled something as insignificant as a broken jar of jam made me appreciate his attention to detail. "You remembered."

A blush glowed on his cheeks. "Actually, it's for your mother, since you mentioned her and your sister. There's also a bushel of oranges. I can drop them off at the next post if you have a letter to send with the gifts."

My mouth opened and closed. He was both kind and generous, two admirable qualities, and while I'd come for a job, the knowledge that he, too, lived and worked at the inn made staying much more attractive. "Thank you. I don't even know your name, and you've already been so kind to me. I'll write a letter as soon as I'm done with work."

"No rush," he said in his low voice. "I'm in no hurry. Just find me when you're ready and I'll set up the delivery."

I sat there, drinking in his lovely golden hair, his stunning eyes, and the tilt of his exquisite mouth, one side slightly higher than the other. His age was impossible to guess, for he appeared both young and wise at the same time. And then there was that aura I couldn't place.

"What is your name?" I asked, my breakfast forgotten.

Leaning toward me, he all but whispered, "If I tell you, you must promise not to treat me differently."

My gaze roved over his tempting features. "Why would I treat you any differently?"

"Because most do once they know who I am." His lips curled up in a half smile, revealing dimples. "Promise?"

Was he flirting with me? A shiver of anticipation went down my spine. Did I want him to flirt with me? Moving closer, I lowered my tone to match his. "Fine, I promise, but Ginger already told me the names of the staff, so I can guess who you might be."

"Oh, is that so?" His gaze dared me to continue.

I grinned. "So far I've met Moses. This morning I went to collect eggs and met Dusty and Giselle. I already work with Ginger and Rachelle, so that leaves Moses' assistant, Marley."

His brows lifted as if he would disagree with my reasoning. "You pay attention."

"I do. Am I right?"

"Ezra, there you are," Ginger's sharp tone interrupted.

The man, whom I'd assumed was Marley, jerked around so quickly the chair almost fell over. His easygoing manner faded, replaced with almost a hardness, an unease.

My mind reeled with the new information. Ezra? As in Ezra, owner of the Dawn? Dreams of attraction and hope of something more crashed and burned. The king in his court, the sun in a room full of shadows—why, of course, he was all those things because this was his domain.

Dipping my head, I distanced myself from him. My chest tightened, and suddenly I wanted to leave the kitchen and hide. I'd been flirting with my employer. Had Ginger seen our brief flirtation? Had he encouraged me, or had I imagined it all?

"Ginger." His tone was clipped and unfriendly. "Do you need me?"

"Yes. We should discuss a few pressing matters before the day grows busy. Do you have a moment now?"

Ezra pivoted toward me and extended a hand. His eyes grew warm again, but his face remained hard. "Mila, it's been a pleasure. Welcome to the Dawn."

And just like that, he was gone.

Unable to eat anymore, I focused on the work, collecting breakfast trays, delivering tea, taking dishes back into the kitchen, and sampling some of the wild strawberries Giselle brought in from the garden. All the while, I tried to ignore the sharp disappointment that sat like a stone in my stomach.

Ezra was the owner of the inn, surprising for one so young, although maybe he had inherited it. Still, I couldn't forget his generous gift, nor the way his eyes had lingered on mine. Perhaps it was something he did with all his staff. Rachelle, who liked to gossip, would be the one to ask. And then there was that odd tension between him and Ginger, which made me curious about their history.

After lunch was a lull, typically when I slipped away to practice. Today I lingered behind the bar, shining glasses with Rachelle.

"Did you meet Giselle today? Wasn't she odd?" Rachelle wiggled her eyebrows.

I didn't want to talk about Giselle, especially her cryptic words regarding the supernatural. Shrugging, I leaned against the bar, holding a towel but doing nothing. "I didn't speak to Giselle long enough to get a grasp on whether she's odd, but I met Ezra today. Does no one call him Lord Ezra? Does he have a title or status?"

Rachelle shrugged. "No one knows, and if you

ask, he'll just tell you to call him Ezra. He's handsome, isn't he, but a bit of a recluse, shy, you know, modest. I hear he's single, never had a wife either and doesn't seem interested. I've attempted to get his attention many times, but he's just so boring."

Ezra seemed far from boring to me, but I tucked her words away. Maybe he wasn't flirting, just being kind, which made me feel worse. "Did he give you a gift when you arrived?"

"A gift?" Rachelle scoffed before her brows furrowed. She put down the glass she was holding and looked at me. "I can't recall arriving. It's like I've always been here."

Her face went slack, and her eyes glazed as she stared. How could she not remember? "Did you grow up here?" I asked tentatively.

"No, of course not." The liveliness returned to her face. "I'll tell you a secret. I'm saving up to leave and go to the city. Didn't you come from Solynn? Why did you leave?"

"I wanted the chance to pursue music."

"I'd assume more opportunities would be available in the city."

"True. But this was an offer I could not refuse. The other option was going to live with my sister and her family in the country."

Rachelle wrinkled her nose. "The city is much better than the country. Besides, I want to be the wife of a lord, or a duke, or maybe even a king. Wouldn't that be lovely? But I can't catch the eye of someone titled unless I go to the city."

"There's no one here?" I asked, thinking of all the travelers who passed by. "Why, a lord might stay here one night and you'd never know."

"You think?" Rachelle asked eagerly, clasping her hands against her chest.

"I was under the assumption that many lords and ladies came to stay here," I admitted.

"True." Rachelle chewed her lower lip. "If only they were more well behaved."

A bell rang before I could ask for more details.

"I'll get it!" Rachelle announced and darted off.

Ginger returned, eyeing me sternly as she slid behind the bar, a stack of papers in her hands. "No practice? You might as well go relax before supper. I don't believe you've seen the gardens?"

Ginger's question left the bitter taste of guilt on my tongue. Unable to tell whether she was upset with me or encouraging me to relax, I explained, "I thought I'd give my fingers a break before tomorrow's performance, but I'll practice more this evening. I've already been to the gardens this morning when I went to fetch the eggs."

"Oh." A faint laugh escaped her ruby-red lips. "No, I mean the botanical gardens. If you continue through the dining hall, you'll reach the ballroom. A door leads outside, and there you'll find the gardens." Her expression softened. "It's a favorite haunt of the guests and my preferred retreat when it's quiet. You might find some inspiration before you practice later."

"Thank you—"

"Please, don't. Like I said before, you are staff, not a servant. No one expects you to be on your feet, working all day. Take some time for yourself, and if the gardens don't suit you, the library on the fourth floor might. Just don't bother any of the guests."

She smiled, and I thought it was a genuine smile as I hung up my apron and left the bar. Library or gardens? I'd been cooped up inside all day, so I opted for the gardens, slipping through the rooms until daylight all but blinded me. As my vision cleared, I stepped out of the ballroom and started down the patio stairs.

My fingers froze on the railing as I saw him for the second time that day. Ezra.

MILA

He leaned against a tree, shaded from the heat of the sun. He waved and strode across the lush lawn. "Hello again, Mila."

My hands went clammy with awareness. Now that I knew he was my employer, I should turn around and go back inside, for I'd heard sordid tales of women who'd fallen under the sway of attractive lords to the ruin of all.

Instead, I walked toward him, reminded of my audition and the blue and gold in the shadows. "Did you ask Ginger to send me out here to meet you?"

"No." He ran a hand through his hair, ruffling it. "But afternoons are usually slow. Will you join me for a turn about the gardens?" He held out his arm, as if I was a lady he was escorting to a ball.

Suddenly I became intensely aware of his height and our proximity, but there was nothing wrong with walking the gardens with him. Cautiously, I placed my hand on his arm.

Pulling me closer, he cocked his head. "You seem uneasy."

I recalled the way his cheek had brushed against mine when he'd carried my groceries up to the flat, and a need to know gripped me. "Why did you come?"

"What do you mean?"

"Back in Solynn. Why were you outside my door? You could have sent anyone, a messenger, or let the letter go through the post, but…" I trailed off, my thoughts jumbled.

"I had business in the city, and I enjoy music. Your performance swayed me to make the offer. Besides, I prefer to meet potential members of the staff face-to-face before hiring them. It helps me insure they are who they say they are."

So it had been him at the symphony hall. Frowning, I pressed on. "You didn't introduce yourself, though, or ask me anything of consequence."

"I didn't need to." Pausing in front of a white gate, he took my hand in his before continuing in his low, smooth tones, "I have a unique ability to read people and sense their intent. I did not sense any ill intent toward me or this inn."

My hand was warm in his, too warm, and I wanted to snatch it away, but I discerned he was giving me clarity. Plunging onward, I said the first thing that came to mind. "What did you sense?"

His lips tilted in the same manner they had earlier, as though he was about to tease me. "From you? Excitement, frustration, some anger, a hint of anxiety, determination, and anticipation."

"All that?" I stared. "Who are you?"

He shrugged. "Ezra."

"No, your ability, it's unusual. Have you always had it?"

"Always."

Those one-word answers were not satisfying. Wiggling my hand out of his grasp, I turned to the gate, which came just higher than my waist. "You're only making me more curious."

"Good, that is the point," he teased as he unlatched the gate.

"How do I get to know you if you won't answer my questions?"

"Oh, you want to get to know me?"

I blushed then, grateful my dark skin prevented him from seeing it. I'd involuntarily started flirting with him again. Worst of all, it was so easy. Unable to make eye contact, I gazed at the gardens. They were idyllic. Daffodils, petunias, poppies, and bluebells waved in the breeze. A twinkling stream of water warbled alongside a stone path before bending out of sight. Ezra held open the gate, giving me a playful bow as I walked inside.

For a moment, I wished he weren't there, because joy welled up so strongly it almost choked me. I strolled down the stone path, thinking of Mother and how happy she'd be to walk through gardens like this. Benches sat in the grass, an ideal spot to sit, dream, paint, or even play. I could bring my violin out here and allow nature to inspire me.

A path curved further into the gardens, but magnificent trees and thick bushes hid the full view of them. Clasping my hands together, I spun to Ezra, who shut the gate behind him. "I've never seen anything like this before. This is a retreat. I'd spend all day in these gardens if I could."

"I'm sure you'll spend many days here," he echoed, a lower note in his tone.

He stood by the gate, arms crossed, watching me. Although his gaze was calm, a darkening in his eyes gave me pause. My breath came quick, reminding me of my decision not to flirt with my employer. Pivoting back to the gardens, I ignored whatever had passed silently between us.

"If you come here early, just after dawn, no one will be around," Ezra explained. "It's about five miles from end to end, but you can wander different paths or sit and read. There's a pond in the very center, where the ducks and turtles swim. I sneak them bits of bread." He chuckled. "The swans built a nest by the pond this year, and they fiercely protect it. Their young will hatch soon."

I refused to look at him, keeping my gaze focused on the greenery, because despite my reservations, a tiny seed of desire had been planted.

"The peacocks live at the far end of the gardens. They are usually calm unless provoked, but during mating season, they are ruthless. Beautiful, though, with their feathers. Namen, the seamstress in the village, comes to collect them for her unique gowns."

"All this is yours?" I confirmed, facing him again. "It is very generous of you to share it instead of keeping it to yourself."

His brows lifted in surprise. "I hadn't considered...it's natural to share my land, to let others come here for some peace or amusement."

Giving a shaky laugh, I stumbled over my words, "Yes. Well. Work first."

"Speaking of work"—he sobered—"I don't want you to think I led you here under false pretenses. I'm aware Ginger asked you to help in the kitchen in the mornings and—"

"It's fine," I said quickly, thinking of the money. "Besides, it's only temporary, and I have plenty of time to practice. I'm afraid I might be bored without the work."

"If you change your mind, come to me."

"I will," I said, wondering about the tension between Ginger and Ezra.

"The summers are busy, full of festivals and celebrations, and I look forward to hearing you play again."

"The violin in my room, where did it come from? Do you play?" I asked.

A stillness came over him before he winked, his manner turning teasing, playful again. "As long as you like it, it is yours to keep. Besides, I can't reveal all my surprises in one day."

He strode down the path, and I walked beside him, examining the gardens. Fat bees flitted from flower to flower, and sometimes a hummingbird would speed through the air with a whirl, incandescent colors brightening the scenery. They were so tiny and fast it made me want to catch one and hold it in place so I could see its beauty.

"At least tell me something about you," I suggested, aware he was more of an enigma than when I'd first met him.

"What do you want to know?" His hands were in his pockets, and he strode casually, as if he did not have a care in the world.

Questions popped into my mind faster than I

could register them. "Do you really live in the ruined tower?"

Ezra laughed. "The staff has been talking about my odd habits, haven't they?"

"A bit," I admitted.

"It's my workshop and private quarters. Most nights I fall asleep there, but I have an office and adjoining chambers in the inn. I keep the books and run operations, make sure there's enough food and wine and money for all this." He spread his arms out to indicate, well, everything, I supposed. "As you might have guessed, Ginger is second-in-command here. She knows how to run everything in case anything happens to me."

"I see," I said, not wanting to talk about Ginger and her lack of warmth. Something was off about her, although maybe in time, I'd understand. "What of your workshop? What do you do there?"

"Oh, come now," he dodged my question skillfully. "Am I going to be interrogated all afternoon? Don't I get to learn something about you?"

"You'll have to wait and see," I quipped. "I can't reveal all my secrets in one afternoon."

He moved so quickly I almost missed it. One moment, I was walking down the path; the next, my wrist was locked in his hand as he pulled me closer, his jaw working. "I see. You toss my words right back at me. Well, then we shall have to do this again."

Lifting my hand, he brushed his lips over my skin.

Every inch of my body tingled in anticipation.

Winking, he released me. "Until next time, Mila."

EZRA

"What are you doing?" Ginger demanded, teeth bared, smokey eyes flashing.

Locking my secret drawer, I rose to see her lithe frame filling up the doorway. An anxious red aura snapped around her. I promptly sat back down, exhausted before our argument began. "What is it Ginger? What do you *think* I'm doing that you don't approve of?"

After marching in, she closed the door. It clanked with finality, like a death sentence. Standing in front of the desk, she cocked her hips to the side and waved a red finger in my face. "It's not what I *think* you're doing. I know because I saw you flirting with her in the gardens. A mortal. You can't play with mortals. They have feelings; they are fragile. If they fly too close to our fire, they will burn."

A sour taste stained my tongue, and my mood darkened. After all the brightness and life Mila had brought, Ginger was determined to keep me in dourness. My shoulders sagged, but I still forced the words from my mouth. "Ginger, aren't you exhausted by this parade? This facade of who we are and who we aren't?"

"It doesn't matter what my sentiments are," she hissed. "It shouldn't matter to you either. We are above such mortal emotions. What happened when you went beyond? Did something change that you're keeping from me?"

Rubbing my temples, I sighed. The beginnings of a headache threatened to return. I needed to play to ease my discomfort. "I have to summon a spirit, a deadly one who will bind the King of Hearts. We have twelve months to either free ourselves or seal our damnation. But you know she will come for me and me alone. I can make it impossible to find you and the others. You can take them and flee."

Ginger was silent, although her chin wobbled just a moment before she jerked it up. "And go where without our leader?"

"You will have to be the leader. You have strength within you."

Ginger crossed her arms. "Another reason the mortal shouldn't be here."

"She has a name," I returned coldly. "Giselle and

Dusty are mortals, even Rachelle, although she has the bloodline and doesn't remember our other life nor wants to. Besides, we host mortals for months—"

"Rachelle will never ask questions because she's blind to it!" Ginger snapped. "The guests aren't here long enough to become aware, and none have seen the inner workings of the inn. Soon things will stop making sense, and she'll start asking questions. How do you intend to explain magic?"

"She's just like one of our guests and won't notice, but if she does, we can explain. She came here to pursue her passion for music. If some of the mystical leaks out, it will be fine."

Ginger snorted. "Keep telling yourself that."

"I will keep an eye on her too. This isn't always up to you, Ginger," I warned. "I have other duties she can perform with me."

Smirking, Ginger paced. "You'd like that, wouldn't you? Keep her close so you can flirt with her. Promise me this is only some minor attraction and you'll get rid of her at the end of summer. Three months is long enough; any longer and she'll grow accustomed to the magic here. And don't compare her to Giselle and Dusty. You are well aware they don't live in the house, and you do your best to keep them out."

Grimacing, I nodded, recalling Endia, our former

hostess. The story we spread was that she'd run away, but Ginger and I knew the truth. "I'll ensure she leaves. She has a mother and a sister in the countryside. I'm sure she'd like to visit them."

"See?" Ginger pointed a finger. "You said 'visit.' I mean 'leave.' Forever. If you get close to this mortal…so help me."

It was cruel, but to defuse her anger, I changed the subject ever so slightly. "I know what happened to your lover, and I'm sorry. But this will not be a repetition of what happened between you and him."

She scowled and went to the window, likely so I couldn't see her tears. "It's not the same. He wasn't mortal, and she is. Have your flirtation, but don't let it go beyond that, and make sure you're clear with her. I don't want to be left with the mess of a broken heart."

I closed my mouth, unable to make promises I couldn't keep. "Will that be all?"

"No," Ginger snapped, facing me again. Her eyes were dark, but otherwise, she'd recovered from her memory of grief. "There's a leak in the cellar that needs fixing, and Moses claimed he heard strange noises. It's worth a look if you aren't busy."

"Tomorrow. Tonight I have to…" I trailed off, unwilling to form the words.

"Yes, work for her. I hope you figure something out, Ezra, and quickly. We've been banished for a long time, and I don't like the constant threat of death hanging over my head."

Right. People were counting on me. It was more than my life at stake. Standing with sudden determination, I strode toward the door. "I need to relight the wards and make sure the guests are all inside and accounted for. We can't have any mistakes tonight."

Like a soldier preparing for battle, Ginger straightened, her defiance gone. "It shall be done."

BECAUSE OF GINGER'S CONCERN, I snuck to the cellar. The air was musty, damp, and I bumped against barrels of wine. When the slurping sound came, a tendril of fear wormed its way around my heart. That freakish sound reminded me of bloodsuckers. Listening, I waited for more, but the sound had ceased. Or perhaps it had been my wild imagination. In the cellar's dark, it was too easy to envision nightmarish incidents. Tree roots that came alive to choke one; bloodsuckers leeching life from flesh, turning one into a rotting creation of death; and worst of all, the evil spirits out for revenge.

Moving quickly, I slipped into the secret tunnel that connected the inn to my tower. The musty press of earth above me increased my pace. The dark was absolute, but I did not bother with lights, for I knew where the path ended. Even my staff found this route too creepy to walk, saying prayers against lost souls or grisly creatures from another portal. I was careful each time I opened and closed a portal, to ensure nothing but myself went through. But there were other masters who could unravel the strings of destiny and undo what I had done.

When I reached my tower, I retrieved my violin, fingers stoking the elegant neck. My heart pounded, but there was no other way. It had to be done. As I recalled the sorceress's demand, my decision firmed.

Returning to the tunnels, I continued further in, away from the lush pastures of my property and into the woods. Moonlight shone in a pale hue when I reached the shrine at the end of the tunnel. Long before my time, someone had built an altar, crowned with black candle wax and rotting vestiges of sacrifice: berries, twigs, leaves, and most disturbingly, bones. I imagined it had once been a place for human sacrifice, the remnants of an old religion where people believed giving a life would satisfy their gods and persuade them to be generous with their gifts.

Careful not to disturb the macabre treasures, I exited the moldering hut. The warmth of the night air was a relief after the stale musk of the tunnel, and I followed the sound of the waterfall to my familiar perch. After taking my violin from the case, I drew the bow over it, creating a long, sonorous tone. The air vibrated as the violin took a breath, its music pouring out, a powerful summons as long as my fingers played the correct notes.

My sense of right and wrong warred within me, something I was unused to but only because I did not wish to summon the spirit. I wondered if the sorceress could summon it herself and yet used it as a threat against me, for she did not want the stain of sin on her soul. Anger flared, but I forced it down, all too aware I needed to focus on the music in order to manifest my desires. I had to forget about my life before this hellish banishment, made gruesome by the tasks the sorceress forced me to perform in her name. But my former life was difficult to forget.

I played a few stanzas to warm up my fingers, the sound muted by the fall of water. Still, it was sweet and syrupy, my own peculiar magic.

My thoughts drifted back to before, when I'd been a knight who'd served the sorceress.

There were many of us under her beck and call, and we swore fealty and honor. We promised to obey, to protect, and one by one, we fell. It all started with the desire to be more than we should be, to possess the power the sorceress held. We experimented with magic we had no business playing with and used it to create. That desire was so potent it blinded us, led us astray, drunk with knowledge and magic.

I still recalled the first knights to disobey and their punishments. It should have been a lesson for me, but I wasn't like them. Foolishly, I believed my superior thinking and determination would save me. I wanted to create and not just see the plants grow and the flowers bloom. I wanted to make life, in my own image, in my own likeness. But knights were not meant to create life, and when my creation took a breath, the monster destroyed everything within reach. Only the sorceress could stop it, and she banished me for what I'd done—binding me to a tower, an inn.

The owner was dying and the buildings falling into disgrace. It was simple for I and my loyalists to take over and establish ourselves in a new world. The sorceress took away our magic except mine so I wouldn't forget. She still needed me, at least for a time, since I was the only one who could open portals into other worlds and travel between them.

But soon she'd found a replacement for me and taken the one thing I couldn't live without. My soul.

I'd get it back when I completed the work and summoned the demon. Only then would I be whole, complete, and mortal. The portals would close, the bonds would dissolve, and I would be free from her, free from magic, and forgiven for my transgressions.

MILA

Nerves consumed me the day of my first performance. I alternated between practicing and pacing, aware I'd never played for an audience before. Ginger had prepped me, telling me I'd be background noise and not to expect attention or applause. Still, I'd be the only one on that stage, though it was small.

A stool was placed upon it, and beside it was a little shelf with a glass of water. I'd play for a few hours, taking breaks between songs as needed. I took my seat long before the hall filled with guests, my instrument tuned and ready. Those who wished to dine in their rooms were given trays, but most came down to partake before slipping away.

My fingers trembled as I tucked the violin

beneath my chin. Taking a deep breath, I lifted the bow and closed my eyes.

The low murmurs of the hall faded, and I felt as though I'd been transported to a field of sunflowers, waving through the breeze while I stood among them and played. The sensation was so strong I smelled the grass, felt the warmth of the dirt between my bare toes and the breeze like fingers stroking my hair. I'd heard of the peak of performance, a Zen-like experience, and yet I'd assumed I wasn't good enough to achieve the heights of musical pleasure, to be so swept away. Reality faded. My fingers flew over the strings, and I moved the bow, the sound coming clear, enchanting.

Maybe it was the permission I had to be myself and play, but I continued, lost in music, a balloon of happiness spreading through me. Along with it came a faint awareness that something mythical about Lagoda empowered me to play better than I had before.

I had no idea how long I'd played until I opened my eyes and suddenly found myself back in the inn. I still sat on the stool, my chest rising and falling from the effort, and the room was full of guests. They talked and ate, and yet from somewhere came a smattering of applause, acknowledging that they appreciated my art. What had happened? Was my imagination that powerful? For no one had noticed anything unusual. They'd carried on, and yet time had stopped for me and I'd been elsewhere while I played.

Taking a sip of water, I reseated myself and lifted the violin again. And as I did, I caught a movement in a dusky corner. My eyes strained, searching, and sure enough there stood Ezra, arms crossed, watching. His face was shadowed, and it appeared as if he was attempting to hide, and yet he was there. That seed of desire sprouted, but I kept my composure, closed my eyes, and let the music take me again.

Later that night, Rachelle hugged me, saying she'd heard nothing like it. I assumed she was being kind as I fell into bed and slept deeply. When a dream came, it was vibrant and lifelike. I walked through a field of flowers, my fingers touching their upturned faces, until a hill led down into the forest. I stepped beneath the boughs, breathing in cedar and spice, and my heart thrilled with anticipation. Suddenly, two arms grabbed me. Hot lips seared mine, breath ragged against my neck, fingers impatient, insistent, tugging at my clothes. His emerald eyes and the passion in his demanding kisses made my heart throb. The want for him was so intense it choked me, and all I could do was moan under his touch, my skin on fire as he consumed me.

When I woke, the place between my legs ached. I lay in bed, relishing, reliving the dream because it solidified what was forbidden. I knew, deep inside, it would be best for both of us if I resisted, if I walked away from the sway of seduction. He was a stranger, and although I was curious about him, in three months I'd return to the city to play for the symphony hall. It would be better if we maintained a professional relationship. Once I got out of bed, I'd forget the dream and avoid him. Yet despite my decision, I lingered in bed, torn between getting up or touching myself to sate my arousal. My hesitation cost me. Shortly after I awoke, Rachelle knocked on my door.

After that, we fell into the rhythm of work, and days passed. I performed three nights a week, and with each performance, my confidence grew. The afternoons spent practicing were beginning to pay off, and my hopes for the future became surer.

The atmosphere of the inn shifted each day. Some guests stayed for weeks, others for a few days. No sooner did we learn the preferences and habits of one individual than another would come to replace them.

One morning, a troubled young woman swept in, curls wild, the hem of her dress soaked. She spoke to Ginger in a low, animated voice before going upstairs. Rachelle was busy seeing to the needs of another guest. So when Ginger came to me, I wasn't surprised.

"Lady Elodie would like a wine from the cellar. A dark red wine. Select a bottle and take it up her, will you?"

"Of course." I nodded, turning toward the kitchen.

"She's in room six," Ginger called after me.

I hadn't been in the cellar yet, and I'd forgotten anything lay beneath the main floor. All old houses had a cellar beneath to store food during the winter, although Solynn boasted food year-round. One could always go to the market or street vendors for a bite to eat.

Beyond the table and the lift was the door to the cellar. Leaving it open, I descended the stairs into gloom. Although torches hung on either side of the stairs, high above my head, they flickered unsteadily, casting menacing shadows on the walls. The air was musty with the scents of old berries and even older vegetables.

On the right side of the cellar, the walls were mud, cooler, I assumed, then the left side, which was made of brick. Shelves lined both sides, but I turned my attention to the wine. The first row had bottles, and I could just make out the pale sheen of liquid inside and guessed it was white wine. The next had bottles of red, and on beyond were barrels.

The entire inn must be completely self-sufficient. They grew grapes, had a grove of oranges, a vegetable garden, sheep and goats and chickens. I smiled, impressed, and my fingers closed around the head of a bottle.

A sound made me freeze. Holding my breath, I listened. A distinct splurging sound came from the darkness, where the light didn't shine. I squinted at the shadows, but the darkness was too dense. Holding the bottle carefully in both hands, I took a step, listening. Unease crept up my spine, and my mouth went dry.

I gave myself a shake. It was childish to be afraid of the dark when it was only the gloom playing tricks on me. A shadow flickered, a shape indistinct and unclear in the semidarkness moved a few paces ahead of me, and a sensation of cold made my fingers numb.

The sound came again. It was lapping or sucking, like a horse drinking from a watering trough. Except this time, it was much louder, as though whatever it was drew nearer. A faint hint of water and decay drifted to my nose, and my chest constricted as a shroud of fear enveloped me.

Instinct told me to run. I caught my skirts in one hand to keep from tripping while dashing back to the stairs. I took them two at a time, heart beating hard in my throat.

When I reached the top, the scent of cinnamon wafted to my nose, calming my initial fright. Peering back down the stairs, I saw nothing but the flickering lamps and the quiet shadows. What had frightened me? And what would make that sound in a cellar? I'd ask Giselle, who frequently made deliveries to the kitchen. She'd know more.

Closing the door, I spun around and practically bumped into Ezra. I hadn't seen him in a while and had thought my attempt to ignore him had been successful. But now, as I gazed up at him, my heart dropped and that desire sprouted again. "Mila?" His gaze shifted to the door, eyes narrowed ever so slightly. "I didn't expect to find you here."

Holding up the bottle of wine, I gave a shaky laugh. "Well, when a guest requests wine, I must comply."

"That's a good bottle. The guest will enjoy," he said, reaching around me to rest his hand on the doorknob.

He was close, too close. Ducking my head, I moved out of the way, wanting to linger but unsure what to say when I had a task to complete. Pointing to the door, I blurted out, "I heard strange noises down there."

He raised an eyebrow. "Like what?"

"A slurping sound, like a beast was drinking something."

I almost missed the flash in his eyes. It was there in an instant and gone the next. He pressed his lips together, and irritation crossed his face. “I’ll look. Sometimes the cat gets trapped down there.”

I opened my mouth to tell him I didn’t think it was a cat, but his odd expression made me change my words. “I hope it’s only the cat.”

A beat passed and stretched before I ripped my gaze away. On the other side of the wall, Moses whistled and Marley, large and silent, chopped.

Ezra opened the door to the cellar, and the musty air flowed in. I gave an involuntary shudder.

“Mila, will you have wine with me tomorrow evening?”

No. Wine with Ezra was dangerous, out of the question, but the idea was irresistible. “Yes,” I agreed breathlessly.

“Come up to my office on the fourth floor, just past the library.”

Nodding, I spun away, thrilled, before he could see the smile that crept across my lips. Ezra wanted to have wine. With me.

When I breezed back into the dining hall, Ginger looked up briefly from her papers, and her eyes narrowed as she watched me pass. Shaking off the odd sensation, I climbed the stairs to deliver the wine.

MILA

"When do you go to town for clothes?" I asked.

It was morning, early, before the guests were up, and I waited for Rachelle in the staff's lounge. She stumbled down the stairs, yawning and stretching. I couldn't remember if I'd heard her in her room the evening before.

Her eyes perked up. "Usually on slow days. I'll go with you because I want some new gowns too. Namen, the dressmaker, is skilled and fast. She makes the most splendid, exotic gowns, and Ezra worked out a deal with her. Because we work here, she gives us a discount."

Ezra. Of course. My blood warmed at the thought of him. "How generous. Will Ginger let us both off?"

Rachelle fidgeted with her thick braid. "I'll ask

her for an extended afternoon. The town is quaint, but I enjoy going."

I'd seen the town from a distance, a row of low-lying buildings, much smaller than Solynn, but I had yet to go myself.

"We'll meet all kinds of people," Rachelle continued. "Did you know Lagoda is known for breeding horses? On the other side of town, there's a pasture full of horses, another reason so many come to the inn."

"I heard it mentioned." I watched her, enjoying the rare moment of introspection from her.

Rachelle went on, her tone wistful, "I used to ride when I was young. My father bought me a pony, and I loved her. One day, he promised me when I was older, I'd get an actual horse. I wanted a stallion, big and proud, not one of those frightened mares. Gentle, yes, but what's the fun in that? I want a challenge, to learn to take charge of the reins and bend a wild stallion to my will."

"What happened?"

She shrugged, and the light went out of her eyes, replaced with that hazy, hollow look. "I was young. I don't remember. We lost everything, and so here I am..." She trailed off, bewildered, before giving herself a shake. "Come on, the bells will ring soon."

Spinning, she marched out of the lounge, ending our conversation. But I was grateful she'd shared, for she, too, had hopes and dreams. Now I understood her desire to marry a lord and gain a position of power, for it would allow her to choose her future instead of being a victim of fate. But why did she get that blank look when she recalled her past? I puzzled to myself as I followed her to the bar.

The day was a busy one, and I volunteered to help during the dinner rush. I took tea to Lady Elodie, who requested another bottle of wine. When I mentioned it, Rachelle volunteered to deliver it, and I let her, unwilling to repeat the discomfort I'd felt in the cellar the day before.

My stomach knotted in nerves as the evening hour approached and my meeting with Ezra drew nearer. I fidgeted with everything and even broke a mug while serving ale, spilling the brew across the bar.

Ginger's hand landed on the rag as I started to clean it up. "Go," she said. "You've worked enough today."

"Thank you," I breathed, grateful she made light of my mistake. Poking my head into the kitchen, I waved at Moses. "I've come for some supper."

"I've saved you a piece of pie," he called. "Have a seat. I'll serve you myself."

When I finished eating, I practically ran back to my room. Bursting in, I went to the wardrobe and studied the uniform black-and-white dresses inside.

They were all simple, none fancier than the other, but I wished I had something alluring to wear to impress Ezra. With a sigh, I stripped off my dress and went to the adjoining washroom to freshen up. At least I'd be clean and tidy.

Standing before the mirror, I brushed my silky hair, admiring the hues of purple. The climate in the mountains agreed with me, for my complexion was clear, almost glowing, and my hair was much easier to manage. There were no more tight knots or frizziness from the summer heat in Solynn.

Finally satisfied, I made way upstairs. I hadn't been to the fourth floor yet, and when I walked off the stairs, my eyes went wide. Lining both sides of the wall were paintings, depictions of varied landscapes in rich, contrasting colors. My rush to see Ezra faded as I stared, twirling to catch the beauty of each painting.

Personally, I'd never been to the seaside or seen the waves tinted coral in the glory of sunset before it faded, or the white sands, with a scattering of shells lining the beach. The wide sky was a concoction of colors, vivid blues and oranges and pinks so arresting it made my heart ache to see it in person.

Another painting captured a field, wild grasses bent over by the invisible wind while white flower petals twirled through the air, creating swirls and shapes as they went. Yet a third depicted a hazy forest, colors muted by gray mist. Shapes appeared behind the clouds, dancers in dresses, skirts and hair billowing, faces unseen. I had an uncanny feeling that if I saw their faces, they would not be what I expected. Something otherworldly, nonhuman.

The thought made me shudder, not with fright but curiosity. I wanted to know if the tales about odd creatures, strangers, and woodland folk were true. The next time I collected eggs from Giselle, I'd press her for more information.

Awed, and slightly giddy, I passed glass double doors that were slightly ajar. Shelves of books caught my eye, and the indistinct murmur of voices and the scent of cigar smoke drifted out. I'd found the library. Making note of that, I continued toward the forbidding door at the end of the hall. It was made of rich dark wood, heavy, I imagined, although it was cracked open. For me?

I lifted my fist, unsure whether I should knock or walk right in. Deciding to do both, I knocked and pushed at the door. Like I'd assumed, it was heavy, and the carpet below it slowed its progress. The air shifted, filled with hints of paper and ink and leather, along with candle wax and a faint note of citrus. My first glimpse was of open doors and a balcony, where that citrus scent drifted in. I was immediately conscious of how I shouldn't be there at all, how plain my dress was, and how rich and ornate everything that surrounded me was.

"Come in, Mila." Ezra's low voice drifted toward me. "I'll be but a moment."

Lingering in the entryway, I studied his office, my feet sinking into the carpet. To my right were two high-backed leather chairs and a rug in front of an enormous fireplace. There was no wood in it, only a collection of ash, since it was summer.

In front of me was an open space and a clear path to the balcony. To my left was Ezra's desk, made of a dark cherry wood, adding to the woodsy, manly theme of the room. Beyond it was a bay window that must overlook the driveway, with a cushioned seat, and on either side of it were shelves of books, scrolls, and loose papers.

A picture in a golden frame leaned against one wall, turned so I couldn't quite see it. Beside the desk was a statue of a creature playing a violin, a female, I thought, but it was hard to tell. I stilled at the sight of the violin, aware it meant something to Ezra, but what?

He finished his work and stood. "I'm sorry to keep you waiting," he said, crossing the room, toward me.

As he moved, I was aware of his height and, even more so, his presence, which filled up the room, reminding me I'd crossed into his domain. What was

I doing? There was still time to refrain from this inappropriate exchange, to quash the flirtation between us, but I wanted to know more about the man who'd given me the gift of music.

Ezra poked his head down the hall before closing the door. It gave a gentle click, and that very sound had a finality to it. Although it would be simple to open the door and walk out again, with my arrival, I'd crossed an invisible threshold. Going back was not an option.

"I'm glad you came," Ezra said, placing a hand on the small of my back to guide me to the balcony. "I selected some of my favorite wines, reds and whites. Do you have a preference?"

"Not that I know of." I shrugged, nervous, as we stepped outside.

The balcony was a semicircle, with a small table to the side of the door, and two chairs. It overlooked the gardens, just enough to see them, but the grove of orange trees blocked most of the view. Still, it was breathtaking, a kaleidoscope of green punctured by tangerine orange and lemon yellow.

He pulled out the chair for me. "Excellent. We can try a bit of everything. I often enjoy a glass after the day's work is done."

"Is that so?" Once I was sitting, my nerves lessened. "I'd imagine the work of an innkeeper is never done."

"Innkeeper, is that what you call it?"

"That's what you are, the owner of the inn?"

"Yes, but the keeper, I'm not as familiar with that term."

I raised an eyebrow as he uncorked a bottle of white and poured two glasses, half full.

"How could you be unfamiliar with that term?" I challenged.

"Well, that would be telling, wouldn't it?" He slid a glass in front of me. "Tell me what you think. It's medium-bodied, slightly tart even though it's fruity, and the finish should be buttery, almost like a sweet cream."

Lifting the glass, I peered over the rim at him. "Are you trying to avoid my question by explaining wine?"

There, that dimpled smile appeared again, making my insides flutter.

"Not at all, just attempting to make my guest feel at home."

I took a sip. He was right. It wasn't sweet, and yet I caught hints of pineapple and spice as it slid down my throat. Smooth. Creamy. Dangerous. Just like him.

The evening breeze ruffled my skirts, and I sat back, scrutinizing him. He was so handsome it hurt. The wind stirred his hair, his expression was shy, but the way his full lips tilted, displaying a hint of imperfection, made him even more attractive. I thought of his generosity and yanked my gaze away.

"Do you like it here so far?" Ezra asked. "I know it's only been a few weeks, but..."

"Yes, very much." Facing him, I took another sip. "I wanted to avoid the countryside because I assumed I wouldn't be able to play music. But Lagoda is enchanting, unlike anything I imagined. It's a lush paradise, and when I walk outside, I'm happy. I don't have to stare at ugly buildings or breath in tepid air. There is so much color here, and it's far from boring. I would have been restless at my sister's estate."

"Did you work in the city too?"

I knew he was just keeping me talking, but the wine surged through me, and my words flowed. "Yes, I worked for an herbalist in the market. Her eyesight was going, and I didn't mind the work, but her daughter came to live with her to take over the business. After my mother sprained her foot, the financial responsibility fell on my shoulders. We had the flat to pay for, the monthly rent, and food, and clothes..." I trailed off, assuming he didn't want to hear about my past troubles. "My sister invited us to move in with her family, but I wanted a chance to pursue music."

"How long have you played?"

"Since I was little. My grandfather taught me how

to play before he passed away." I smiled at the memory, my small fingers stumbling over the notes. "It was his violin I played at the audition, but it carries more sentimental value than actual use. I appreciate the new one."

"You play well," he praised me, his tone so low it was almost seductive. "The symphony did not give you a fair chance, and you've improved since you've been here."

I stared at him over the rim of the glass, tingling from his compliment yet eager to change the conversation. "Thank you for giving me a chance, but what about you? Where are you from?"

"Not here." He ran his fingers through his golden hair, ruffling it. After draining the last of his glass, he poured himself another. "Coming here has been an adjustment. The rules, the culture, it's all very different, but I wanted to create a haven to give guests a respite from their troubles."

"That's noble of you."

"No," he chuckled. "This place is too lovely to keep to myself."

"It is like a paradise. The paintings in the hall, do you collect them?"

His eyes brightened. "I do. Nature speaks to me, and I enjoy seeing it depicted in various ways."

"Is that what you do in your workshop?" I pressed. "Collect art?"

"No." His smile slipped a bit. "I don't have the talent to paint, aside from colors on a canvas, but I carve. There's something gratifying about taking a raw piece of wood and transforming it."

"I'd like to see your creations," I told him honestly, setting down my empty glass.

He leaned over to refill it. "More white? Or would you like to try a red?"

"I enjoyed this. More white, please."

He winked at me as he poured, and I laughed in return. The wine felt good, as did the conversation, a perfect cadence of back-and-forth. Tilting his glass to me as if in a toast, he took another sip. I grinned, and as I did, my hesitations faded.

We talked a bit more as the sky darkened. Lightning bugs came out, bright spots in the sky like stars, but the glow of light from the study kept us from sitting in pure darkness. It was pleasant and warm, and things awakened within me. I knew this: I wanted to explore it further.

"It's getting late," I said, draining my glass.

The buzz of wine filled me, and I was afraid I'd say or do something unforgivable if I kept drinking with him.

"Yes, may I walk you back to your room?"

"No." I half rose, feeling the room swirl ever so gently around me. "I'm fine; it's just down a few stairs."

“Oh, Mila,” he sighed, rising to help me stand.

I didn’t want him so near, and yet I could not resist. It took all my strength to pull back.

“We will do this again soon,” he insisted.

I couldn’t tell whether it was a request or a statement. “Yes,” I agreed. “Thank you, Ezra. You didn’t have to.”

“I know, but I simply do as I please.”

The enchantment ended as he guided me back inside, and I felt the loss of it keenly.

“I can walk you down. It’s no problem,” he said.

“Maybe next time.”

“All right then, good night.” Catching my hand, he pressed it to his lips before releasing me. “Until next time.”

MILA

The stairs creaked under my footfalls, and although the halls were lit, glimpses of the silver moonlight helped my passing. My thoughts flickered back to Ezra, and a tight ball of hope sat in my chest. I shouldn't hope, I shouldn't want, but I did, and it was mutual.

What, exactly, I needed or wanted from Ezra I did not have clarity on, but I couldn't help but feel a faint sense of guilt, reminding me not to rush into anything. My sojourn at the Dawn was only for three months, and the first month was almost over. I pushed away that thought, and as I did, Aveline's words drifted back to me: *You never know where you'll find love. It is beautiful, life-changing, better had for a little while than not at all…*

But this wasn't love, only a brief flirtation.

Reaching the main floor, I padded to the door that led into the staff lounge.

A sound came from behind me, a faint murmur but not a voice. I had the distinct feeling a presence watched me. I spun around fast. Pressing my back against the door, I peered into the shadows. Even the flickering lights did not fully illuminate the hall, and something, anything, could be out there.

My thoughts raced back to the slurping sound I'd heard in the cellar, and as if reacting to my fear, a shadow moved. It was a shape—I was sure of it—hulking, bent in half as though in pain. It moved, a dark blur, and my heart leaped into my throat. I burst into the lounge and closed the door behind me, tight.

Pressing my ear against the wood, I listened, determined to hold the door shut with my body. Why wasn't there a lock on this door?

The warm and friendly air of summer changed, and a foul coldness seeped around me. A distinct smell of decay made me wrinkle my nose. Why hadn't I taken Ezra up on his offer? If he'd walked me back to my room, I could have avoided this situation, or I would have felt safer if he had seen the shadow too.

I waited, but nothing chased me or tried to open the door. After a few moments, my racing heart rate slowed, and I doubted what I'd seen. Had it been my fanciful imagination? An effect of the decadent wine?

Letting go of the door, I backed away, waiting to see if anything would chase me. Nothing did. That eerily cold sensation faded, and I went up to my room, unable to shake the unease.

I peeked into Rachelle's room when I arrived. She'd left the door cracked, but her bed was empty. Again. Where did she go these evenings? It wasn't particularly late, but I wanted a word with a friend to ease my discomfort.

After closing all the doors, I locked my room and put on my nightgown. Pulling the covers over me, I lay still, but my mind would not relent. The slurping sound, the hunched, lurking shadow...was the paradise of the inn too good to be true? Was something else going on that I didn't know about? Eventually I drifted to sleep and dreamed of dark things.

OVER THE NEXT couple of days, the inn was busy, and I did not see Ezra again. I stayed away from the cellar, practiced violin, and limited my time alone after dark. I also studied Ginger and Rachelle for unusual behavior. If something malevolent dwelled in the inn, surely they would know. They both acted as if nothing was wrong. At least Rachelle did, but it was impossible to read Ginger. She brushed in and out, sharp-edged and abrupt, other times waving me away, giving me more time to myself. I recalled her words. We were staff, not servants; we weren't expected to work ourselves to the bone.

I wondered if those were Ezra's words, not hers as I speculated about her relationship with Ezra. He claimed she was his second-in-command, but why her? It wasn't jealousy, for the few interactions I'd seen between them had been stilted, almost hostile. What was the history between Ginger and Ezra? I resolved to find out.

On Tuesday morning I went to fetch the eggs. Rachelle was grateful I'd taken over that task, and I was growing used to Giselle. After lacing my shoes, I hurried down the stairs and slipped out the back door.

The sheep and goats had done their work, for the grass on either side of the path was short again. The animals grazed in the distance, balls of off-white fur and lumps of brown, moseying their way through the meadow. Humming a tune, I glanced at the tower, offset on the hillside, a lonely tribute.

Was Ezra there now, working on another carving? Or had he slept in his office? Innkeepers weren't rich, yet the paintings outside his office told the story of a wealthy gentleman. Next time I saw him, I'd ask about the carvings and the paintings. If my luck held, he'd invite me to his workshop. The thought made me smile, and my guilty conscience eased the more I entertained being in his presence.

I found Giselle in the barn. Just like Rachelle had said, one side was painted a bright red. The vibrant color made me smile as I moved to the open door, the scent of animals washing over me. "Giselle?" I called, poking my head inside.

"One moment," she hollered. "The cow is giving me some trouble."

A few moments later she appeared, carrying two pails, hay sticking out of her curls. She looked so funny I burst into laughter, clamping a hand over my mouth at the last moment. "I didn't mean to laugh at you," I apologized.

She smirked and set down the buckets. "Let me guess, I have hay in my hair."

I nodded.

"It's not the first time it's happened. That cow is temperamental." She jerked her chin over her shoulder and rolled her eyes. "Some days she gives me milk; others she wants to fight about it. She best give up, because I always win. You're here for the eggs."

It was more of a statement than a question, since I came for the eggs weekly. "Yes, and..." I twisted my fingers together, wondering how to word my question. "I'm curious about some things here. When we first met, you told me Lagoda is the land where strange things happen. Why is that?"

My mind went back to the slurping sound in the cellar, the shape in the dark, and the coldness that had accompanied both of them. I'd felt that oddness when I'd first arrived too but hadn't shared my hunches with anyone, afraid it might simply be my imagination.

Giselle grunted, folding her arms across her chest. "Most of it is talk, and I haven't seen anything to confirm, but often what happens to people is based on belief." Her face softened as she talked. "The Lagodians claim odd things happen here. According to legend, it all began when a flash of purple light illuminated the sky and a violet star fell onto the island in the lake. Some grew wealthy, some grew poor, and some people even disappeared. The theory is that something landed on that island, making the veil between worlds thin."

I listened to every word, still skeptical but aware that even superstitious talk might have a hint of truth in it. City folk claimed people who lived in the country were touched in the head. Their lives were so focused on survival—food, clothing, and shelter—that they worked until they were naught but skin and bones. That kind of hard life changed them, making them think of new ways to amuse themselves, and so the stories of the supernatural developed.

"What do you believe?" I asked.

Giselle narrowed her eyes, studying me. "I believe it's smart to keep an open mind, but tell you what. If you want to know more, come to dinner tonight."

My immediate reaction was to reject her invitation, but it wasn't my night to play, and I was curious about what else she'd tell me. "I'll come," I agreed.

Giselle's entire face lit up when she smiled. "Good, we eat a bit late, but come over when you're done at the inn."

I smiled back, grateful I was making a new friend. Taking the basket of eggs, I started back to the inn. The lake shimmered as I passed, the waters rougher this morning. I noticed the dock I'd overlooked before, for the way it was angled made it visible from the barn. It was a short strip of wood with a small boat tied up beside it, oars sticking out of the sides.

When I saw Ezra, my heart skipped. He was stripped down to his trousers and taking things out of the boat. Two enormous fish, almost as big as him, lay on the dock. Monstrous fish. I gaped, aware it would be polite to look away from his nakedness, but the sun made his skin dazzle in the light, and the sight of his toned body made desire twist within me.

I should keep walking before he caught me staring. Biting my lower lip, I quickened my pace, moving up the trail until he was out of sight.

"Mila?"

Turning around, I shielded my eyes against the sun. Had he seen me watching him?

Ezra strode toward me, tugging a loose white shirt over his toned chest. His eyes brightened as he overtook me. "Going up to the inn?"

"Yes." I held up the eggs. "It's Tuesday. Egg day."

"So it is," he said, taking the basket from me.

"I can carry it," I protested.

"I know," he retorted. "But just because you can doesn't mean you need to. I'm going up to the house anyway. I caught fish for the week, but I forgot the knives to debone them. I need to borrow a pair to properly gut and slice them up for Moses."

I stared up at him. "You catch fish for the inn too? Is there anything you can't do?"

"Yes," he laughed, "lots."

Somehow I doubted that, and my expression must have said so, for he went on, "This is my inn. I feel a duty to make sure it thrives in all areas. Which includes food."

"And what other things?" I pressed.

"Many things," Ezra said easily, his long strides slowing as he spoke. "Did you know there are four key categories to survival? Er, not survival but to living a well-balanced life. There's health, which is knowing where your next meal is coming from, having plenty of food and water, shelter, and safety. Then there's purpose or a goal, the knowledge that we are contributing to something vast. Leave someone alone for too long and they become bored, which leads to unhappiness and that never-ending sadness because something is lacking. There's the spiritual, a connection with something greater that is outside of ourselves. And finally, there is connection, usually through relationships, although it varies—family, friends…lovers."

He paused on that last word, drawing it out in such a way I could not mistake his meaning.

I sucked in a breath, determined to ignore the way my face warmed. "You've thought about this long and hard. You almost sounded like a philosopher."

"Are there philosophers in Solynn?"

Laughing at his surprise, I raised an eyebrow. "Still living? I don't know, but surely your early studies included some of their works. I'm no scholar, but even what I learned hinted briefly of the wisdom of philosophers, the meaning of life, the pursuit of happiness, and the hollowness of pleasure without a greater purpose or depth."

A faint blush rose on his face. "Like I said, I'm not as familiar with the customs here. I was raised far away, and what I studied and learned was different. I would like to know more about the philosophers here. If you tell me their names, I'll order some scrolls from the city."

Scrolls? "You mean books. Their words have been transcribed from ancient scrolls into books."

"Mm, of course." He was odd, in an endearing way.

"So the four categories of life, did you make that up on your own or is that common knowledge? Where you come from, of course."

"Is that a question, or are you teasing me again?"

I giggled; I couldn't help it. His presence surrounded me with lightness and ease. "I'm sorry, it's just sometimes the words you say sound outlandish and it amuses me."

"Does it?" He gave me his dimpled smile, and my heart melted.

As we arrived at the inn, a gray cloud passed over the sky, blocking out the light just for a moment. Ezra looked up, and alarm crossed his face, forgotten when he returned his gaze to me. "What are you doing tonight?"

"Giselle invited me to dinner, but—"

"Don't change your plans on account of me. Giselle and Dusty are excellent company. You'll enjoy your time. Come find me tomorrow afternoon, in the gardens."

"I will. If I can get away," I corrected, not wanting to appear too eager.

"If," he repeated.

Moving closer, he touched my hair and trailed one finger down my bare skin.

I shuddered under his touch, stepping closer, wanting more.

But just like that, he was gone, and I knew I'd go to the gardens tomorrow afternoon.

MILA

The sky was still bright with the afterglow of a storm. It had rained all day, a gentle mist coating everything in gray. A sensation twisted through me, that in the drizzle, without the sunlight, there was no knowing what moved out there. Fog descended, and I feared it would be impossible to find my way to Dusty and Giselle's hut. Right at the last moment possible, the sun came out, slicing through the mist like a blade and burning away the fog.

I stepped outside and took a breath of fresh air. It was damp, musty, smelling mostly of wet sheep with faint hints of floral and citrus. But the water shone like crystals on the grass, twinkling like gems. Tiny creatures whizzed back and forth, almost too fast for my eyes to see. Still, a fanciful thought came to mind, that they were miniature people who came to harvest the raindrops.

Shaking that thought away, I made my way to the hut.

Before I could knock, the door swung open, and Giselle waved me inside. "You came!"

"The rain stopped just in time," I said, eyes darting across the hut.

It was one wide room, the stone fireplace at one end, with a black pot simmering over it. The rich scents of food and spices made my mouth water. A square table set for three sat in front of the fire, and a bright-yellow rug covered the floor. A multicolored quilt blanketed the bed, which was tucked into the opposite corner. Two rocking chairs sat under a window along with a shelf of books and several projects—knitting, woodworking, quilting—stacked neatly in baskets. It was simple, a melody of love, and my heart stilled.

In Solynn the poor coveted the estates for the expansive rooms full of luxuries, but the one-room hut was simple and yet fuller than any estate. I sensed the aura, peace and joy.

Giselle beamed. "It's not much, but we need little, since we're outside most of the time. This keeps us warm during the winter and gives us a cozy place to sleep away from the elements."

"Oh, I think it's perfect," I told her truthfully. "In

the city people believe they need so many things, but here, I can feel the happiness in this place."

"Can you? See, I knew I liked you." Giselle grinned. She'd changed into a light-blue dress, and her red curls were loose, dancing about her shoulders. "Dusty will be in shortly, just went to check that the animals are secure. It gets quite dark out once the sun goes down, so we both agreed we'll walk you back after supper. Besides, I enjoy a moonlit stroll."

"That's kind of you. I accept," I said, feeling even more at ease.

"Have a seat. Supper's almost ready. Ezra went fishing today and brought us a large one. I've been letting it simmer all day long with vegetables and spices."

"You cook too?"

"I do a bit of everything, but Dusty and I share the cooking. He has his family recipes, and I have mine. Somehow it just doesn't turn out right unless we personally make them."

I took a seat at the table, watching the embers around the fire. A loaf of round bread sat in the middle. It looked like the ones Moses had made. "Can't you get food from the inn?"

Giselle laughed as if I'd said something funny. "Moses is too generous, but we like to have our own food here too. No one can make bread like he does, though, when he has a mind to do it. Sometimes we go to town. Have you been yet?"

"Not yet. Rachelle is going to take me to the dressmaker. I want some nice clothes that aren't for work."

"Oh, Namen is excellent. She'll treat you well, and she's fast. She always gets it in her head you'll need something fancier than you think you do, but she's right. She has the sight, you know." Giselle tapped her head.

"As in she can see the future?"

"Not the future, but she has a hunch about clothes, and you'd be best to follow her advice."

"I'll keep that in mind."

The door opened, and Dusty came in. After taking his hat off his head, he hung it on a hook near the door that also had coats and scarves, with boots sitting below it. "Welcome, Mila," he called, his face ruddy from being outside. "I brought some elderberry wine. Would you like some?"

"Yes, I'm not picky."

"Good." He wiped his hands and ambled across the room to give Giselle a kiss on the cheek. "This bottle was made right here in our own vineyard."

After going to the cupboard, he poured each of us a generous serving of wine, while Giselle dished up bowls of steaming fish stew. It simmered in a red sauce, with chunks of white fish floating in it, surrounded with mushrooms and round cherry tomatoes. All the food in Lagoda tasted far better than the food in the city. Was it the air, the freshness, or something else?

We ate and drank heartily, laughing and talking until my skepticism about them faded. It was a refreshing change from the inn and quite different from my time spent with Ezra. I thought of him briefly, wondering what he would have invited me to do tonight. As my thoughts drifted to him, I steered the conversation in that direction. "How do you know Ezra?"

Dusty wiped his mouth with his napkin and folded it on the table. "I do a bit of woodworking, more as a hobby than anything else, but I know wood. One day, Ezra came looking for a specific piece for his collection. We started talking, and next thing I knew, he was telling me about the inn, the property, and how he needed help working the land. He shared his vision for the orchard, the gardens, the vineyards, and it sounded like an ideal opportunity."

"Just like that, you decided to work for him?"

"We did." Giselle nodded, beaming at Dusty. "I was making quilts back then, selling them at market along with Dusty's wooden creatures. He was a woodsman. It was good work, honest, but not what we wanted to do. Ezra's invitation to work the land came both as a challenge and something we'd dreamed of doing. At the time, we were saving up to buy land, and I wanted a larger garden. Then we came here. With the lake, the barn, this hut, and the big house up the hill, it's everything we dreamed of."

I watched them hold hands at the table, grinning at each other. My eyes misted over with wistfulness. Since I'd grown up without a father, it was rare for me to see acts of love between partners. Ezra had helped them realize their dream, and unexpectedly, my thoughts went to Rachelle. She had goals and was unwilling to talk about them. Life, in all its beauty, was about work and chasing a whimsy that could never be achieved. Yet Dusty and Giselle were happy, living their dream every single day.

"How long have you been here?"

"Hmm…five or seven years." Dusty shrugged. "I can't rightly recall. It took a few years to figure out the rhythm, to get the garden growing, purchase livestock and plant the vineyard, but now it's second nature. We've got to get another cow and perhaps in time, raise some horses and give the other horse breeders in the valley some competition."

"What about Ginger? Has she always been here?"

"As far as I can tell," Giselle puzzled. "I don't know her very well. She likes to keep to herself, but she does a good job running the inn."

I had to agree, but it was odd that Giselle and

Dusty, who had been there for years, didn't know very much about her. "Where did she come from?"

Giselle gave Dusty a confused look before turning back to me. "I don't know that either. My guess is she has a past she doesn't like to talk about and she's afraid of getting too close to anyone."

Nodding, I voiced my other thought. "What about Rachelle? How long has she been here?"

Giselle shrugged. "She and Ginger have always been here. I admit, when we first arrived, I mistook Ginger for Ezra's wife and Rachelle for his daughter."

A chill went through me at her words. Wife. Daughter. But Ezra was so young.

Seeing my expression, Giselle laughed. "I was wrong though. Ezra's always been single, a bit of a loner but a hard worker."

I let out the breath I'd been holding. "What about the woman who was here before me? The one who ran away?"

Giselle exchanged a glance with Dusty. "Should we tell her?"

He went to the fireplace, retrieving a pipe and tobacco from the mantle. "Might as well," he said quietly.

Giselle leaned back in her chair. "Remember how I told you strange things happen here?"

I nodded once, doubts swirling.

"Well, I don't think she ran away; that's only the official story. I think something happened to her. Her name is…was…Endia, and I hope, if she's still alive, she found a better place. Shortly after we moved here, she arrived, fleeing from an abusive family. At first she was shy and quiet, but as she worked, she blossomed. She was animated, dedicated, and she didn't want to leave. I don't believe she left willingly, because she told me a hundred times how happy she was to have found the Dawn and how much she enjoyed spending time with the guests."

A wistful look crossed Giselle's face, and I imagined that they'd been close.

"Did she play an instrument?" I asked.

"No, but she was the kind of person everyone loved."

Odd. Since Rachelle had never mentioned her. I settled back while the scent of tobacco wafted through the cottage. Taking another sip of the crisp wine that tasted rather like berries, I asked, "Why do you think she didn't run away?"

"Something scared her," Dusty spoke up. "In the days before she disappeared, she came here often, talking about shadows in the dark, someone stalking her in the inn, and…what was the other thing she always said?"

Giselle snapped her fingers, trying to recall. "Ah, it was the air. She was always cold."

I swallowed hard. Shadows. Stalking. Cold. Pushing away uneasy thoughts, I pressed for more information. “Did you believe her? Did you ever see lurking shadows?”

Pressing her fingers to her lips, Giselle shook her head adamantly. “That’s what’s odd about it. We’ve been here for so long we’d know if something unusual was happening. I feel terrible we weren’t able to help her, and I still want to know what happened to her. There were no clues, and with the work here, we searched as long as we could without finding answers.”

A knowing gripped me. An unsolved mystery was here, and suddenly I wanted to find out what had happened to her, for I had similar inklings and I wanted to know why.

“I’d like to help, if I can,” I offered, aware the warmth of the wine in my belly made me brave.

Giselle waved her hand. “That’s kind of you, but there’s no need. It’s over now. Tell us more about Solynn, your mother and sister, and your love for music.”

And just like that, the threads of the unknown slipped away, and I spoke about my familiar past. Dusty filled our glasses with wine, and our conversation turned round and round, as if to avoid the solemnness of a missing woman.

Time slipped away, and as the scent of tobacco

was faded, I realized the lateness of the hour. "I should get back." I rose, although the wine had made me tipsy, and I wanted to curl up with a blanket and close my eyes.

"Goodness me, is that the time?" Giselle asked, peeking out the window.

"I'll get the lantern," Dusty offered.

The three of us stepped outside under the silvery glow of moonlight. It cascaded about us, white and radiant, as if I was in a fairytale.

"If you aren't playing, come with us to the harvest festival," Giselle said. "The dance takes place outside, under the moon."

"I'd like that," I said, although at that point, I would have agreed to anything.

As we crested the hill, the inn lay before us, a dark shape the moonlight was unable to penetrate. Dusty and Giselle took me right up to the door that led to the lounge, and I was grateful they'd walked me back. Crossing the meadow by the light of the moon sounded magical, but not alone. Unlocking the door, I turned back to them. "Thank you for a wonderful evening."

"Our pleasure." Giselle grinned.

"Come back anytime," Dusty agreed, touching a hand to his cap.

I slipped inside, then peeked through the window

as they walked off, hand in hand, across the moonlit field.

A sigh of contentment filled my heart as my feet carried me up to bed, and this time, there were no dreams to haunt my sleep.

MILA

I didn't realize how late I'd stayed up until Rachelle shook me awake. "Come on, sleepy-head. What were you doing last night?"

"Dinner with Dusty and Giselle," I told her, yawning and stretching.

"You actually enjoy hanging out with them?" Rachelle asked skeptically.

"I do. They have marvelous stories to tell from before they came here, and legends from the countryside. Besides, they are creative and happy. I've never met a couple like them. Most people give in to arguing and complaining, but I haven't heard them share an unkind word."

Rachelle frowned. "After one night, I suppose not. They were probably on their best behavior for you. Everyone is good at pretending in front of others."

"Is that what you think?" I asked calmly, combing my fingers through my tangled hair. "Everyone is pretending?"

"They do it for different reasons, to hide their vulnerabilities, to appear smarter, more confident, prettier, skillful. There are lots of reasons to pretend everything is good when it's not."

She scurried away to finish dressing. I pondered her words as I got ready for the day, noting the slump of her shoulders, the lethargic unease she moved with. Something was wrong, prompting her words. Perhaps she was the one who was only pretending today. A silent cry for help.

Once I was ready, I went to her door. "What's wrong, Rachelle? Did someone make you unhappy?"

Rachelle slumped on the bed, and her face crumpled. "It's all my fault. If I tell you, you'll think so little of me."

"I promise just to listen," I assured her, sitting beside her. I had no room to judge, and no matter what she said, I resolved to keep my thoughts to myself.

"There's a man who comes here every year, right around spring and summer. I...I got to know him, and he promised to take me with him to the city. A few days ago, he told me he needed money. I guess I thought he was a man of his word and that because we were lovers, he wouldn't trick me." She stared at her hands. "I didn't love him. I just thought he could give me a different life and I wouldn't have to be here all the time. It turns out he already had a wife and child, and his stallion threw him on his way home. He's dead, the money is gone, and…I'm stuck here."

My heart thumped in my chest, and a thousand thoughts rushed through my mind. It was a tale I'd been warned against time and time again. But Rachelle was alone. She didn't have anyone looking out for her to warn her against those who sought to take advantage. Taking her by the shoulders, I looked her in the eye. "Rachelle, you were tricked, and that is nothing to be ashamed of, but I'm sorry. I'm deeply sorry this happened to you."

She sniffed, then fell into my arms with a sob. "You're sorry? If I'd told Ginger, she would have scolded me. I knew it was a stupid risk, but I wanted, and I will always want, more."

"It's not a terrible thing to want more."

"I was going to be gone by the end of the summer, and now look where I am, without the money I've stored up. I'll have to stay here forever."

"Maybe not forever. Maybe another opportunity will arise."

Reaching for a handkerchief, Rachelle dried her tears. "Maybe, but doubtful. There aren't many opportunities for young women who are alone in the world. You ought to know that. Look at you and me and Ginger, alone, working in an inn. Not everyone has a happy ending like Dusty and Giselle."

Her last words rang out bitterly, and I realized it was jealousy. Giselle and Dusty had achieved the dream. The rest of us, well, we were still searching for ours. I wanted to do something to help Rachelle, but I didn't know what.

"Come on, then." Rachelle wiped her eyes. "Let's go before Ginger comes looking for us."

From breakfast through lunch, Rachelle pretended everything was fine, although now and then, a vacant look came over her eyes. I didn't know how to comfort her, and my questions concerning Endia were not appropriate to bring up, especially considering the fact a man was dead.

When Ginger dismissed us for the slow afternoon, Rachelle quickly disappeared. I considered following her. Yet the tantalizing idea of meeting Ezra in the garden was too tempting to ignore. If I were wise, I would go to the library or elsewhere, but Ezra's presence made me feel euphoric.

As I opened the gate, my eyes were drawn to the flowers, which shone more vibrant than before, and the greenery seemed bigger since last night's rain. I caught a flash out of the corner of my eye as something thumped to the ground in front of me. A round fruit rolled to a stop at my feet like a gift. Picking up the fruit, I craned my neck back. One of the trees was heavy with rich, ripe oranges, and its branches hung low over the gardens' entrance. I breathed in citrus, realizing that scent would always remind me of Ezra. Holding the orange, I strolled the path, searching for him.

Visibility was limited by the green bushes that grew taller than me, but otherwise, the wide path was peaceful. Eventually I came to a fork in the road. Unsure which way to go, I randomly selected the left path. The gardens were more of a maze, each corner revealing more exotic flowers. Although I enjoyed their beauty, my heart sank as I peered around each curve and did not see Ezra. Was he in the gardens this afternoon, or had he been called away on business?

Swallowing my disappointment, I slowed my pace as the path ended in front of a pond. The blue-green surface rippled as ducks floated across it, bobbing underwater to eat. Weeping willows gathered around the far bank, some with their roots sticking out of the mud. Sure enough, an ivory swan perched among the willows, black eyes watching to ensure no one would come near her treasures. Lily pads floated on the pond's surface, with white-and-pink blossoms. A frog hopped off one, creating a tiny ripple in the water. The scenery was charming, idyllic, and the bench in front of the pond encouraged me to rest before returning to the inn.

"Hello," a husky voice called.

Eyes wide, I spun around, relieved as Ezra walked out from the path I hadn't taken. He carried a basket full of oranges, and as he neared, I saw his eyes were red-rimmed, as though he hadn't slept.

Tongue-tied by his sudden appearance and my potent relief, I waved. "Hi."

Holding the basket higher, he explained, "The oranges are in season, and I was picking some for tomorrow's breakfast."

"I found one on my way here." I held it up.

"If you found it, it's yours to keep. Will you sit with me?" He gestured to the bench.

"That's why I came," I quipped playfully.

His eyes brightened as we sat, although a proper amount of space remained between us. "How was supper with Giselle and Dusty?"

"Wonderful," I told him earnestly. "As you said, they are delightful. I hope they invite me again, after I catch up on sleep." I suppressed a yawn.

Ezra chuckled. "They do like to stay up late, talking."

I wondered if it would be appropriate to bring up Endia, but my bravery faded. "Giselle and Dusty also told me you invited them to come work here, and as it turns out, they'd always hoped to do exactly what they are doing. How did you know?"

Cocking his head, he gave me a sly look. "I told you before, I can sense people's desires. Besides, I like them. They make me feel comfortable."

Right. The odd thing he did. I wondered if he could sense my desire for him, and my cheeks warmed at the thought. Swallowing hard, I considered asking him about Ginger, but it seemed too intrusive, so I hurried on. "This morning I had a brief conversation with Rachelle. Her spirits are low…"

"Yes, she is sad."

I wasn't surprised he knew that, but was relieved I didn't have to explain further. She trusted me with her secret, and I did not want to break her trust by sharing with him what had happened. "I want to cheer her up, although I don't know her very well. All I know is that she likes horses."

"Hmm. I'll think of something. Dusty mentioned breeding horses, and while I don't think we have the space for it, we could take on a few more. I'll speak to him about it."

"Thank you," I breathed. It would be delightful to see Rachelle smile again without having to pretend. Although a horse was no substitute for the city, perhaps she could get what she wanted by staying in Lagoda.

"What about you? Are you happy here? Do you have any needs? Wants?"

How could I tell him what I desired? I had clothing, food, shelter, and music. I wasn't sure if he wanted an actual request or if he was humoring me. "I'd like to visit your workshop sometime and see what you do there."

Ezra said nothing for a long moment, and his expression was still as if he was turning over my simple request.

I opened my mouth to take it back and then paused, letting it hang between us. I'd crossed a line, I was sure of it.

"It's not that I don't want you to come to my workshop; it's simply that I'm not sure if I'm ready to be perceived in that way. The closer people get to me, the more their opinions shift and change. I'm not like most people, and it comes out in my work."

His voice was low, steady, and when he looked at me, his eyes were a shade darker. I wanted to tear my eyes away, but his gaze held mine.

"Mila, I like you. I want to get to know you, and I want to spend more time with you. But some of the heavier aspects of myself I'm not ready to reveal. Not yet. The time will come."

"What are you saying?" I whispered, not daring to look away. His words gave me hope, and yet his secrets dashed it away.

With a sigh, he stared off at the pond, then rose.

My fears surged. He liked me, but he wasn't willing to share. He liked me, but he wanted to keep me in the dark, to pretend.

He knelt in front of me, knees in the dirt, and took my hands in his. The sun gleamed on his golden head, and my breath caught. He was handsome in an otherworldly way, the set of his jaw, his sensual mouth. I had the sudden compulsion to lean in and kiss him, to feel his lips against mine and his hand, warm and strong, around my waist, embracing me. Could he sense those wants?

"Mila, this inn has given me the chance to do something new. I named it the Dawn because it's like being reborn, a second chance at life to do things right, and I don't want to ruin it by introducing all the layers of myself to you too quickly and frightening you away. I don't know you well yet, but from what I've seen, you have a kind and generous soul, you're curious, you make me laugh, and I appreciate your honesty. I also sense you are bold and not afraid to ask for what you want. One day, I'll take you to the workshop and let you see through the lens of my art, my craft. But for now, I just want to talk to you, to show you. Will it be enough?"

My voice trembled when I spoke. "Yes, it will be enough."

His shoulders relaxed, but instead of letting me

go, he turned my hand palm up in his and pressed his lips against the inside of my wrist.

A thrill shot through me along with the faint memory of my dreams of him. Strong hands encircling my waist, impatient fingers unraveling clothes, hot and heavy kisses in the woods. My entire body shuddered, wanting that dream to be real, craving his warm mouth against my skin again.

"You are quite lovely, Mila," he murmured. "I want to be worthy of you."

With those cryptic words, he stood and released my hands.

I wanted him to stay, to say more, but words would not come. He smiled at me, although I detected sadness in his eyes.

"The orange harvest is this week. I've hired a few lads from the village to help with it, but after, I want to spend time with you. We'll make a day of it, go out on the lake, pack a picnic, and I'll show you this place."

"I'd like that," I told him, standing.

He ran a hand through his hair. "I'll find you soon," he promised and left.

MILA

I slept poorly that night, my mind awake, puzzling over what had happened in the gardens. Suddenly a rush of strings filtered to my ears, as though the sound was lured by the wind, to my window. Pushing back the covers, I tiptoed on bare feet to the window and opened it. My view overlooked the rotunda, and the night air was crisp, as it often was in the foothills. Hot, summery days cooled by the balmy breeze of night, almost enough to make one shiver.

Hints of cedar drifted to my nose, odd, as if it was a smell from somewhere else. There were no notes of fruit or the sweet fragrance of flowers, just some haunted tune being played and the night gathering around to amplify it.

Closing my eyes, I listened to the lonesome song

continue, a series of notes played on a violin, frantic and reverent. The pace quickened, the song increased, and the tempo made me want to sway. It wasn't a song to dance to, for it was too wild. It was a call, a summoning, as though it was attempting to waken something buried deep and bring it to life again.

The song paused, and I opened my eyes, as if seeing would allow me to hear more. Something moved, flickering in and out of the pale light. I leaned further out, hoping to glimpse the violinist. Instead, a shadow stepped from the trees. It was just a shape, hunched over, sinister, and suddenly the air went icy. I trembled as the shadow moved, somehow staying out of the patches of moonlight as it walked through the trees. A vile odor filled the air, the scent of death, decay, and my heart leaped into my throat.

I stared, unable to look away as the form slithered, drifting into a grove of trees, and did not reappear again. My hands shook violently as I yanked the window closed and pulled the curtains tight. Pressing a hand to my mouth, I stopped the cry of hysteria and took a deep breath. It was nothing, just my imagination. A guest or one of the staff was out on a midnight walk, and the darkness made it impossible to see clearly. That was all. I should go to sleep. Evil did not exist here; nothing was haunting the inn.

But each time I closed my eyes, I saw the hunched shape again, felt the cold air, and smelled that foul scent. I couldn't help but think of Endia and what had happened to her. What if something ominous and evil was out there? What if it had taken her?

FOR THE NEXT FEW DAYS, I couldn't shake the sensation that something was wrong. But the rhythm of the inn continued despite my trepidation. A few new lads were staying at the inn to help with the harvest of oranges. The ripe fruits were everywhere, sent up to the guest rooms on trays, an enormous basket planted in the staff lounge. More were stocked in crates and loaded into wagons to be taken to the city. It was smart of Ezra to have so many avenues for revenue.

The sweet fragrance should have made me happy, but all I recalled was that dark shadow. Briefly my thoughts went to Mother and Aveline, but I decided against writing them a letter with my frightened notions. While I wanted their advice, they could do little to comfort me from afar. Besides, nothing had happened to me, just fears that were all in my mind.

At last the weekend came, and Rachelle and I went to town to visit the dressmaker. Giselle came with us, driving the wagon, but an awkward silence stretched because of Rachelle. I felt I couldn't speak plainly in front of her, and Giselle hummed in peace, either ignoring or oblivious to the tension.

The town was less than an hour from the inn, a fair bit to walk but nothing to the horse's quick trot. Like Rachelle had mentioned, it was two intersecting streets with rows of buildings. It was quaint, small, and not for the first time, I wondered why the inn was so set apart from it.

The buildings were old and weather-stained, but the dressmaker shop was a spot of bright color, almost as if it did not belong. Giselle pulled up in front of the shop. "I'll be back in a couple of hours," she called before clicking her tongue behind her teeth and setting off again.

I vaguely wondered what she'd be doing, but Rachelle tugged at my arm, pulling me inside.

I'd been in dress shops in Solynn, ladies fussing at one another, yards of fabric everywhere, and dresses hanging up showing off the latest fashions. In contrast, here a small woman sat behind a table, needles sticking out of her mouth as she sewed. Her dark eyes studied us as we entered, and then she rose. She was old and wrinkled, with golden-brown skin and a tight bun of midnight-black hair pulled back from her face. I guessed her to be close to Mother's age.

"Ladies, what can I do for you?" she asked.

"This is Mila. She's been at the inn a month but needs new clothes," Rachelle said. "I've returned to pick up clothing and request a few new pieces."

At that, the dressmaker came from behind the table and assessed me, her beady eyes roaming up and down my body. "Namen," she announced. "It would be an honor to create a wardrobe for you. I have just the thing that will go well with your luscious hair."

"It's a pleasure," I told her, wondering if she could see what clothing I should buy. I wanted to say more, but Namen turned away.

"Rachelle, welcome back. I made some alternative pieces for you, and before you protest, take them. I sent the bill up the hill, and Ezra has agreed to pay it."

Rachelle blushed, flattered, not embarrassed.

"Same for you." Namen wagged her finger at me. "I make. You take. Don't worry about the price. Now stand here while I help Rachelle."

She went to a curtain that separated the room, and waved Rachelle back. I waited while they talked, Namen scolding yet motherly, Rachelle with a tremor of excitement in her tone.

After a while, it was my turn to go behind the curtain.

It was a bright room with lots of windows.

Instead of asking me what I wanted, Namen walked around me, taking measurements, asking me to hold my hands up and shaking her head fiercely when I tried to speak. She wrote notes on a pad of paper, my name scribbled at the top with the numbers I assumed were my measurements.

"You work at the Dawn," she stated.

I nodded, almost hesitant to speak in her presence.

"But you have enough work dresses, yes?"

My face warmed under her assessment. "Yes, I have work dresses. I'd like something to wear when I'm…not working."

Namen arched an eyebrow. Her shrewd eyes missed nothing. "After work, hm. To impress a man, no doubt."

"Something comfortable," I said quickly, "that is nicer than my work clothes."

"And a dancing dress too," she agreed. "Leave it to me. You shall be stunning." She waved a hand at the piles of material behind her. "Purples and blues will suit you, perhaps some red, a hint of yellow, ah, and gold embellishments."

"Nothing too extravagant," I told her, not wanting her to send an absurd bill to Ezra. I'd have to ask Rachelle more about paying for the dresses and whether it came out of our wages.

Namen winked at me. "Let me do my work. Now go and come back in one week."

Pressing my hands together, I moved to leave, when something else caught my eye. Little golden statues sat at the corners of the room, each one holding a different instrument. Their features were marred, as though the designer had put little thought into anything other than the instruments. One played a violin, another a piano, the third a harp, and the fourth a flute. "What are those?"

Namen followed my gaze, and for a moment, her face brightened in surprise. I wondered if anyone had taken an interest in her for who she was beyond a skilled dressmaker.

"Gods of the seasons." She pointed. "Spring, summer, fall, winter."

I followed her finger. Spring was the flute, summer the harp, fall the violin, and winter the piano. Interesting. I knew nothing of those gods. Perhaps another folktale?

"What about the instruments they play? What meaning do they have?"

Namen studied me out of narrowed eyes. "Do you not know the histories?" She snorted in disbelief. "The gods use their instruments to change the weather and call forth the blessings of each season. If you are curious, you should read more or listen to your elders."

I stared at the statues again. For some reason, I sensed there was something I should know. “Will you tell me about them?”

“No time now.” Namen waved her hand. “Ask when you return, or speak to Giselle. She knows the truth.”

Giselle, who was friends with everyone and knew everything. I determined to ask her as soon as possible.

MILA

Rachelle was wandering about the store when I reappeared, fingering different materials, a smile on her face. She seemed happier than earlier, as if new clothes were a momentary distraction.

She smiled as we left. "Isn't Namen great? I mean, she's a little strange, but the clothes she makes are lovely. I'll have to send all mine back though. She made evening gowns and riding outfits, all clothes meant for a grand lady. I guess I hoped that because she was making them, I'd become that lady, but now I'm just here." She shrugged.

"Maybe you will," I suggested, well aware of the dangers of planting false hope. "Is it common for Namen to do what she wants without input from you?"

"Yes, and you'll love everything she makes you."

"What about the bill? Does it come out of our wages?"

Rachelle bit at her bottom lip. "I don't recall. I never pay much attention."

Nodding, I decided to ask Ginger. It would be less awkward than asking Ezra. Besides, it was Ginger who ran everything, and with that thought, a thread of unease shivered down my spine. I had a hunch that the key to finding out more about Ezra included Ginger. She was some sort of unmovable force in his life, but her importance and the reason were impossible to gauge.

Giselle pulled up just then, the wagon empty, all smiles. "Productive morning?" she called.

"Very," Rachelle responded.

We clambered into the wagon and started back to the inn. When we arrived, Dusty came around to take the wagon back to the carriage house, and Rachelle drifted away. I tried to catch sight of the workers in the grove, but it was difficult to see them through the trees.

"You've been thoughtful." Giselle nudged me.

"I have a lot on my mind," I told her.

"I'm always open to talk. In fact, why don't you come to the vegetable garden? I have some new seeds to plant and could use some company."

"I'd like that," I said immediately.

"As long as you don't mind getting dirty," Giselle said.

"I'm not afraid of hard work," I told her.

I'd walked past the vegetable garden countless times but had never been inside. Rows of vegetables poked up, some shooting taller than me. We passed rows of golden corn, and I imagined playing hide-and-seek in them. That was what Aveline and I would have done when we were young. I'd never been remorseful about my upbringing, but as I walked past the green tomatoes and the vines of peppers, I wondered what life would be like in the countryside for children. There were places to run and play without being stifled inside, waiting for the next outing.

Giselle knelt beside a bare patch in a far corner and patted the freshly tilled dirt. "Look at that," she said. "Dusty already tilled it for me."

A wheelbarrow sat beside the patch, full of tools and brown shapes with white roots.

"Potatoes," she explained. "They grow all the time, but I figured it would be good to plant them later this year, in time for winter. No one wants to eat potatoes all summer, and they are a hearty food."

I recalled winters with potatoes and how Mother would make them in different ways. If one got creative, there were plenty of ways to make filling meals from soups, a hearty baked potato, or mashed potatoes to go with a portion of meat or fish.

"We'll just bury each one in the ground, cover it with a mound of dirt, and that's it. I'll come around and water them later, since the sun looks like it wants to stay out all day today." Giselle plucked a root from the wheelbarrow and buried it. Soon her hands were covered in dirt up to her wrists, but she didn't seem to mind.

I joined her, working quickly. It was hard work but rewarding, since I knew I was contributing to the garden. Butterflies hovered around us, and the humming of bees pollinating the flowering vegetables was comforting. Occasionally a breeze blew, lifting the sweat from my neck.

"What's on your mind?" Giselle asked gently. "You're a bit more skittish than normal and constantly looking over your shoulder. Has anyone harmed you?"

Was it that obvious? "No," I blurted out. "Nothing like that. I saw someone walking through the orchard in the middle of the night. There are so many guests it's hard to keep track of them all, and someone I don't know could have curious habits." I tried to shrug it off, for that was the story I was sticking to. I wasn't like Endia; I wasn't seeing things that should not be. "When I was in the dress shop, I saw statues, and Namen told me they all have stories, the gods of the seasons. Is that another legend?"

Giselle sat back on her heels and wiped her forehead with the back of her hand, leaving a smudge of dirt behind. "Yes, it is an old tale. The gods come at the turn of the seasons to play music that inspires nature to change. When the world was young, the gods did so freely, coming to this land to play the music that would sway nature. With each seasonal change came blessings and miracles. But little by little, the people stopped believing in the gods, claiming the seasons changed naturally. With the work of their own hands and the inventions they created, they no longer needed blessings or miracles from the gods. As you can imagine, this angered the gods, and so they stopped coming and demanded worshippers and rituals and sacrifices to encourage them to return. Lagoda became divided between those who wanted to honor the gods and the old ways, and those who wanted to ignore them and focus on the new ways of invention. Those who believed conducted rituals, including blood sacrifices, ceremonies, and all kinds of foul things. According to the tales, it was a bad time. Feuds and battles broke out, creating bloodshed and murder. After a while, it all ended, and no one heard the song of the gods again. Every now and then, someone claims to, but it's something to keep to themselves.

In fact, I'm surprised Namen had her statues on display. Usually one wants to keep them hidden for fear of incurring the wrath of others. I suppose it's all old legend now though. I'm not sure anyone believes anymore."

I knelt in the dirt, still as I listened to her story. Song of the gods. I recalled the violin I'd heard, far off, beautiful, played with a skill I did not have. If I could play like that, I'd never lack again. "What do you believe?"

"Mila, because I like you, I will be frank with you. Regardless of what people want to believe, the gods haven't forsaken us. That's the thing about faith. People claim it is subjective, but is it? Truth is truth, no matter how much people attempt to bend it to align with their selfish desires. Gods aren't petty like humans, nor are they bound by the logical impediments of this world. It is easy to be jealous of one with immortality and vice versa. Perhaps they are sick of dealing with small-mindedness and stupidity. Yet I can't explain it, but at the turn of each season, I sense an old, otherworldly presence. Perhaps it's because of where we are located and how the veil between the world of the gods and our world is thin up here, but I can't shake the feeling they are watching over us and those who believe will still receive blessings."

I let her words sink in, realizing I'd never considered faith in gods, the unseen beyond us, the makers of this world and all life. As I weighed Giselle's words, things Ezra had said floated back to me. He, too, had mentioned a spiritual connection and how it was an unavoidable part of life. Did he believe in the gods too? Did I even want to address this topic with him?

Ever since my time with him in the gardens, my feelings about him were conflicted. I knew what it was though: fear of getting to know him and finding out whether he was as good as he appeared or a disappointment. Wasn't it normal for relationships to have imperfections? Quiet arguments, miscommunications, and moments when the other person did not feel seen or heard. All those things could be overlooked in the big picture of a long-term relationship that, in general, made one happy, or at least as happy as they were allowed to be. Did I want to find out if that could be possible with Ezra?

"I've never heard stories about the gods," I told Giselle. "But I think I understand your faith in them. You spend so much time in nature, and out here it's much easier to believe. It's harder in the city, where there's the rush and constant noise of city life. It's hard to be quiet and think for oneself among the barrage of information and the instruction of teachers and professors who are wiser than others."

Giselle snorted. "People always have excuses for

why they will or will not believe in something. That's just the thing though. They don't care about truth; they only care about feeling good about themselves."

"How does one distinguish truth from what makes one feel good?"

"Now, that's the right question to ask. It's conviction. You'll feel it in your soul that it is the truth and not something you're regurgitating because a teacher or family member or even a comrade like myself told you. You'll discover it for yourself, and your finding of the truth will be so strong and pure that you'll know."

Knowing. Was it that simple though? Giving a shaky laugh, I tried to lighten the conversation. "I don't know what to think. Are you trying to convince me the gods are real and I should search for them myself?"

Giselle patted the last potato into place and stood, surveying our work. Her face was earnest when she spoke. "I'm not trying to convince you of anything, Mila. You have enough smarts to figure out things. I'm simply answering your questions and giving you more to consider as you make sense of what you learn here. When I was young, I went to school, and there were many teachers, but my favorites were the ones who encouraged me to ask questions about the world and not to sit back and simply take their word for it. It changed my perspective, and I'm only doing the same for you."

"I appreciate that. You've given me a lot to think about."

Giselle nudged me with her elbow. "You're quite agreeable, you know that? You don't have to be. You can speak your mind and I won't judge you for it. The point of these conversations is to ask, to discuss openly. We'll still be friends even if we disagree."

MILA

Giselle's words stayed with me a long time, and I pondered them, turning over impossibilities in my mind. Were the old gods real, and did I hear them? If so, what about the darkness I saw?

I heard the violinist more often. Sometimes at midnight, other times at dawn, but I dared not peek out the window, too frightened of what I might or might not see. I wanted to blame it on the air in the mountains; it was thinner, lighter, and made my mind more fanciful. Perhaps it also affected my vision, making me see things that were not there. I asked Rachelle if she ever heard a violin playing, but she shook her head. That vacant look returned.

I'd heard tales of people going mad. It started with seeing things that weren't real, and they were convinced it was. The insane lived in a remote asylum near Solynn, where no one would bother them and the doctors worked to find a cure, or at least keep them from self-harm while they lived out the rest of their days. I promised myself I wouldn't end up like them, and the resolve built and grew. Instead of cowering in my bed, I needed to find the source of the music and have my questions answered once and for all. But how could I walk about at night if there were shadows creeping through the inn like monsters?

After a considerable time spent thinking, I decided I needed a knife. If I had a weapon, I'd feel safe, and if anything tried to harm me, I'd cut it first. However, wandering about outside during the middle of the night was too risky. It was dark, and it would be easy to lose my way or fall in the unfamiliar landscape. I'd only seek the violinist if I heard the music during dawn. As I was satisfied with my plan, a bolt of anticipation went through me. Soon I'd find the truth, whether it was a prankster or an old god. I laughed at myself. Perhaps I was going mad. Who had the audacity to believe they could sneak up on a god?

One morning, after the breakfast rush died down, I stood at the bar, thinking over how to steal a knife. Moses and Marley were always in the kitchen, and they were organized. They'd notice the moment a knife went missing, and I wasn't sure where any others might be hiding. A shadow darkened the doorway, and a moment later Ezra slid inside, calm and well dressed, his eyes soft with sleepiness. My heart warmed, and all my plans fled. I could simply ask instead of snooping around.

Smiling, he came to stand in front of me, and I realized I was the only one at the bar. Ginger had stepped into the kitchen to have a word with Moses, and Rachelle was collecting the last trays from upstairs.

"Mila, just the person I hoped to see," Ezra greeted me, leaning his elbows on the counter.

It had been a while since I'd seen him, what with the harvest of oranges, and afterward I'd assumed he was busy. I'd missed his presence more than I wanted to. I didn't mean to say the words out loud, but they slipped off my tongue like water off a cliff. "It's been so long since I've seen you."

His eyes clouded. "I know, work, but I haven't forgotten. Anything." Standing straight, his gaze shifted around the bar. "Where is Rachelle? I want both of you to come to the barn with me, immediately."

I frowned. We never went to the barn. "Is something wrong?"

"No." He winked. "I just need some help."

Rachelle appeared a moment later, trays in hand. Arching an eyebrow, she breezed through to the kitchen and reappeared with a cinnamon bun. "What?" she asked, staring from Ezra to me.

Ezra gestured to the door. "Will you accompany me to the barn?"

Rachelle took a bite of the bun, wiggling her eyebrows at Ezra. "This sounds quite naughty. Why are we going to the barn?"

My face warmed, both at her words and the way she'd said them, the innuendo clear in her tone.

"I need some assistance, especially from you, Rachelle," Ezra replied evenly.

"Only because you're in charge," she quipped.

I was surprised she spoke to him like that. It was borderline disrespectful, but Ezra didn't miss a beat.

We followed him out of the inn and around to the carriage house that perched just beyond the staff quarters.

Ezra escorted us in, taking the entrance that led to the horses. I'd seen it from a distance but hadn't gone inside myself. The scents of hay and horses filled the air, along with those of sweet grass and the mustiness of oats. It was a surprisingly homey, comforting combination of smells.

"Dusty wants to get into horse breeding," Ezra explained. "I told him we don't have the staff for it and we'll need to hire some help, plus we'll be competing with Lord Ensworth, who is a well-established name in horse breeding. However, Dusty would not relent, and I promised to look for help. If either of you would be interested in assisting with the horses, it would be most helpful. They'll need to be walked, fed, and ridden daily. I know it's a busy season in the inn, but I'll speak to Ginger and see if—"

"I'll do it!" Rachelle blurted out, dropping her half-eaten bun in the dirt. "It doesn't matter. I can help with the horses and work inside too. I'll get up at dawn. I'll ride them during the afternoon."

Her eyes were shining as she clasped her hands together, almost like a child begging for just another sweet before bed. Slowly, I lifted my gaze to Ezra, for I realized what he'd done. He hadn't forgotten a word I'd said, and he'd given Rachelle horses in the only way she would accept. My throat went tight at what he'd done, making her happy, lifting her sadness. I was sure she wouldn't forget about being a lady married to a wealthy lord, but at least she had something to throw her heart into.

She was already at the stables, reaching out a hand to one of the horses. It sniffed her, and she rubbed its nose, her voice soft. "My father had horses, and I loved them. He taught me everything about them…before…"

"You'll have help too," Ezra said. "I mean what I said. I don't want you to work yourself to the bone, but I'll have to find suitable help here."

"I won't let you down," Rachelle promised.

We left her there, standing in the barn with the horses. I followed Ezra back outside, and once we were in the sunlight, the lump in my throat melted away like thawed ice. "Thank you," I whispered. "You gave her something special."

A shy smile lit up his face. "And what would that something special be?"

"Hope."

He held my gaze a beat longer than necessary. "You gave me the idea, Mila, so in fact, you were the one who gave her hope."

I stood there, grinning at him while the sun beamed on his head, making him appear like a sun god. "Does it always feel this good?" I asked.

"What?"

"Making people happy?"

He gazed at the orange trees. Their branches, now light from lack of fruit, swayed in the breeze. "Yes, it feels closer to redemption, closer to being forgiven."

I wondered why he'd used those words, and caught a trace of sadness. His past was part of the mystery of him, and perhaps he'd open himself fully to me.

"Tomorrow afternoon, come join me at the lake," he said.

"Is that a request?"

"It's an invitation. Like I said earlier, I have forgotten nothing. I still want to spend time with you, to get to know you, if you will have me."

"Yes. I will."

"Well, now that's settled, off I go to find a friend for Rachelle to work with."

"A friend?"

He gave me a sly grin. "A friend, maybe something more. Everyone needs someone."

The retort died on my lips. He was right. Everyone needed someone. Even if they believed they didn't.

MILA

The lake was glistening, and my stomach flip-flopped as I stood on the dock. The idea of sitting on a carved piece of wood in the middle of water was somehow both disconcerting and exciting.

Ezra hefted the picnic basket inside and held out his hand to me, one foot on the dock, the other balancing on the boat. "Have you ever been on a boat before?"

I laughed nervously. "No, why do you ask?"

"The way you're eyeing it. I promise it won't bite."

"It's not the boat I worry about." My gaze went to the waters.

"In that case, I promise I don't bite either, at least not too hard."

My eyes snapped to his, and I could think of no

incident where he would bite me. It struck me as so ridiculous a laugh burst out of my throat.

Taking my hand, he guided me into the boat. It rocked back and forth under my weight, and for a moment, I clung to him as he guided me down. When the rocking stopped, I took a deep breath, calm again.

Ezra untied the boat and picked up the oars, pushing away from the shore.

"I'll take one," I told him, holding out my hands. He shook his head, but I pressed on. "I like to keep my hands busy."

Begrudgingly, he passed over the oar. It was warm from his grip, but the wood was smooth. When I dipped it into the water, it flowed around the oar gently, and we moved. Grinning, I glanced up at Ezra as we rowed in sync, but quickly my eyes were drawn back to the water. It was translucent near the top, and fat fish with black scales wiggled below the surface. We passed a school of tiny silver fish, and I laughed when one leaped out of the water.

The air on the lake was cooler, and although the sun beat down, it wasn't too warm, but I imagined as summer wore on, the heat could be quite oppressive. Once we were out a bit, I could see the island and on it a tangle of bramble, heather bushes with a slight opening, a path leading further in. I stared at it, wondering. From my purview on the lake, it looked like a bay instead, the dense foliage backing up to the blue mountains in the distance.

"That's the island, isn't it?" I asked. "Can we go there?"

"There? Now?" Ezra raised an eyebrow.

Tucking a loose strand of purple hair behind my ear, I grinned at him. "Unless you have some other destination in mind."

"No, my only thought was to enjoy your company, and that can be accomplished in the boat or on the island. You'll have to follow my lead with rowing though."

"Following," I agreed, holding up my oar.

"It's not an island, not really. The fastest way to reach it is by boat, but one can access it from the mainland."

I scanned the rise of the land, the way the tower loomed above the lake, giving Ezra a lovely view from his workshop. Behind the dock a set of stairs were carved into the green hillside, leading right up to the tower. Beyond the bulk of the tower, I couldn't see, for although the path rolled downhill again, old trees blocked the way and most likely the path to the bay. My heart skipped a beat. What if the individual who played the violin was on the island? I could reach it on my own without taking out the boat. Next time I heard the sound, I'd seek answers.

"Mila, your oar!" Ezra's voice jolted me out of my

thoughts just as the boat tipped dangerously. With a yelp, I yanked at the oar, dragging it back in as I righted myself, grabbing onto the edge.

Water splashed over the side, soaking the hem of my dress and my shoes.

Ezra pulled in his oar, laughing. "What did you see out there? You looked so serious."

"Nothing," I said, flustered. "I just…I've never been on a boat, and the landscape is so curious here. It's quite a shock from the city."

"Is it?" he said, reaching for the oar.

I let him, although his gaze seemed to penetrate me, finding the untruths and unfurling them.

"No," I admitted. "That's not what's bothering me. I've been listening to Giselle's stories about this place, the old legends and superstitions that surround it. I admit, I am curious. Which is why I want to go to the island, to see what it's like to step on sacred ground."

"I'll take you, but know that it's just land, quieter than the farmland though. I believe it's the silence that gives it the sacred aura."

His voice had gone soft, and for a few moments, the waves gently lapping against the hull of the boat were the only sound. Was he trying to tell me something? Or was I reading more into the situations than I should? If I had to guess, I'd assume something about the island bothered Ezra, but his expression was closed. Difficult to read. Had I spoiled something?

"We don't have to go. I'm just curious."

"I'd rather take you myself," he assured me. "It is the ideal place for a picnic."

A few minutes later, the boat bumped against the beach with a gentle jolt. Ezra splashed out into knee-deep waters and tugged the boat further up the shore with surprising strength. Returning to the side, he held out his hand and bowed. "May I assist you?"

I took it, his grip warm, and a tingling sensation went through me. A moment later, my feet were on the island, and I waited for a shift in the air, something to change. Sand-brown rocks covered the beach. A few feet away were a tangle of bramble, bushes, and trees, a shadowy forest waiting to welcome the forest queen. I breathed in deep, enjoying the hints of mint, lavender, and wood. Something was here. I sensed it, and although it was uncanny, it also made me desire to explore further.

My hand tightened around Ezra's as he drew me closer, as if the magic of the island filled him too. In the distance was a chirping, not quite birdsong but something else, delicate and sweet, and a rushing, crashing sound like faint thunder on the horizon. "What is that?" I asked, delaying the inevitable.

"There's a waterfall in the distance. You can hear

its song from here." He studied me, pulling me closer until our bodies were inches from touching. I lost my breath somewhere, but I couldn't tear my gaze from his forest-green eyes. They were calm, hypnotic, compelling. His movements were slow, intentional as he let go of my hand, his fingertips moving up my arm, his other hand resting on my hip, steering me closer.

I rested my hands on his arms. My lips quivered as he pulled me firmly against his hard body. Longing filled me, and I tilted my head, mouth raised, knowing what was to come next. His fingers brushed hair back from my brow, his calloused fingertips grazing my cheek as he cupped my face. When his wide, smooth lips touched mine, a jolt passed between us like steel striking flint, lighting a flame. He held the kiss a beat, and then he slid his lips across mine again, gently prying my mouth open with his tongue. As I acknowledged and accepted his advances, the kiss expanded, like a flame burning the edge of a match, growing bolder, brighter, stronger. I opened my mouth to him as his tongue dipped beneath the seam of my teeth. He pulled back, teasing, skimming my lips with his before taking me again, kissing me hard and long.

My grip tightened on his arm, and the gentle Ezra I knew transformed. Each kiss sent another bolt through me as though I was a small fire and if he kept kissing me, tasting me, teasing me, I'd become a blaze. My breath shifted to hungry pants as his arm wrapped around my waist, pulling me tighter against him until a shrieking sound erupted from the forest.

We stumbled apart, and I took advantage of the moment to recover. Ezra's breath was ragged as his gaze darted up at the treetops. When he faced me again, his eyes were glassy, and he reached for me, drawing me back into his arms. "It's a mating call," he told me, so close our foreheads almost touched.

I couldn't help but think how appropriate it was, especially while we were kissing. I'd never been kissed like that, and my entire body hummed at his touch, my lips burning to be taken, devoured by him again.

"A mating call," I repeated, giving a shaky laugh.

"Would you like to see the island now? Or do you prefer the shore?"

"As long as we can return to the shore," I admitted, my fingers closing around the hard muscle of his arm. My legs were weak, and an ache between them made my face flush. I wanted more, much more of Ezra. He'd only given me a taste, a delightful taste, but it wasn't enough.

Leaning closer, he brought his mouth right next to the curve of my ear so his heated breath sent shivers of arousal through my body. "We can always return to the shore."

Then he stepped back, as if unshaken by what had happened between us. Taking my hand, he laced our fingers together and walked toward the shaded path into the forest, leaving the boat and the picnic basket by the shore.

"I've heard romantic relationships here are more reserved than I'm used to, and I was very forward back there. You'll have to tell me if I go too far."

I squeezed his hand. "I admit, you took me by surprise, but I enjoyed it." The fire inside threatened to flare up again. "Don't change anything."

He stopped, facing me. "'Don't change anything.' Sometimes you say things and I don't think you know how wonderful you are, but tell me if you change your mind. I don't want you to have any hesitations or reservations about speaking your mind to me."

Lifting my hand, he pressed it to his lips, and I suppressed a moan. It was bold of me, but I wanted him to lean me up against a tree, lift my dress, and take me right there in the cool shade of the forest, where the only watching eyes were those of nature.

He did not. Only his eyes danced between mine and my lips.

"I have no reservations," I told him, and as I spoke those words, I realized I did. Or at least, I had. He was my employer, and a relationship with him should be forbidden. But after that kiss, I wanted to peel back the layers of who he was, unveil him for myself, to understand the depth and idiosyncrasy of his character. And more than that, I wanted to know where he was from and why the customs of the land were uncommon to him. Perhaps it was simply his culture, and I wanted to understand that too.

"Good," he said, and we continued.

The forest path led us deeper in, and not more than five minutes passed before we arrived at a grassy clearing. A ring of trees surrounded it, and blue flowers grew like a royal carpet. Red toadstools with white dots sprung up in clusters near the trees, and dew glistened like gems. "What is this place?"

"It's the dancing glade. If you've listened to Giselle's stories, surely she told you this is where those who still believe in the old ways come when the seasons change."

I stared, wanting both danger and the thrill of excitement. "Do you believe?" I dared to ask.

"I believe many things," he told me, skillfully avoiding answering my true question. "At least enough to come here, sometimes."

"It is beautiful, and the air is sweet. Does the island carry any other secrets?"

"This enchantment isn't enough for you? You want more?"

I tilted my head, smiling at him. "I don't see a

path out of this glade. How does one reach the waterfall?"

He shook his head. "You don't. The terrain here gets rough, which is why it's best to come with someone who knows the lay of the land. Mila, I know you are curious, but don't come here without me. The routes are confusing, and it's easy to lose your wits. Alone."

My wits. I bit my lower lip, thinking of Endia, the shadows I'd seen, and my concerns about my sanity. Those were not words I wanted to hear, and the edge in his voice held a warning. Pulling away, I walked to the perimeter of the circle to clear my mind. "Ezra, you keep telling me you're not from here, but where are you from? Do you have a family? Brothers? Sisters?"

"I'm from another land…" He trailed off as though weighing his words, determining how much he wanted to tell me. "My parents were farmers, peasants, poor. They tilled the land in serfdom to a lord, and I…I wanted more for myself. They were complacent with their lives. The little we had, barely scrapping by, was enough for them. It didn't matter if we weren't warm enough in the winter or whether we had full bellies or threadbare clothes. I was their only child who lived, and I know I should be sad about it, but I can't remember the others; their lives were too brief. Now, looking back, I think the loss made my mother hard, and my father only focused on the work. They had no joy, no life, for that kind of existence is not life at all but servitude to the land. I don't recall the lord we worked for, but I have an impression that although he was not unkind, he simply did not understand the needs of his serfs, and why would he? He'd never been in our place. It made me bitter. It made me long for more, and so as soon as I could, I joined the knights and served a great and powerful..." He hesitated, choosing his next word carefully. "A woman who would be called a queen here."

"What happened then?"

Ezra twisted away from me, walking to the middle of the circle and staring up the blue sky. The clouds drifted slowly through it, like a leaf caught in still water, floating yet barely making progress in its journey back to land.

"Mila, it is not a happy story." When he faced me, his eyes were dark and his jaw set in a hard line. "Many things happened. I served, I moved up the ranks, and all that power went to my head. I broke my vows, and I was banished because of my wrong-doing. Now that I'm here, I'm focused on putting the past behind me to live in a way that is honorable. This time, instead of being greedy for power because of the lack I grew up with, I want to enjoy every moment of this life. I want to work the land with my own hands and reap the harvest. I want to share my wealth with those who need it. I want my life's purpose to bring people joy, not devastation."

His raw words dropped away, replaced with a heaviness. A piece of him had been unraveled, and even though I didn't know the details, the broad strokes of his life were enough. Still, my mind went to dark places. What had he done to be banished? Had he stolen something? Murdered someone? But those were questions I could not ask him, and I sensed there was more I would find out as I spent time with him. His eyes were stormy as I approached and reached for him. His hands were curled tightly into fists as though he was holding back a rage that burned inside.

"I know it wasn't easy to share, but thank you."

His fists loosened. With a groan, he swept me into his arms. My hands rested on his chest, and the fire within ignited again.

"I tell you about the darkness of my past, and all you say is thank you? What kind of wondrous creature are you?"

My breath caught. "Because I'm so used to people pretending, and you, you tell me the truth, even when it's difficult."

I wanted that kiss, but he withheld it. Standing there, he scanned my face as if testing the validity of my words. "I don't want to hurt you," he said finally.

"There's more, much more, about me you don't know yet. I promise I will reveal all, bit by bit, but I don't want to frighten you away."

"I'm not frightened. I'm here."

"I know," he said and released me.

MILA

We returned to the beach, where Ezra pulled out the picnic basket and unpacked it as we sat in the grass. I leaned back on my elbows, watching the water lap at the boat, and the serenity of the island filled me with peace. Ezra had recovered from our conversation in the dancing glade, and a lightness returned to his movements.

"I cook sometimes." He passed me a bowl of food. "But since Moses took over the kitchen, I leave him to it. He does a much better job than I do."

"I'd like to taste your cooking sometime." I grinned mischievously.

"Only if I get to taste yours."

"You'd have to arrange a kitchen for me. I'm sure Moses would not want us to borrow his."

He raised a finger in warning. "When I decide to

invite you to my workshop, you can use my kitchen there."

I wasn't sure if I should tease him about that, but I tried anyway. "Oh, you are considering it?"

"In time." Unwrapping the packet, he pulled out a sandwich. Before he took a bite, he looked at me over it. "Tell me something about you, Mila, something I don't know."

To give myself time to think of what to say, I unwrapped my sandwich and smelled it. The tang of fresh tomatoes, the peppery spice of basil, and the heavy scent of bacon met my nose. I took a bite, almost slobbering on myself in my haste. I swallowed and cleared my throat. "This is delicious, and I'm not sure what to tell you. You know what's most important to me, music and family. Mother and Aveline were my entire world growing up, and the three of us have always been close. I was lucky, I suppose. I always knew I had to work for a living because the idea of marrying a wealthy lord did not appeal to me, nor were there any opportunities. Coming here for music is the one thing I decided to do for myself, for a chance at adventure, a new challenge to rise to."

"You don't like to talk about yourself, do you?"

"Why do you say that?"

Ezra fished an apple out of the picnic basket and pointed it at me. "Everything you just told me I already know, but I want to know you, deeper, beyond all that. What do you lose yourself in? What makes you happy?"

I froze. Ezra sat across from me, attempting to peer into my soul. It was like being bare before him, a risk I wasn't sure I was ready for. Yet here we were, sharing, trusting each other, being vulnerable together. Putting the sandwich in my lap, I took a deep breath, willing myself to be open and honest as he had been earlier. "Music has been my passion for a long time, but I know it goes much deeper than simply the act of playing. It's the emotions that build within me, the feeling that as I play, I'm growing closer to myself, my truth, and my soul. When I play, I transform. I don't know how to explain it, but it's like an out-of-body experience, and when I'm around art, the same emotions well up. Art makes me feel alive, like I'm connecting with something greater, beyond myself. It happens when I play music, sometimes when I've dabbled with paint, and when I walk the gardens."

"The way you explained it is lovely. Did you feel the same sensation when you saw the paintings outside my office?"

"Yes," I said eagerly. "They were inspirational, and yet it was more, as if there is a deeper meaning the artist was trying to capture and portray. Take the statute in your office, oddly similar to the statutes in

Namen's shop. I felt like the artist was afraid of being seen, of being too detailed and descriptive. So only the musical instruments are carved, and the rest is a vague blur, as if it shouldn't be seen."

When Ezra spoke, his voice was low. "You saw statues in Namen's shop?"

"Yes, the old gods. She explained how they use their music to call forth the seasons. Well, Giselle explained in full, but I was interested in it, the history of it, why people used to believe and then they stopped. Inventions shouldn't halt belief, so why did they?"

Ezra's mouth opened and shut. Running his fingers through his hair, he shook his head. "You have an exquisite mind. There's one thing I've noticed about you, and I don't know if you realize this or not, but you have a gift. You see people for who they are. You take the time to get to know them and reserve judgment. That is unique."

Ezra's words left me feeling almost as warm as his mouth did, almost. My emotions shifted and twisted, moving into dangerous territory. I decided I was going to enjoy him. Come what may.

MY CLOTHES ARRIVED the next week in a bundle Giselle brought in from town. Among them were lovely dresses, fine and stylish, more expensive than anything I would have picked out myself, and I was thankful she had chosen for me.

I felt like a lady of the court as I tried on dress after dress. They were all light, silky, and some clung to my body more than others, dipping and curving. Namen had blessed me with two new work dresses, simple and efficient, trousers and a linen shirt to ride in, three evening dresses all different shades of pastels. When I looked in the mirror, I realized she'd chosen colors that complemented my bright-purple hair and rich brown skin. She'd done her job well. The last garment came with a note pinned on it: *Wear this for the harvest festival.* I smiled. She'd thought of everything.

I took advantage of the calmness to write to Mother and Aveline, my fingers pausing as I thought of Ezra and our time spent on the lake. He'd made it clear what he wanted, but should I tell them or wait? The original plan had been for me to spend the summer at the inn, for that was during the busy months. Fall was less busy, and in winter, people did not want to leave their cozy homes to brave the snow and ice and visit the inn even though it was only in the foothills of the blue mountains. Winter, I intended to stay with Mother and Aveline, back in the country house, before returning to the inn again, if they had need of me. In fact, I hadn't considered past the summer, but the idea of leaving Ezra was painful.

Turning those thoughts over in my mind, I took my violin and went to play for the dinner rush. The room buzzed with life, and it was difficult to find my focus. Even when I placed my bow on the strings and closed my eyes, I couldn't concentrate. Instead of drifting away to a meadow where flowers lifted their faces to my song, I remained in the room, aware of the guests laughing and talking, the sound of mugs clinking while the music drifted in the background. Ignored, I played but not well, and all the while, a lump of disappointment settled in my throat. Summer was almost half over, and if I did not improve, what would be next?

When I finished, the guests carried on as if I was not even there. Usually I received a bit of applause but not tonight. Shoulders heavy, I made my way out of the room when Ginger called, "Mila?"

I chewed my lower lip as I faced her, aware my performance hadn't been my best.

"It's busy tonight. Would you mind taking a bottle of white wine up to Lady Elodie? After you put away the violin."

"Of course," I said, relieved she had nothing to say about my music, but then, she never had.

The bells rang, and Ginger moved away with a sigh. I sensed it was busier than usual, and instead of taking the violin to my room, I slipped into the lounge and placed it on the table.

I usually avoided the cellar, but Ginger hadn't bothered to bring up a bottle of wine. Reminding myself I'd seen nothing untoward in the cellar, I bravely opened the door and started down the stairs. Musty air greeted me, and the torches were well lit. Determined not to see anything odd, I focused on the shelf of wine. In my haste, I grabbed a bottle of red, only noticing when I turned to go back up the stairs. With a sigh, I spun around, replaced it, and more carefully this time, selected a white wine. It was the same I'd shared with Ezra on the balcony. My heart beat faster. Would I see him tonight? Would we trade kisses in the dark?

Pivoting to go up the stairs, I froze when the hair on the back of my neck tingled. Swallowing hard, I turned around. The air had shifted in the cellar. It was dense, hard to breathe, and the familiar mustiness was replaced with a foul rot. My fingers tightened around the bottle, and I lifted it, as though it was a weapon. My heart kicked as something moved. I was sure of it, a flicker beyond the light. Something was in there. I felt the awareness in every fiber of my being as I backed toward the steps. What was it? There came a faint glow and then red eyes. They were no more than orbs, glowing in the darkness, a film to them as they stared at me. I didn't wait to see what would happen next. Turning, I ran up the stairs, slamming the door to the cellar behind me, and breathed, hard.

"Easy there," Moses called from around the corner.

I couldn't say anything. My breath was gone. Instead of taking the lift, I slunk out of the kitchen to the stairs, hoping no one had witnessed my fright. As I walked, I mulled over what I'd seen. Something lurked in the cellar, some beast, and it wasn't a cat at all. Now that I'd seen it with my own two eyes, I knew I wasn't losing my sanity. My throat was tight as I climbed the stairs. I needed to tell someone, and I desperately wanted an explanation. Would Giselle tell me more? Or should I go directly to Ezra? It was his inn. Surely he knew what happened in it and the truth about what had become of Endia. I went cold just thinking of her.

On the second floor, I went to Lady Elodie's room. She'd been at the inn for a while and mostly kept to herself. Rachelle brought Lady Elodie breakfast each morning, and she usually went through a few bottles of wine a week. Sometimes more.

When I reached her door, it was cracked open. I knocked gently and called out, "Hello. Lady Elodie? I brought a bottle of wine."

The door swung open further under my touch, revealing the sitting room. A tray sat on a low table before the fire. Further back would be the bedroom and the adjoining door to the washroom. They were tight quarters but nice for those who stayed for more than one day to have their share of privacy or carry on business behind closed doors.

"I'll just leave it here," I called out.

No response came, but I was in a hurry, so I placed the bottle on the table. I didn't mean to pry, but a book lay in one chair, wide open, spine cracked as though it had been laid down in a hurry. A letter sat beside it along with a bottle of perfume and an extravagant diamond necklace. The jewels glistened in the firelight, and my eyes widened. Diamonds like that spoke of untold wealth, but Lady Elodie seemed to be running from something. Since it was none of my business, I stepped back and frowned. An odd odor permeated the room. A hint of iron and something else, like a sweet liquid. Forgetting about her things, I stepped further into the room, and that was when I saw it.

Dark-brown spots dotted the floor. Blood. My heart raced, although I reminded myself it could be her monthlies and she'd rushed to the washroom for rags.

"Lady Elodie? Do you need any more assistance?" I called.

There was silence, and an icy dread filled me as a slurping sound began. At first it was small, quiet, far away. I listened, and there it came again, just like the eerie sound I'd heard in the cellar. Clenching my hands into fists, I resolved to be bold and brave. Surely there was a reasonable explanation for it if I was hearing it upstairs. It might be the piping in the inn, with so many washrooms and guests coming and going. After all, the floors creaked oddly too.

When I reached the bedroom, the adjoining door to the washroom was open, and I hesitated. Was I intruding on her privacy? The slurping sound came again and then an inhuman hiss. Something dark moved behind the door, suddenly and violently, followed by the smack of skin striking skin. It came again. And then a low moan.

My heart thumped wildly in my chest, and I took a step toward the washroom. It moved in a blur of shadows, but when red eyes met mine, I spun. Heart in my throat, I left the door wide open and thumped down the stairs, barely avoiding a collision with Rachelle.

"Watch it!" she called.

"Sorry," I threw over my shoulder, rushing into the bar.

Ginger was in the kitchen, organizing bottles of wine into a crate. She looked up sharply when I rushed in. "Mila? What's wrong?"

"Room six. Lady Elodie's room. Something isn't

right. There was blood and a dark being in the washroom, and I heard her moan…"

Ginger stared at my hands, then at my face. Her expression changed, and fear shone in her eyes. "Take a deep breath."

"There was a sound," I gasped, my voice high-pitched, as I was almost in tears. "A slurping sound and a hiss. I called out to see if she needed help, but she didn't respond. It all felt very wrong, so I came here…" I trailed off.

Ginger squeezed my arm. "You were right to come to me. I'll take care of this. Sit, have a drink, calm down."

She swept out of the room while I collapsed at the table. My entire body trembled as I recalled what I'd seen, first in the cellar and then in Lady Elodie's room. What was it? What had happened? Rachelle joined me shortly to eat her dinner, while I sat stock still, sipping on a glass of wine, waiting for Ginger to return. Taking a deep breath, I asked Rachelle the one question I hadn't dared to ask. "Rachelle. What do you think happened to Endia?" I whispered.

Rachelle's brow furrowed. "Who?"

"Endia. Remember, she used to work here, with you, until she ran away."

Rachelle looked up at me, a frown turning her lips down. She shook her head. "I don't remember an Endia. I don't remember working with her. Why did she run away?"

I stared. "I was hoping you could tell me, since you were close."

Rachelle shook her head and finished her meal. "I don't know what you're talking about. I've never heard of anyone named Endia."

As she stood to leave, I wondered if something was wrong with Rachelle. Why couldn't she remember? I sat in the kitchen for a while longer, feeling safe as Moses and Marley cleaned up. Moses whistled as he worked, and the sound was calming, reminding me despite the terrors, I wasn't alone. I finished another glass of wine as I waited, but Ginger did not appear again.

MILA

At dawn, the haunted tune of a violin filled the air, and I rose from my uneasy sleep. All night long I'd been wakeful, afraid to close my eyes, the fear of the dark very real. I couldn't shake the feeling that something terrible had happened, but the inn was quiet. I listened to the tune play, but even it could not placate my fears. I had no desire to rush out and find it.

When I opened the adjoining door to wake Rachelle, she was already gone, likely to the stables. My shoulders slumped. As of late, not only was she distracted, but sometimes she woke earlier than I to go into the barn before breakfast. Feeling alone, I dressed and brushed my hair automatically, chewing my lower lip, but I couldn't shake the uncanny shroud of gloom.

Scanning the shadows, I went downstairs, but nothing odd moved, and there were no strange sounds aside from the familiar creaking of the inn. A few guests were already eating in the dining hall, and I imagined they were the ones who would hurry off on business. Moving behind the bar, I made my way into the kitchen.

Ginger sat at the table, short black hair tucked behind her ears, drinking a cup of tea and finishing a blueberry muffin. Her eyebrows rose when I walked in. She gestured to the table and spoke, keeping her voice low so as not to be overheard by Moses on the other side of the wall. "Mila, come, sit and eat. I hoped we might have a word alone today."

"About last night?" I guessed, my heart lurching at the thought. "What happened to Lady Elodie?"

Ginger frowned. "When it comes to matters that concern the guests, I expect you to behave with the utmost integrity and understand this isn't something that should be discussed again, not with anyone else, not even Rachelle."

I sat rigid in the chair. "I understand."

Ginger folded her hands under her chin, red lips pursed as she stared at me. "Lady Elodie had an accident. Something made her very sick last night, which is why she was in the washroom when you went up. I was able to assist and, as she wished, helped her pack up and leave."

"Leave?" I said flatly. Who left when they were sick? If she had been that ill and if she was the one making those sounds, a doctor should have been called. The one in the village would have ordered her to rest, not leave.

"Yes," Ginger interrupted my thoughts, her voice firm. "She did not wish to be seen in her condition and wanted to be off as soon as possible."

Perplexed, I twisted my hands together. "But why? If she was sick, it would have been better to rest here, in the privacy of her room. Besides, my room is right by the window. I didn't hear any carriages last night."

Ginger's eyes narrowed. "I'm sure you wouldn't have heard a carriage when you were sleeping."

The warning in her tone gave me pause, and at the same time, something within me hardened, for her tale did not ring true. Was she trying to frighten me? Was she telling me the truth?

"It's over and done with," she went on. "You did the right thing in calling me, and I have dealt with the situation. We will not speak about this further."

The insolent fever rose in me along with a hint of anger. Tapping my finger on the table, I glared back at her. "What about the shadow, the creature with red eyes, and the slurping sound?"

Ginger's steady gaze flickered, and her lips curled back, almost into what might be a snarl.

"I heard a slurping sound. The first time I heard it was in the cellar and then again in Lady Elodie's room. I also saw a shadow and glowing red eyes. I don't think the lady was ill at all. I think something attacked her." It was the first time the idea had come to me, but now that I'd said it out loud, it felt true. Emboldened, I continued, "Is this what happened to Endia? Did something terrible happen to her and you told everyone she ran away?"

Ginger did not respond. In fact, she let the silence stretch between us, and we stared at each other, unwilling to budge from our points of view.

At last, Ginger relented, her snarl morphing into somewhat of a sneer as she stood, leaning forward to tower over me. Her voice dropped even lower as she spoke. "I think you've had too much wine and it's addled your mind. It is as I said, and I will not repeat myself. The situation last night was dealt with. The lady left, and there is nothing to base your suspicions on. In fact, why don't you take the morning off, go get some fresh air, and think of how ridiculous your claim is? This is an old house. You're likely to hear strange noises, and you have a vivid imagination. Suits you, though, with your purple hair."

The last words she dropped as if something was wrong with me. I bolted up, but she stepped away. "I'll see you later, Mila."

I sat down heavily after she left, surprised at the turn of the conversation and the cold aloofness with which she had sneered at me. My hand went to my hair. Her slight felt like a thorn pressing into my side. My face crumpled, but I wouldn't let myself cry. Taking a deep breath, I waited until I was calm, then stood. My eyes went to the cellar, and I was half tempted to walk down there and wait for the creature to reveal itself again. Those red eyes and the disconcerting slurping sound had haunted my dreams last night. If I wasn't going mad, I had to prove to myself that it was the house. But what was it hiding?

Rubbing my eyes, I swiped a muffin off the table and left, brushing by Ginger quickly so I didn't have to look at her.

Keeping my head down, I walked to the gardens. Sitting by the pond would make me feel better, and I was grateful it was early. I wanted to sit quietly alone and decide what to do next.

The scents of citrus and flower blossoms pulled me from my melancholy thoughts. Was Ginger right? Had the lady gone off in the night and what I'd interpreted had just been my imagination? No, I knew what I'd seen this time and the other times too. A menace crept through the inn, and Ginger knew about it. But if Ginger knew what it was, wouldn't

Ezra know too? The thought made me cold. I wanted answers, needed answers, but would I like what I found?

"Mila?"

Startled, I glanced over my shoulder. My heart kicked with irrational fear, then flip-flopped as Ezra neared. Again I was stunned by how much he looked like a sun god in all his glory. His gray shirt was untucked, hanging over his trousers as if he'd dressed in a hurry. His golden hair was still wet and slicked back from his forehead. The sun cascaded upon him, highlighting his chiseled jaw and the depths of his green eyes, like pools of water. I stared openly, my pulse throbbing.

"Ezra," I breathed, my voice only a whisper as I rose to greet him.

My gaze fell to his arms. I wanted to be in them, my face pressed against his hard chest—his embrace melting away all my fears.

"What's wrong? You're usually not out this early."

I sat back down and twisted my fingers together. I wanted to tell him, but it would cast doubt on Ginger, the woman he trusted to run the inn without him. His second-in-command. What sway did I have over a long-term, deep relationship of his past? Despite the budding attraction between us? An attraction I desperately wanted to explore. But the shadows flashed before me, and I knew the price of remaining silent was my sanity.

Ezra sat beside me, giving me space as he said, "I can't help if you don't talk to me."

"I know," I said, staring at the swan, which sat on her nest. Her life was happy, uncomplicated. "There are things happening that I don't understand, and I can't explain them, but I feel…I feel like there's a truth hidden from me."

Ezra moved closer until his hip pressed against mine. Using one finger, he caressed my chin. "Tell me."

I sucked in a breath and told him. It came out in a rush, the noise in the cellar, the red eyes, the shadow creeping through the orchard in the dark, the shape in the hall, and then what had happened last night. He listened, although his expression shifted, turning to raw concern. "I didn't want to bother you with this in case it was just my imagination," I admitted. "But I know what I saw last night, and Ginger dismissed it. I don't believe the lady was sick, and I slept badly last night. I would have heard a carriage…"

"Mila, all these secrets?" Ezra scolded gently. "You should have come to me."

"I didn't know I could. Ginger and Rachelle have

been here much longer, and they noticed nothing amiss. And what's wrong with Rachelle? She doesn't even remember Endia, and why did she run away? Did something terrible happen to her too?"

A muscle in Ezra's jaw twitched, but before I could study his expression further, he pulled me into his arms, pressing my head against his heart. Listening to the slow and steady beat, my worries faded. He believed me, didn't he? He'd have a reasonable explanation, and I could count on Ezra being honest with me. When he released me, I sat up, flustered.

"Mila." He held my gaze with his somber one. "I need you to know that sometimes, strange things happen here. It's not simply an old legend. It's the truth."

Blood rushed to my ears at his admission. "I believe you."

"Much of what Giselle told you is true, which makes me think there is an undesirable roaming the property. I thought I'd been careful." He whispered the last words, as though he was talking to himself and not to me anymore. Straightening up, he stood and cleared his throat. "I'm going to talk to Ginger, and then I want you to spend the day with me."

I stood. "What about everyone else? Will they be safe?"

"It depends on what Ginger did to fix the situation, which is why I must speak with her. But if it is what I think it is, there is no need to worry during daylight."

I trembled, for his words did little to comfort me. The fact that he knew what it might be was even more disturbing. He turned to leave, then spun around, reaching for me. In one motion, he pulled me tightly against his chest, his hand pressing against my back. He kissed me. Hard. Crushing my lips against his. I tasted a burst of orange flavor, and I parted my lips, wanting more than a breathless moment of heated passion.

Ezra broke the kiss slowly, his teeth nipping at my bottom lip as he dragged himself away. His eyes were glassy as he whispered, "Don't leave."

After running his thumb over my lips, he turned in the direction of the inn.

I stared after him, a pool of desire spreading through my body. I wanted to unravel the mystery of who he was, where he was from, and I wanted to know him fully. I was teetering on the edge of the unknown, and if I went over the brink, I'd sink into bliss, and when it broke, it would burn like a blazing fire. Wrapping my arms around my waist, I sank back down on the bench to wait, turning his words over my mind.

"Don't leave."

What had he meant? Don't leave the garden, or don't leave the inn? Because how could he have known I'd considered packing my bags and running to my sister's estate, where it was comforting and familiar?

MILA

By the time Ezra returned, I'd finished feeding my uneaten muffin to the ducks and turtles. They gathered around, swimming in circles, waiting for another crumb to fall. Even the orange-and-white koi in the pond swam near the surface, their mouths moving up and down, begging for more.

Ezra appeared silently, hands tucked into his pocket as he came to stand beside me. His face was pale, and there were dark circles under his eyes that hadn't been there before.

"How did your conversation go?" I asked.

Pressing his lips together, he considered my question. "Poorly, I think. Ginger and I don't always see eye to eye."

"But you trust her?"

"In most things, yes."

"So what's the truth, Ezra? What happened?"

He was silent a long time, staring out at the pond, a look of misery on his face. His stillness frightened me, and I wanted to ask, to press him to tell me, and I didn't want to at all.

"I've run so far, trying to hide from the past, yet it always chases me and finds me. If I were truly self-less, I'd tell you it's too dangerous for you here. You should leave, go live with your mother and sister. If I tell you the truth, I fear you'll go, and I want you to stay."

A flame of heat ignited within me at his words, and the air between us hummed with tension.

"I'll stay," I whispered.

"But you can't promise to stay without knowing the truth. You bring light and life and happiness everywhere you go. Your aura, your spirit, shines so brightly it draws me to you, as if by basking in your presence, the rest of my darkness will burn away and I'll be whole, complete, pure again. You make me want to be more, to be better than my past."

"You are better than your past." I took his hand, clasping it with both of mine. "I've seen you. You work just as hard as everyone else here, maybe even more. You put the staff's needs in front of your own, to ensure they are happy, and you are generous both with your time and your wealth. You're more than your past."

"I'm not," he choked out, words rough and hard. "Every time I think I'm free, something happens."

His fingers curled around mine, but I sensed the trembling within his body. "Ezra, what's going on? What are you trying to be free of?"

"Of her," he said.

Her? The powerful queen he served? "I thought your punishment was banishment."

"No."

He was quiet again, even longer this time, and I perceived the warring within. My heart sank as the silence continued and I realized if he shared his secret with me, there would be no turning back. Perhaps this was what he'd meant about the layers of his personality, about it changing how I perceived him.

At last he blew out his breath and sighed. "What do you believe, Mila? About the supernatural? About magic?"

I wasn't ready for the question, and I stumbled back to the bench. "I…I don't know."

"Magic surrounds us here in Lagoda. It is the cause of many, many things, but especially of what happened last night. Most of it is my fault. When I was banished, my punishment came with stipulations. If I don't comply, someone pays the price."

I swallowed hard because he was speaking in

riddles again. "Is that what happened to Endia? And to Lady Elodie?"

"Yes, in part. Mila. This isn't easy to say, but both of them are dead."

Dead. I hadn't expected that, and my limbs trembled. I wrapped my arms around my middle and rocked back and forth. Fear was sharp and dread cold within. "How? Why?"

"Endia did run away, and we never found her body, but I know where she went. She ran to the islands and got lost wandering the paths. There are cliffs, wild animals, and it was winter, too cold for her to survive there for long."

I felt numb even though Ezra was giving me the answers I'd long sought. "Why would she go there?"

"She believed that was where the shadow creatures came from. She thought they were haunting her and if she could find the source, they'd stop."

My eyes snapped up, because it was what Giselle had said, shadows and cold. So Endia had assumed the island was the source… A prickling sensation went through me. "Why Lady Elodie? What did she do?"

"Nothing. She was in the wrong place at the wrong time, and I know how one of those shadow creatures got in. There's an old tunnel that leads from the cellar of the inn to an ancient shrine. It's a malevolent place, and I assumed the creatures that haunted it were long dead. I was wrong. I will block the tunnel to make sure nothing can access the inn through the cellar. The guests will be safe, and more importantly, you will be safe again."

"But the shadow creatures, what are they? Where do they come from?" I pressed, unable to keep the tremor out of my voice.

"We are in the foothills of the Lagoda mountains, where the veil is thin between worlds. Sometimes beings we can't explain come across. Once I complete my work, my task, the barrier will be sealed, but until then I promise to protect this land. I am determined to succeed, to gain freedom and earn your love."

I stared at him. Had he used that word? Had he said "love"? Since I was mute with shock, nothing else would come out as he sat beside me.

"There, now you know the truth. Let's not talk of dark things anymore."

Everything he'd told me should have been a deterrent. Two innocents had died, and shadow creatures haunted the inn. Dimly I was aware I should pack my bags and leave this place that threatened my sanity. He had explained, and perhaps it was the grief, the idea of love, fear, or a mixture of all that made me sit and stare.

Before me blazed a man like the sun god, and I knew if I stayed, if I said yes to this, there was no going back. But I wanted to experience the depth and breadth of love, the wild waves of feeling, and more than anything, I wanted to fall in love with him. He was so beautiful and so perfect. With the anguish behind his eyes, I wanted to do something, anything to see that crooked smile on his face again. Instead of standing, making my excuses, and leaving, I leaned in and brushed my lips against his.

EZRA

After the incident, I avoided Ginger as much as I could, knowing what she would say. Still, on the third day, she barged into my office and shut the door behind her. Her face was pinched, jaw clenched as she tucked her hair behind her ear—an action that seemed normal, but I, knowing her for so long, knew it was a nervous tic. Ginger was better when her hands were busy and she had something to do. Still, I didn't wish for her to take out her rage on me.

"You've been avoiding me," she declared.

I nodded in agreement. "I have because all we do is fight and I'm weary of arguing."

She snorted at that and moved to the cupboard to pour herself a glass of wine. "It's because I'm right, isn't it? I warned you what might happen if we kept the mortal. Mila. And now you're too fond of her to make her leave. Wine?"

"Yes." I held out my hand for the second glass she poured.

"Bringing her here to play music. What were you thinking? You know the spirits awaken with music, especially the notes of the violin."

"Her music is pure, raw, beautiful. She's not skilled enough to awaken anything, and I enjoy it," I snapped in her defense. When I'd first heard her play in Solynn, the rawness of it had entranced me. I'd felt that way once—young, fresh, pure—before magic marred every note. "Besides, this happened before with Endia. It was my playing that awoke the spirits, and my negligence of barring the tunnels. It is done."

Ginger perched on the edge of the desk, staring at me. "For now, yes, but what happens when you must use the magic? It will start all over again, and you can't save everyone."

Swirling the wine in the glass, I sighed. "No, I can't save everyone, but I can try. What I need is a break. I've tried, and it's not working. With the harvest coming and the shift of the seasons, I should have a chance."

"All Hallows' Eve," Ginger said, her tone ominous. "And if you fail?"

"Then it's up to you." I met her thoughtful gaze. "If I'm going to die, I want to live first, finish living at least. I want to love boldly, unashamedly, without the regrets of our former life."

Ginger set down her glass and leaned over. "Did you ever consider what she wants?"

"Every day."

If only Ginger knew how much I'd restrained myself. Leaning back, I closed my eyes, thinking of the taste of her lips, her bright spirit in contrast to my darkness. I'd already come so close to losing her even though I'd been careful to reveal who I was slowly, to get her used to one surprise before introducing the next. Now everything was fragile, and I'd had to encourage her to stay, alleviate her worries by telling her the truth. Half truths, at least, for if she knew what I had to do for the sorceress, she'd run, as she should.

Silence stretched between us, but it wasn't as heavy. I sensed Ginger was giving me her blessing and her support even though she disagreed, and that made everything easier. I remembered when she'd entered my service, determined to do what no other woman would. Fight. At first, I'd denied her, but she was fierce, angry, hurt, and wouldn't stop. I realized it was a way of dealing with her past, using anger as a shield and her sword as a way to get back at those who'd wronged her. She'd been the first loyalist, later followed by Moses and Marley. They were the three who'd survived after the sorceress came after us. Rachelle's father had been an unfortunate casualty, and I owed it to him to protect his daughter, especially because of the trauma she'd endured. She'd rather forget than remember those who were lost, and although forgetting was easier, I didn't want to lose my determination.

"How is everything else?" I asked finally, aware we were both sitting lost in thought.

Ginger shrugged. "As expected, the guests haven't noticed what happened. We were lucky Lady Elodie kept to herself and they took me at my word concerning her departure. Rachelle is oblivious, as always. What are you going to do about Mila? Summer's end in near, and I'm guessing you're going to invite her to stay?"

"Yes. I assume you no longer need her help in the mornings?"

"I would prefer it if she left, but now I see that will not happen, and no, I don't need her in the mornings. If you want her to stay without going mad, you need to make sure she doesn't spend every single day here inside the inn. She already knows too much."

"I told her about Endia," I admitted.

Ginger's fingers tightened around the wineglass. "What did you tell her?"

I repeated back the story, almost word for word.

"And she believed you? That the island is haunted

with monsters?" Ginger's laugh was brittle. "She's smarter than you give her credit for, Ezra. One day, she will unravel all your secrets and you'll be faced with telling her the truth."

I pressed my lips together. Ginger was right. I would be wise to step away, keep my word, and let Mila go at the end of summer. Her music had improved, and what I had to do was risky and could destroy many, but it wasn't just my freedom I'd gain; it was the safety and freedom of many more. Perhaps when it was all over, I could find her, later, woo her, make her mine, but for now I had to let her go.

That evening, I went downstairs to watch Mila play. She sat straight-backed on the stool, eyes closed, violin tucked almost lovingly under her chin. Her music was light, sweet, with none of the heavy, sonorous tones I often heard from the violin. She must have sensed the aura of the inn, the need for a distraction to take the guests' minds off heavy things. Folding my arms across my chest, I pressed myself into the shadows, repeating the words over and over in my mind: *Let her go. Let her go.*

It was not good for her to be here. I had to let her go, but as she played, a selfishness consumed me. Why should I deny myself the bright spot of happiness that cast sunshine into the shadows reaching out to drag me into despair? Instead of waiting, I should snatch my chance at happiness, and even more so because I felt her desire every time I was around her. At first, there'd also been hesitation, but that had long gone, although I often perceived her curiosity about me. Ginger was right. I had to tell her the truth before she unraveled my secrets. I could only pray she wouldn't run away.

Scattered applause broke out as Mila finished playing, and she bowed, a satisfied smile on her face. My fingers twitched as she exited the dining hall, and I resisted the urge to go after her. But only for a moment. There were many things I could tell her about the violin, simple tricks to improve her skills. I was doing her a disservice by not telling her, and yet I liked her exactly the way she was.

My long legs carried me quickly through the hall, and I stepped out into the entryway. She was opening the door to the staff's lounge, and I called out, "Mila."

The very air shivered around us as she spun, gasped, and then smiled. Her aura of excitement brightened the entire hall, and I crossed the floor to her in two steps, all thoughts of pushing her away disappearing like shadows under sunlight. "I enjoyed your music tonight," I told her.

"I thought of you as I played," she admitted, eyes shining.

My gaze flicked to her lips, then back to her eyes. She noticed, and a small sound escaped her throat.

"Listen"—I tilted my head—"I know I originally invited you to stay through the summer, but I'd like you to stay for a while. At least through fall. Play in the evenings and spend your days with me. The harvest is coming up, and I'll be busy, but afterward…"

I trailed off and drew her into my arms rather awkwardly, since she still held the violin. She tilted her head up at me, thinking, her brow furrowed.

"Will you stay?"

She pressed one hand against my chest, fingers curling around my shirt. "Yes. I'd like that."

Relief rushed out of me, and with a sigh I kissed her, claiming her lips, licking, tasting, sucking, and then, remembering where we were, and who I was, I pulled back. It was tempting to push into the lounge, carry her up the stairs, and take her. But I wanted to wait and draw out the delicious moments between us. The right opportunity would come soon enough, and I'd gotten her to stay. I'd take it one step at a time.

MILA

As the weeks passed, things changed. Although I expected death to cling to the inn like a shroud, the warmth of the summer sun burned away all traces of evil. As Ezra had promised, the shadow creature with the red eyes was gone. I refrained from going into the cellar, but even when I walked the inn after sundown or peeked out my window at midnight, there were no hunched shapes or lurking shadows. The kiss of coldness and the stink of decay did not greet me again, and soon the foul presence seemed nothing but a nightmare.

Silently, though, I grieved for the two women who'd lost their lives, and while I knew what had happened to Endia now, it seemed unkind to tell Giselle and plunge her into fresh grief. I wondered if

Ezra and Ginger stuck to the tale of her running away not only because it was the truth but also because they hadn't found a body to confirm her death.

Summer descended into fall, and I grew more comfortable in my role, playing the violin. When Mother and Aveline wrote, asking when I was coming to the estate, I replied that Ezra had invited me to stay through the fall. I'd come for winter.

Rachelle was content and happy again. Ezra explained she had a condition that made her forget everything but her most important memories, which was why she had to stay at the inn. Always. But she had the horses, and when a young man came up from a nearby village to work in the barn, she was quite taken with him.

Ginger remained aloof, and I no longer worked behind the bar in the mornings. I was relieved to put more distance between us, although sometimes I'd offer to work if there were more guests than usual. But the height of the summer was over, and slowly the inn became quieter.

The harvest was a busy time, and I barely saw Ezra. I played almost every evening, sometimes with another group of musicians. Fresh ale and wine flowed freely, and the workers celebrated along with the guests. During the most unexpected times, Ezra would find me. All smiles, he'd tug me into a shadowy corner and kiss me until my lips were swollen. I burned for him.

MILA

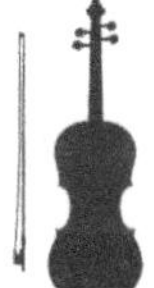

"What are you wearing to the festival tonight?" Rachelle asked, breezing into my room and flinging herself on the bed.

"Namen made me a dress specifically for tonight," I said, wrapped in a towel as I walked to my wardrobe.

I pulled out the dress and held it up, careful not to let my wet hair mar its beauty. The gown was more revealing than I would have liked. The pale-pink skirts, although falling to midcalf, were lacy sheers that showed off my legs. The top of the dress left my shoulders bare and hinted at cleavage. It clung to my torso and fanned out around my waist.

"It's beautiful." Rachelle bounced on the bed. "You'll look like a princess wearing it."

"It's different from what I usually wear," I admitted. "And I'm not sure how to do my hair."

"Let me," Rachelle gasped. "Come, sit. I'll make you look like a queen. I only wish I had flowers to weave into your hair. White ones; they'd complement the purple."

Obediently, I perched on the bed while Rachelle combed through my wet hair, weaving it into a crown of braids on top of my head. It reminded me of being young, when Aveline and I had taken turns braiding each other's hair before going to school. A lump swelled in my throat as I thought of her and Mother. Winter was far away, and as happy as I was in Lagoda, I missed them. Thoughts of them sharply reminded me of my arrival and the sound of the violin I'd heard for weeks in the beginning. But it had all stopped after the incident. My thoughts sped up, colliding. Why had everything stopped? The shadows, the fear, the coldness, and the violin. Were they all related?

I recalled my brief voyage to the island and Ezra's words of warning, reminding me not to visit it myself, and yet…I felt as though a mystery was still hidden from me and I could only find the answers on the island. Was that what Endia had run away to find? Answers? My pulse quickened. There was still something odd and off about the Dawn, and the paradise of Lagoda carried secrets. I didn't feel like I knew them all yet...but Giselle had told me her stories. I knew all the legends and folktales, but there was nothing in the library to confirm those tales. At least, nothing written. Giselle had explained that most tales were told by those who could not read and write, and unless one copied them down, there were no records, only word of mouth. I knew what Ezra had told me about the island, not to go alone, but the shadows were gone, and I was tempted. Something was still hidden from me, and I wanted to know the truth.

"Are you going to the festival with Rabon?" I asked.

"Yes." Rachelle blushed. "Tell you a secret. I think I'm falling in love. It's odd; I've had lovers before, but I've felt nothing like this. I have no desire to go to the city anymore. It is enough to work with horses and Rabon and take care of the guests here."

"I'm glad you're happy," I told her honestly, relieved she'd found what she was looking for.

"What about you?" Rachelle poked my side. "You're going to stay here, aren't you? It won't be the same without you and your violin."

"Yes, I'll stay." I wondered if I should tell her about Ezra. But my eyes went to the violin, and I tapped my finger against my thigh. While it was rewarding to play almost every night, something was lacking, something more. Would it be better if I returned to the city to play with an orchestra? Would I improve faster if I was challenged? But this was paradise, and yet I couldn't shake the feeling that something was off.

"I'm glad of it," Rachelle went on. "When this room is empty, it feels like someone is missing."

Endia. Rachelle missed her in her own way, although not knowing who she missed. I shook that thought away, determined to enjoy the celebration and not think of morose things like death.

"There, done!" Rachelle pulled me with her into the washroom and planted me in front of the mirror. "What do you think?"

I smiled, eyeing the braid wrapped around my head like a crown, while the rest of my purple hair fell in a cascade of waves around my shoulders. All I needed was a garland of flowers, or fall leaves, and the look would be complete. "It's perfect," I told her.

We dressed quickly, but even before we finished, I heard the music, the wild pulse of drums and the quick rhythm of strings. A twinge of guilt pierced me. I should play too, but Ezra had told me to take time off to enjoy the evening. I thought of his heated kisses, and my core fluttered.

Rachelle and I slipped downstairs. Giselle had informed me that Ezra hosted the harvest festival at the inn each year, and the dining hall, the ballroom, and the gardens were transformed. The villagers came, dressed in their best, along with the guests who'd chosen to stay throughout the festivities.

I knew nothing of harvest schedules, but it was only late August. Giselle told me the second harvest festival took place at the end of October, and that was when the last harvest was brought in from the fields. There was another celebration but nothing as big as this one.

The inn was more crowded than I'd ever seen it, and a hum of excitement tingling in the air made my heart beat faster. Rachelle ducked away, used to all the commotion, leaving me alone. Anxiety bloomed, but I reminded myself that Giselle was outside, waiting for me near the gardens. I weaved through the throng of people, men drinking, women preening at them from behind fans and pretending not to care.

When I reached the ballroom, I paused, my eyes drawn up to the drapery that hung from the ceiling and the chandeliers shining. It was lit up in there, as bright as daylight. A stringed quartet played a waltz, and a few couples danced, beaming at each other as they moved through the rhythm of steps. I crept along the wall until I reached the door leading to the balcony and then further outside.

It wasn't any cooler in the open air, with the hot sun beating down, but the scent of pumpkin and spice drifted to my nose, and I relaxed.

Giselle had told me to find her, but it took me a

while to weave through the crowds before I spotted her at a table laden with food, pouring a peach-colored drink. A bright-yellow dress left one shoulder bare, accenting her red hair and dark skin. She grinned and waved.

"What is that?" I asked.

"Fruit wine, or dessert wine," Giselle laughed and poured me a glass. "It's sweet and will make you feel like dancing. You're just in time. The music is starting up."

"The musicians are already playing indoors." I pointed back at the ballroom.

Giselle snorted. "Nonsense, that's for the posh lords and ladies. Out here, the music is for the wild ones. You'll see." She winked at me and drained her glass in one swallow.

Sure enough, a rhythm of beating drums began, a steady thud that made my pulse quicken.

"Come on." Giselle grabbed my arm and ran, taking me past the garden and into a grove of trees. Beyond it, a meadow opened up, and the scent of lavender tickled my nose. I stared, for it was a field, surrounded by daffodils, and yet it reminded me of my daydreams. Flowers and long grasses grew alongside the trees, and spots of yellow bloomed beneath those boughs. I drew in a deep breath.

The villagers gathered in a semicircle. They were younger than the ones I'd seen inside the ballroom.

Wild. Curious. Just like me. The trees were dark above me, and the wind roared, but as the sky darkened, lanterns were lit around the trees. Giselle paused by a laden table, passed me another glass of elixir, and giggled, "It begins!"

The wild dance was a drastic transition from the events in the city, with carriages arriving at large estates to drop off lords and ladies. The beat of the drum, the sweet air, the pulse of something otherworldly made my blood sing.

I drained the glass Giselle had given me, and the sweet elixir bubbled through me. My feet moved on their own, tapping in rhythm to the beat.

Giselle grabbed my hand, and suddenly we were in a circle, dancing around a bonfire that leaped and crackled as if it was alive. Staring at those orange flames made my eyes water and my vision blur. I imagined shapes jumped out of them, each of them a god with a musical instrument in hand, playing along to the drums. The resonance of a harp, the sonorous tone of a violin, the call of a flute, and the vibrations of an organ. One by one, each sound blared like a crisp clap of thunder.

My hand went sweaty in Giselle's, and I lost her, but the throbbing of the dance did not cease. Someone handed me another glass of the fruit wine, and by then I was too thirsty to question it. I drained it, tossing away the glass, my back sweaty. It was hot out there, among the dancers, the drums, the music. Silver moonbeams shone, and something simmered within me.

Lifting my arms to the light, I spun around and around, laughing as a wave of sheer joy hit me. Everything was perfect, serene, and life was an unending glory. If I could but hold on to my emotions at this exact moment, I'd harness complete and incandescent happiness.

And then two arms went around my waist, and my spinning slowed as Ezra caught me. Placing my hands against his hard chest, I pressed my body against his. I knew exactly what I wanted. What I'd craved since the day he'd appeared on the steps.

"Why are you looking at me like that?" he breathed into my ear.

"Because I'm happy," I laughed, all my feelings bubbling like boiling water in a kettle, impossible to keep to myself.

He kissed me while I laughed, but his lips only caught the corner of my mouth. It was so fast I didn't have time to appreciate it. Pulling back, he swept my hair off my shoulders. The cool air kissed my skin, pursued by his heated kisses along my neck, down my collarbone, and over my shoulders. I shuddered. "Ezra," I moaned.

At the sound of his name, he paused and drew back, his chest heaving as he caught my eye. A wicked glint lingered there before he twisted his fingers through my hair and kissed me hard. My fingers fumbled for purchase, and I couldn't breathe, couldn't see. I was lost, swept away in a sea of him and only him. Impatience made me tug at his clothes, barely aware of the dancers and merriment a few feet away.

Ezra laughed, his lips grazing my ear as he whispered, "Later. For now let's enjoy the dance, the moonlight, and the sweet elixir."

With that promise, he pulled me back into the dancing circle, his firm hands holding me steady as we twirled, spinning, caught in the endless dance. It felt like a wave that we were unable to escape. The pressure built, moving us back and forth. More wine was pressed into my hands, and a sweet tang shuddered down my spine.

Eventually odd creatures appeared at the edge of the glade. Women with antlers sprouting from their heads, men with hooves for feet, and bearded men no taller than children. People who were not possible. Violet rays swayed and flashed, but I didn't care as long as Ezra's warm hands held mine.

The night deepened, and as time passed, I could not tell where I ended and the other dancers began. The throb was both within me and outside of me, and I couldn't stop laughing at everything and everyone. My breath came ragged and harsh, and I was thirsty, oh so thirsty and warm. Even the breeze couldn't cool what lay inside, a surging passion that fizzed and built until it exploded. Pops of brilliance shone in my eyes before the world turned black and I fell down, down, down into bliss from which I wasn't sure there would be an awakening.

MILA

The pounding of my head woke me, and agony pulsed through my veins. I moaned, pressing my hand over my eyes, as if that movement could pause the drum that beat inside my mind. Every muscle in my body was sore, and my feet ached. Slowly the night returned. Dancing. Drinking. Kissing. Ezra!

Squinting, I peeked with one eye open and saw a dim room. The curtains were drawn, which was a relief. I closed my eyes again and with a jolt realized, from the briefest glimpse I'd seen, I was not in my room. Even the bed was different, soft and gentle, luring me deeper into comfort. The pillow felt like silk, and the sheets were cool beneath my body. My dress was bunched around my waist and had slipped off my shoulders. It was likely creased, maybe even ripped.

Lying still, I took slow breaths until the pounding receded into a dull thud. Squinting again, I opened both eyes this time. It was an enchanting bower with heavy dark curtains covering the window. Pillows were piled around me on the enormous bed, and a painting hung on the wall in front of me. It was of the dawn golden-and-pink rays shining over glistening waters. My heart softened at the sight of its beauty. The room was cozy, quiet, smelling of lavender and wood. That was what it was. A faint hint of wood surrounded me.

Testing my body to ensure the headache wouldn't return, I gingerly sat up. A leaf fell out of my hair, and twigs were on the floor. What had I done last night? My throat ached. I was desperate for water. The door was open, leading to a hall beyond. I glanced around one more time. I'd been with Ezra last night. My heart constricted. Was I in Ezra's tower? In the workshop he'd promised to show me but only when he was ready?

I stilled, for I wasn't in the right mindset for secrets, but perhaps water would refresh me. I scanned the room once more, my eyes landing on a robe lying on the foot of the bed. Quickly I wiggled out of my dress, leaving it on the floor. The hem was muddy, and it looked like it had been wet at one time. How drunk had I been? Tying the robe over my nakedness, I attempted to untangle my hair but soon gave up.

After traipsing across the floor on bare feet, I peeked out of the door, eyes going wide. Daylight crept through the windows of a circular room, displaying the clean stone floor, a water pump and sink, a pile of clean dishes, a cupboard, and root vegetables hanging from the rafters. A round table, covered in scrolls, sat in the middle of the room, and on it was a pitcher, full of water, I hoped. Crossing the floor to it, I was relieved to see it was water. After pouring myself a cup, I drained it dry and was starting on a second when I heard a step.

An arched door on the other side of the room swung open, revealing a spiral staircase leading down and Ezra.

"I didn't expect you to wake so soon," he said, shutting the door behind him.

He looked magnificent, dressed in loose trousers and a light shirt. He was barefoot, and I'd never seen him so relaxed and comfortable. Running a hand through his hair, he gave me that dimpled smile, and my heart melted. I wanted to embrace him, kiss him, then have him rip off the robe and make love to me on the floor. Something inside my chest was ballooning and expanding. The irony of my situation was not lost on me, with my desire not to fall in love or repeat the mistakes my mother had made. But every step with Ezra was perfect. He was unique, although a bit of mystery remained. "I was so thirsty, and…I…er…don't remember everything that happened last night."

"It's the wine. It's sweet but goes straight to the head." He tapped his skull. "We danced, we drank, and when you passed out, I brought you here and put you to bed."

"Is this your tower?"

He winked. "Yes, we are on the top floor. I like the views from here, but I built the bedroom to allow me to sleep, even during daylight."

Suddenly I felt shy. I was in his home, wearing his robe. It smelled like him. "You finally decided to show me where you live."

"Yes." He tilted his head, studying me, then crossed the room to me.

Sliding his arms around my waist, he pulled me close and held me tight.

"I haven't washed." I cringed.

"You smell like the forest," he told me, "like a wild dancer. I like you like this." Leaving one hand on my hip, he moved his other to the ties of the robe. "Are you wearing anything under this?"

Suddenly bold, I said, "No, but maybe you should check, just to ensure I'm telling you the truth."

His eyes lit up. "You are a tempting creature." He gave the knot a tug. "Let me feed you first. You must have a headache."

"The water is helping."

"Food will help more. Sit, you're my guest today."

"All day, no work?"

"No work. It's the custom after the harvest. We worked hard for days, and today is a day of rest. Moses makes a generous meal and leaves it on the bar, where guests can help themselves. No one is required to do anything, aside from recover from the night's antics."

"Recover." I rubbed my head ruefully. "That wine did things to my vision. I saw horned creatures and women with tails."

"Yes, you saw what you saw."

His tone made me peer sharply at him. "Are you saying it was real?"

"This is Lagoda, and the veil between worlds is especially thin on nights like these. It is plausible some of the fair folk came out of hiding to dance with us, but you'll never find them again, even if you try."

I stared at him, trying to wrap my mind around it. He'd been trying to tell me this all summer. Other beings were real, and I'd seen some last night. My headache began to pound again, and I gave up thinking. It was much easier not to believe even though I'd seen the creatures with my own eyes.

"I see," I said and smiled at him, although it turned into a grimace.

Shadow creatures and fair folk, a veil between worlds. What was the veil hiding, and what was on the other side? And then another question rose, one I'd never considered before. Had Ezra been there? I studied him while he worked, his slim figure hiding taut muscles, the fall of his golden hair, sometimes with hints of a reddish orange, depending on how the sunlight fell. No, I came to the conclusion he was human through and through. Nothing made me think he might be one of them.

Ezra served a meal of fruit, eggs, bread, and jam. Fig jam, I noticed with a smile, wondering if it was popular here or if he'd done so to humor me. We ate in a comfortable silence, and he was right. As soon as the food hit my belly, I felt much better, especially after washing down the bread and jam with peaches. Yet another fruit that was rare to find in the city, or at least for those who were commoners. The titled, of course, used extreme measures to supply all their needs.

Not for the first time, I thought of Mother and Aveline and wondered how they were faring in the countryside. They'd written letters, of course, but words only went so far. Seeing them in person would be lovely and perhaps break the enchantment, the spell that seemed to hold me here at the Dawn.

"What are you thinking?" Ezra asked, his low voice luring me out of my thoughts.

Taking another sip of water, I studied him, a lightness returning to my heart. "Of my mother and my sister. They'd love it here."

"Tell them to come sometime. They are welcome here," he said.

The words rang true because it was Ezra, because he was generous and kind and… "You're so good to me," I whispered.

"You make it easy." He leaned so close our knees touched under the table. His eyes were dark, sincere, and shimmering with yearning.

I parted my lips to respond, but my words faded under the intensity of his gaze. What was between us was potent, powerful, intoxicating, and although I'd given myself wholly to his kisses, nothing had happened beyond that. I wanted to submerge myself in him and experience the extent of passion and pleasure.

He placed a hand on my knee, fingers inching up, close to my inner thigh.

I bit the bottom of my lip but held his gaze. This was what I wanted. Something curled deep in my belly, and I didn't think it was simply lust for him. It was more. An awakening, a desire for something deeper that went beyond sharing picnics on the lake or taking walks in the gardens.

"Ezra?" I whispered.

"Mila," he responded, "I'm done waiting."

MILA

Ezra stood so suddenly his chair fell over and crashed to the floor with a boom. The look in his eyes was indescribable and his movements a blur as he practically lifted me out of the chair, one hand squeezing my bottom, the other splayed against my back.

The calm, sweet man I knew shifted and morphed into something more dangerous and dominant. Before I could catch my breath, his lips were on mine, hot, insistent, the sweet nectar of peaches on his tongue. The blaze within me ignited, replaced with an ache for more. I squirmed in his arms, my fingers fumbling, tugging at his shirt as he spun me around. A moment later, my back was against the wall, and he lifted me higher until I could wrap my legs around him, the robe falling open.

Ezra drew back with a hiss. My face hovered above his, just inches away from his delicious lips. "You are naked, aren't you?"

"I told you," I teased, my fingers curling around the nape of his neck.

I dipped my head to taste him again, and he welcomed my advance, kissing me gently and then not gently at all. He pressed kisses against my jaw, sucking at my neck until I panted, bucking against him. Desperate.

Breaking contact, he pinned me with his dark eyes. When he spoke, his voice was rough. "Do you know what you do to me?"

"Show me," I ordered, a wildness growing inside, warning me I was on the verge of losing all control.

His grip tightened, and suddenly the wall was gone as he carried me into the dark bedroom. A faint glimmer shone in from the curtains, providing just enough light for us to see each other but muting everything else.

Ezra laid me on the bed, positioning himself between my legs. When I propped myself up on my elbows, he reached for the knot of the belt and pulled. The belt slipped down my hips, but the robe remained closed, like a gift, waiting for him to unwrap it. My breath hitched, but instead of touching me, he pulled off his shirt and tossed it over the side of the bed.

He was slim, his body hardened from his days as a knight. A crisscross of scars covered his torso, coming around his rib cage like the claws of a great monster. I reached for him, paused. But he stilled, waiting.

Encouraged by his patience, I sat up, and the robe slipped from around my shoulders. When I pressed my hand against his chest, heat radiated off his body. His fingers slipped under the robe as he bent his head to kiss my neck.

Soft lips sucked at skin, and his teeth nipped playfully. My breath caught in my throat as he moved his head further down, fingers closing around my waist, sliding to my hips.

When he kissed the swells of my breasts, I moaned, and a bolt of desire twisted through me. I opened my eyes as he pulled the robe off and let it slip onto the floor. "Ezra," I whispered, "this is my first time."

His breath warmed my skin as he met my eyes. Liquid desire pulsed there as he dragged his tongue across his bottom lip. "Do you want me to stop?"

"No…I…I thought you should know."

"It makes you all the dearer to me," he admitted. "If, for any reason, you want me to stop, just say so."

"Don't stop," I begged, wrapping my fingers around his biceps.

And then, because I wanted him to know how

ready I was, I reached inside his pants and squeezed his hardness. He jumped, hips bucking toward me. His tone came out strangled. "You're sure this is what you want?"

"It is," I said. "Ezra. Just take me."

He closed my mouth with a kiss and then laid me down. Removing his pants, he let me see him in all his glory. He was long, hard, and just that brief grasp had given me a glimpse of just how big he was. My entire body throbbed, imagining how he'd feel inside. I needed to be filled, to be taken. Bending my knees, I spread my legs, shyness replaced with need, and he sensed it too.

"I want you to be ready for me," he said, fingers sliding up my thigh, parting them further to his eager fingers.

Then he bent his head, bringing it near my wetness, and licked me. One slow lick, so light I barely felt it, but my whole body arched and my eyes rolled back in my head. My fingers tightened on the sheets, curling into fists as he licked me again, this time applying more pressure.

With a gasp, I tilted my head back and closed my eyes, enjoying every delicious sensation. His tongue was everywhere, exploring me, licking me, going deeper until he found my nub and sucked on it.

Sensations fired through me, one after the other, coiling, twisting, taking me to the brink of ecstasy. I couldn't get enough. I arched and squirmed, desperate to reach that epic summit. He paused and slid inside of me, one smooth, slow motion. My body opened, adjusted to him, and although a jolt of pain flared, the pleasure burned it all away. Wrapping his arms around me, he held me tight. Our bodies pressed together as we moved in sync, like musicians playing a rhythm, like dancers moving to a beat.

I clung to his broad shoulders, my body shaking and shuddering, submitting to him. A cry formed up inside me, bursting from my lips, impossible to hold back. The orgasm that rocked through me was too strong to hold back. His groans answered my screams as he convulsed against me. For a moment, I was outside of myself, beyond our lovemaking. That one act had caused me to transcend, and from there would be no return. What Ezra and I had done had bonded us, fused us together, and I had the distinct feeling that from now on our fates would be entwined.

MILA

We fell asleep in a haze of satisfaction. Contentment buzzed through me, soft and warm and sweet. Among the glow of lovemaking, everything was infinitely perfect. It was a moment to bask in, hold on to, and perhaps, one day, look back on and know that I fully enjoyed. I was happy, with no regrets.

I woke before Ezra, thirsty again. The light had grown muted, older as the day wore on. How many hours had we slept? Untangling myself from the blankets, I retrieved the robe and padded out for more water. My legs wobbled under me, and there was a faint ache between my legs. A giggle escaped, and I pressed a hand over my mouth, careful not to wake the golden king.

After satisfying my thirst, I tiptoed back to the

doorway, leaning on it as I watched him sleep. He lay on his back, long lashes closed, face calm, although one side of his mouth curved up in a smile. His chest rose and fell, and his hair was wild and disheveled. My chest ached with how striking he was, so perfect and irresistible. If a painter could catch the image of him, just like that, I'd hang it in my room and wake every morning to it.

Dark-green eyes opened. Turning his head, he gazed at me. Slow. Steady. "What are you doing over there?"

"I was thirsty." I smirked.

He glanced at the window as though it would tell him the time, before standing. The twisted blankets fell away, revealing his nakedness and his cock, still hard. Unable to tear my eyes away, I stared, heart racing, cheeks flushed. The ache between my legs wasn't pain; it was desire. I wanted him again.

A wet sigh escaped my lips as he dressed, hiding his scars from me. Still barefoot, he approached, sliding one arm around my waist. Tilting my head, I looked up at him, mindful of our proximity. The very act of lovemaking had made me more aware of him, of every gesture, every expression, every word that hung on his lips. Making love was supposed to satisfy the need, not strengthen it.

"Still thirsty?" he asked.

I wasn't sure if he was talking about water or

something else. I cocked my head and resorted to teasing to hide my trembling desire. "Satisfied for now, but I might get very thirsty again soon."

He laughed, although it sounded more like a snort. His lips brushed mine as he spoke. "Well, what do you want to do?"

I wondered if he perceived that being with him was enough. It didn't matter what we did or where we were. His presence filled me. If he spoke, I'd listen. I wanted to share everything with him, and a sensation grew, so compelling and strong within me that it hurt. Clearing my throat to hide my emotion, I leaned into him, inhaling his scent. When I'd regained enough of my senses to speak without my voice cracking, I asked, "Now will you show me your workshop?"

He took my hand, leading me out of the doorway. "I will. I cleaned up the wood shavings this morning so you can walk around it barefoot. I will not tell you more but let you see for yourself and decide."

I wasn't sure what to think of his cryptic words, so I let them lie there as he led me to the staircase. It spiraled straight down, pausing at three different landings before we reached the main floor. My mind whirled, wondering what was behind those doors.

The bottom floor was an open space, with unbridled daylight pouring in. Dust floated like motes of light, and the staircase was in the middle. With my feet resting on the bottom stairs, I took in my surroundings, my breath catching at the revelation of Ezra's secret.

An army of statues covered the floor, some carved out of wood. Others looked like silver, gold, marble, granite. They were a combination of people, creatures, wild and varied. A woman stepped out of a tree. A man held a pipe to his lips, but horns grew out of his head. Instead of feet, he had hooves. A child held up an apple, but her hair was like snakes, writhing around the crown of her head.

Others were more horrifying, a hunched beast with fangs and drool coming out of its mouth. A shrouded shadow, faceless, holding a hand out as if reaching for the soul. A dog with three heads, each one more terrifying than the other. Row after row of creatures were frozen there, and the detail with which they were carved was both admirable and frightening. Realistic, as if they were creatures who'd lived and breathed once but now they were soulless statues.

Suddenly, the carving I'd seen in his office and the ones in Namen's shop made sense. The features were blank, while the instrument was detailed.

I sat heavily on the last stair, staring in mute disbelief. But it was all possible. It was all in front of me. Ezra was oddly still and quiet beside me. Shy, considering what he displayed. He'd been right to hide his gift away for so long, but why?

"This," I spoke at last, my voice a thin thread of awe. "This is your gift?"

"This is my gift."

"Ezra, this…this is the most remarkable thing I've ever seen. They're so lifelike, so real…how?"

I tilted my head up at him, expecting to see his face pink from my praise. Instead, his shoulders were hunched and his face drawn into a sadness I did not understand.

"It comes to me," he said slowly, carefully. "The ideas creep up on me, begging to be reborn. They serve as reminders of what I've seen, where I've been, what I've done. This is the only level of creation I'm allowed to have. No more."

The way he whispered the words was haunting, as if he'd done something once and this was an apology. Again, I wondered at his history, at the vague story of darkness he'd told me. What had he done that was so wrong it had required banishment?

Turning my attention back to the statues, I stared at them, one by one. The detailed ones were like the creatures I'd seen last night in a drunken blur…creatures he'd told me were real. And a dawning awareness came over me. Slowly. Like the setting sun in the evening, the moments so sure and steady one almost never notices until it's completely dark. All this time, had Ezra been trying to tell me who he was? He was one of them. Not from here. From another world. Gifted. Magnificent. Strong. My sun god. What had he done?

"How long have you been able to carve like this?" I asked. It was a lifetime of work, and I couldn't even imagine how long it had taken him to shape and form each creature.

I recalled one of my conversations with Dusty and Giselle. Ezra had found them on his quest for wood, for this, his creations.

He sat beside me, his shoulder brushing mine. "I started when I was young, to pass the time, not that there was much time. In a miserable life, where I controlled nothing the one skill I had was the ability to mold something beautiful out of clay and, as my skill grew, wood. I worked with my hands but hid my gift from my parents, not that they cared. Once, I put a carved hummingbird in my mother's window, thinking it would make her smile. But she was too far gone by then. Nothing lit up her spirit. By the time I became a knight, it was already an innate skill, a way to ease the passing of time when traveling. I made nothing as complex as these until I gained my own tower."

He trailed off, and though I waited, he did not speak again. I stared at the child with the waving hair. Snakes. A shudder went down my spine. "What do they mean to you?"

Running his fingers through his hair, he sighed. "They are reminders of who I once was and who I want to be now. Redemption is possible, and if I stay on the right path, I will attain forgiveness."

I took his hand in mine, lacing our fingers together and holding tight. "Ezra, you speak of such darkness, of sorrow, and of a past you are unwilling to share about aside from vague hints. But all I've seen of you is goodness. You are kind, generous, considerate. All those things can't be an act, because I've seen you daily, working to ensure the happiness of others. You serve without apology, and I can't help but believe whatever held you, whatever darkness that had a grip on you, is gone. You have changed, and it's your goodness that intrigues me, that makes me start to fall in love with you."

Eyes wide, he faced me, his voice low. "You aren't frightened, are you?"

"It is surprising, but I realize you've seen much more than I have, wild creatures and varied lands, and I'm willing to trust you."

His eyes brightened, and he leaned closer, pressing a hand against his heart. "Do you know what your words do to me? I thought I was beyond having anything worth living for here on this side of the barrier, beyond the scope of what I've known, but you, you're always surprising me. I don't deserve you or your love, but I know that's not how love works."

"No," I agreed. "Love is a choice."

"You are wiser than your years," he breathed, studying my face. "It is a choice, and I choose you."

I kissed him first, tasting the fire in his words. Even though the creatures surrounding us had lifeless stares, I sensed we were not alone.

MILA

The inn was quiet after the harvest festival, and the next evening, I slipped outside to walk to Ezra's tower. Craning my head back to eye the carriage house, I spied Rachelle and Rabon outside of it, laughing. They'd probably go on a moonlit ride, and I wondered who would be later to bed, myself or Rachelle?

Nerves fluttered in my belly like the wings of butterflies as I hastened up the path to the tower. Blooming flowers lined the walkway, their white faces upturned to the light. Tiny yellow bees hummed, darting in and out of the delicate petals. Daylight hovered on small stones that poked up from the grass. At first, I thought they were boulders, markers of some sort, until I saw the writing on them.

Squatting, I studied one, brushing away the grass to give myself a better view. A series of lines was carved into the stone, runes, and they glowed faintly, just a hint of gold in the sunlight. Brow furrowed, I stood upright and continued to the tower. Why would someone put runes on stones, and what did they mean?

Ezra waited for me, leaning against the doorframe, hands in his pockets. The sunrays caught him just right, and I let out a breath, staring unabashedly. He was breathtakingly handsome. The angles of his face and body, perfect in every way. As I neared, my skin flushed at the reminder of what he'd done to me only the day before. What would he do to me tonight?

"Searching for wild strawberries in the grass?" he called.

"What? Oh." I laughed. He must have seen me inspecting the runes. "No, there are drawings on the rocks, and I was curious about them."

Taking his hands out of his pockets, he straightened. "Yes, a bit of superstition, but they add some landscaping to the scenery. I thought they'd be best left where they are."

"Superstition?" Another old tale. "Of what?"

Ezra's fingers trailed down my arm. Taking my hand in his, he pressed it to his lips. "They are old wards to protect against evil spirts and unwanted intruders."

My mind went to the wild creatures he'd carved out of wood and the shadow I'd seen in the cellar, but he drew me into his arms so quickly I didn't have long to dwell on them. Instead, I leaned into his embrace, feeling secure, happy, wanted.

"What do you think of water?" he asked, releasing me to shut the door.

I shivered as I walked inside, even though I'd mentally prepared myself for stepping into his workshop again. Although the statues stood frozen, they seemed real and lifelike, waiting for a soul to give them life. They were disturbing, regardless I'd promised myself to come to terms with it. Facing Ezra, I answered his question with one of my own. "Of water? What kind of question is that?"

He chuckled. "Do you like water?"

"Yes…" I drew out my answer, confused, as he led me up the stairs.

"Good. I have a surprise for you."

More surprises? "It involves water, doesn't it?"

"Correct, but you will not entice me to say more," he teased.

I raised my eyebrows as we continued past the second landing. "What is behind these doors?"

"Storage, odds and ends." He shrugged. "But I

think you'll like this." We stopped on the third floor, in front of a simple door. "Close your eyes."

I studied the mischievous expression on his face as he let go of my hand. Obediently, I closed my eyes.

The door swung open with a slight wind, and soft fragrances came to my senses.

Water, citrus, and wax.

"Open," he breathed in my ear.

Blinking, I stared at a pool of water. Gray stones surrounded the bath, which sat on the floor, with steam rising from its surface. A series of broad steps led down into it, like an invitation, welcoming me to the depths. It wasn't large, just enough for three or four people to sit in comfortably, but around the edges, candles burned and vines trailed up the wall to the ceiling. Towels and robes hung off hooks in the wall, and there were a few low-lying seats. A tray perched by the water's edge, carrying a collection of fruits, cheeses, and wine from the vineyard.

"What is this place?" I whispered, enchanted.

Ezra pulled me further into the chamber, where the stones were slick with water. Standing behind me, he wrapped his arms around my waist and held me there, his breath tickling my neck. "This used to be an old bathhouse where those who lived in the tower came to rest and relax when they were off duty. I imagine they had feasts here and many long nights full of food, drink, and merriment. I've never had much use for it. It's lonely here, just myself and my thoughts. Although, it is a good place to sit and think. The water is always warm, a phenomenon I cannot explain. It relaxes my muscles after a long, tense day."

I wondered what long, tense days Ezra had as owner of the inn, but among his share of work, managing the books, and taking time to fish and carve and pick fruit, he was quite busy.

"Now that you've seen it, what do you think?"

"There were steam houses in Solynn. The lords enjoyed them, and while some claimed they discussed politics, from the guests that were invited, it was clear something else was going on."

Ezra's voice vibrated against my skin. "Something else like what?"

Squirming out of his arms, I reached for the clasp of my dress, loosening the ties and buttons that clinched it around my body. Smirking at him, I backed away. "It would be easier to show you."

After yesterday, I was past the point of shyness with him. I wanted him to see me unclothed, unbound, to look upon my bare body and desire me as much as I desired him. Shimmering out of my dress and small clothes, I folded them on a nearby bench. Keeping my back to him, I enjoyed the slow hiss that left his lips as I walked down the steps, into the water.

It was warm, almost hot against my skin, but it felt good. The waters weren't still; instead, they moved, foaming and creating bubbles like fingers to massage my skin. A seat ran alongside the wall, and I perched on it, my feet floating up. I giggled at the weightlessness I felt and faced Ezra.

He hadn't been idle and was already waist-deep in the water, floating toward me.

"This is amazing," I told him as he sat across from me, a satisfied smile on his face. "It's inappropriate for a woman to spend too much time in the water. At least, in the city."

Ezra frowned in confusion. "How is water inappropriate?"

Tucking my hair behind my hair, I explained, "Inappropriate for women. In the city, there aren't many natural bodies of water. Most of the pools and lakes are man-made or on estates. Children can play in them when they are young, but to find a woman bathing in public is a crime because of the nudity. They say it tempts men and a true woman would never use water to tempt a man to take her virtue."

Ezra snorted. "That is preposterous. It sounds very much to me like the government in the city is given over to ridiculous rules."

"They are," I said. "Most of the time it's because

someone wealthy complained, and because their funds hold sway over politics, they often get their way. Is it not the same where you come from? Doesn't money rule the whims of men?"

"It depends. Usually power is stronger than money, and strength."

With the way he spoke, I had the distinct feeling he wasn't talking about power from authority but something else, invisible, unexplainable. But I did not ask for clarification as he poured me a glass of wine.

Passing it to me, he moved closer. "Tell me, what was it like growing up in the city?"

I shrugged. "I have nothing to compare it to, so I have no complaints." But even as I spoke, the haunting memories came whispering back. The teasing voices, the fingers pointed at Aveline and me for being peculiar, poorer. We hadn't had maids in the house, nor could we have partaken in the extracurricular activities the wealthy did. Even though Mother had spared us, we'd gone to work as soon as we could contribute. I was much happier outside of the classroom, grown up and able to pursue my own passions. And I would not let the lingering bitterness of the past mar the pleasure of the present.

Ezra watched me closely before taking a sip of wine. "We do not have to speak about the past."

Oh. I'd forgotten how he could sense feelings. Perhaps he perceived the shadow that had hung over me just then.

"The scrolls of the philosophers you told me about arrive today."

"Scrolls. Not books?"

Ezra rewarded my teasing with his smile. "Yes, well, books are more practical, but I like the idea of scrolls, unrolling parchment to see the words laid out for me."

"Are you studious? Do you aim to write your own manifesto as those great philosophers once did?"

"Perhaps I shall, when I understand life more fully," he quipped. Moving to the edge of the pool, he lifted a strawberry off the platter of fruit. "For now, I am content to share the delicacies of this life with you. Have you had fruit dipped in chocolate?"

I let the sweetness of the wine hover on my tongue before swallowing it, and tingles raced up and down my spine. Between the wine and the water, I felt as light as a feather, as if I would float away. "I've had fruit, and I've had chocolate, but never together."

"Well, you're missing out. Let me fix that."

After dipping the strawberry in a bowl of melted chocolate, he held it to my lips. I took a bite, and a symphony of flavor exploded in my mouth. My eyes widened as I stared at him, and I devoured the rest whole.

"That is marvelous," I said, mouth full, not caring.

Ezra chuckled. "Have another."

We dined on fruit and chocolate, and soon I lost count of the glasses of wine as we spoke about mundane things and basked in the water. And with each glass of wine, I moved closer to him, hungry again for his lips, his touch, as though it would never be enough.

"Your hair is purple," he said at one point, his fingers lifting the wet ends out of the water. "Why is that? I told myself when I first saw you, the woman with the purple hair, 'That is unusual and attractive. I must know her story.' Why purple?"

Heat covered my chest, and it wasn't from the water alone. I inclined my head toward his, my pulse pounding. "I've always stood out. As a child, as a young woman, it was hard to fit in with others. Especially women my age. I decided, once and for all, to solidify how different I am. I've never wanted to be anyone other than myself, and the way people judged me before they got to know me did not feel right. At least let them judge me for being bold and sure of myself. I went to the gardens and gathered Maiden's Blush. Aveline helped me soak the roots and dye my hair. Afterward, no matter how many times I washed it, the color never came out. It grows purple now."

He gazed at me with his soulful eyes. "Do you regret it?"

"Never," I breathed.

His eyes roamed over me. "It's beautiful. You're beautiful."

When he kissed me, the truth of his words seeped into me, and I floated into him, allowing him to take me, possess me. The thought occurred to me as we broke apart, gasping, that I did not want a short-term fling. A brief attraction fueled by lust, mistaken for love.

I wanted something real and beautiful and passionate. Something I could not walk away from. I stared into Ezra's forest-green eyes, for he was the answer, the missing part of my soul. That knowledge was both intensely terrifying and riveting. I knew, beyond a shadow of a doubt, I wanted him.

MILA

The wild cry of the violin played, low and sorrowful, haunting. I gasped, then leaped out of bed and opened the window. Enchanting music drifted to my ears, music I hadn't heard in weeks. It was wondrous. Beautiful, making my heart yearn for more. How could one play with such soul, such aptitude?

The haze of falling in love and the glow of finding where I belonged lessened as I recalled why I'd come to the Dawn. It wasn't to fall in love or discover its secrets; it was to pursue music, and somehow, along the way, I'd lost sight of my goal. I'd become complacent instead of focused on bettering myself. Even my afternoons of practice had become shorter and shorter as I'd walked the gardens or assisted Giselle or daydreamed about Ezra. The distant violin reminded me I could be more. Given the right motivation, I could go beyond the shallow knowledge I possessed and learn how to play from the soul.

An idea struck me as the cool breeze floated in. Originally, I'd wanted to find the person who played, and had believed the music came from the island, one of the fabled gods, because there was something sacred and magical about the land. And the shadow creatures had reminded me there were creepier things, horrors I could not fully explain even though I'd seen them with my own eyes. If I found the player of such music, I would ask for a gift, an impartation that I, too, could play from the heart.

With that thought, I dashed to the wardrobe and flung on my dress, but just as I reached for my shoes, the music drifted away. Gone. I waited, but a blanket of silence coated the air. Sitting heavily on the bed, I sighed. I was too late, and streaks of the sunrise were already gracing the inn with light. Next time, I'd have to wake earlier to discover the secret of the music. Since I was already up and dressed, I decided to go to the barn to visit Giselle.

As soon as I walked outside, my eyes were drawn to the tower glimmering in the pale light. My gaze was pulled beyond it, and my feet moved of their own accord, reminded of something Ezra had told me long ago. The island wasn't an island at all but a bay, connected to the mainland by a path. I'd never attempted to access it, for there hadn't been a reason, but today I glanced over my shoulder and started up the path to Ezra's tower.

Rune stones glowed like beacons as I neared the tower, but the stones continued beyond it, like a guide for lost travelers. Heart racing, I continued, hoping that Ezra wasn't home, watching me explore. Beyond the tower, the path slowly descended, leading back to the lake. I followed it downhill, all the while aware of the tower rising high above me, an ever-present guardian, watching, waiting. I wasn't trespassing, but my body heated and I quickened my pace, not wanting anyone to spy my curiosity.

The teal waters of the lake shimmered gold in the morning glory, and although the narrow trail beside the lake was muddy, the rune stones clearly marked it. Why hadn't I seen them before? The path zigzagged like a worm alongside the bank before turning inward into a clump of thickly wooded aspen trees. Green leaves surrounded the wood like a halo of fog, hiding the secrets of the island from intruding eyes like mine. Goose bumps pebbled on my arms, and my mouth went dry. Rune stones stood like guards on either side of the path into the wood. Had Endia run here to discover the secrets of the island? What had she known that had led to her death?

Wind stirred, blowing through the shades of green, creating a low roar of music as I stood on the path, indecision twisting through me. Was the island hostile or friendly? A clear path led into the gloom. If I stayed on it, it would be impossible to become lost. But there was no music, no reason to enter those shaded boughs.

A blur of blackness weaved between the trees, reminding me of the creature I'd seen in the cellar, and my heart skipped. My fingers tightened into fists, and I stepped back, my bravery gone. It was nothing. Just a bird or a beast, for wild animals lived on the island, and I'd almost trespassed into their territory. Still unsettled, I hurried uphill, back to safety.

I discovered Giselle in the barn, humming as she worked. It was warm inside, smelling of animal musk and sweet hay, scents that made my nose itch with sneezes. "Mila, what brings you here this morning?"

Shrugging, I sat on a bale of hay while she weaved a basket together. Giselle's fingers were always busy. "I heard a violin playing, and since I was already awake, I came here."

Giselle raised an eyebrow. "A violin?"

"Yes." I nodded. "Does anyone else play around here?"

She dropped her gaze back to her work. "Perhaps it was a musician who spent the night after the harvest festival."

I doubted it. "I've heard it before and then silence for weeks, but now I've heard it again. I don't know where, or why."

"Strange things happen in these parts," Giselle said, studying me. "If, though, you're so curious, maybe you can find out who plays."

"That is what I intend to do when I hear it again. Have you heard it?"

"No, but the supernatural does not reach out to all of us the same way."

I chewed my lower lip, wondering if she was thinking of Endia, whom Ezra suspected was dead. But there wasn't a body to prove it, so she could be far away and happy. "Have you been to the island?" I asked.

Giselle cocked her head. "Of course."

"No, I mean not using a boat but the path along the bank that leads into the forest?"

"Oh, that side of the island." Giselle shook her head. "I have no desire to be lost in the forest. I hear the path only takes one so far before it plays tricks on the mind. Besides, the wild animals still live there, and Ezra asked that they not be disturbed."

I tucked that knowledge away, aware that Ezra warned people away from the island.

"What about the rune stones? What can you tell me about them?"

Giselle smiled. "There's a tale concerning those

too. The stones were carved with runes to protect the villagers from evil spirits and unsavory types that lived on the island. When the gods of music came to change the seasons and the people did not welcome them, they plagued them with grief. Darkness appeared. Some claimed the dead came back to life and spirits made of shadow and bone crept out from the island and haunted them."

Even though it was full daylight, I shivered at the story.

"To protect themselves, the people took stones and went to someone who could carve runes to protect them from evil. They were placed around the island, creating a path to prevent the spirits from escaping, and they are still here today."

"So if one stays on the path, or near the rune stones, they are protected?"

"That is the idea," Giselle said.

I thought of the red eyes and the shadow. "What if the runes don't work?"

Giselle snorted. "Some things only work if you believe in them. Now, it's only an old tale leftover from tradition. In my years here, I've seen nothing I could not explain."

Nothing? I'd only been here for three months, and even I'd seen things I couldn't explain. Another thought struck me even though I couldn't explain why. "Giselle, have you ever lived in the inn?"

"Bless me, no, I've always been out here."

I nodded and brushed the thought away. For why would the inn have anything to do with the supernatural?

Giselle poked my side. "I saw you with Ezra during the festival."

My face heated. "Yes, we were dancing."

"Looked like more than dancing." She winked.

She'd seen us kissing, which had been anything but chaste. I fixed my gaze on the hay, unable to meet her eye. "Yes…I know…well…"

"I'm only teasing," Giselle said. "Ezra is a good man, and he's always been alone. It's good for him to have someone like you."

My heart softened as she validated our relationship with words I had desired to hear. Still, I wondered with a pang if indeed she knew him truly. The version of himself he presented to the world differed from the version he presented to me. He was more mysterious, with secrets that were being slowly unveiled to me. Did she know about his workshop and the statues that appeared so alive? The shadow of darkness that haunted him? His banishment? Yes, he was a good man now. But who had he been before?

MILA

"You shouldn't work for me anymore," Ezra said as we left the inn.

It was afternoon, and he'd found me in the staff's lounge. I had been on my way upstairs to practice, but his presence was too tempting to ignore. Besides, I wanted to ask him about the violin I'd heard that morning, but his words about me not working for him stole my excitement. "Why?"

"Given our relationship, I don't want you to feel you have to work here. You should be free to come and go as you please."

"And do what?" My pulse pounded, and my fingers twitched. I gazed across the rolling meadow, the blue mountains in the distance, and my throat went dry. Without waiting for Ezra to answer, I continued, "Ezra, I enjoy working here. It gives me a schedule, something to do. I'm not the kind of woman who can sit in a room doing nothing. I need a goal, a purpose, activities to challenge my mind. If I wanted to do nothing, I'd be at my sister's estate. Here there is my music, the garden, the animals, the lake, the guests, the inn itself. There's always something to do, and each day is new, exciting, and fresh. If you take away my work, you take away the excitement, the reason I came. It's staying busy that makes me appreciate the time we can spend together after the work is done."

He stroked his chin. "You're quite passionate about this."

"Yes." I wondered what was going on in his mind. "I know I don't have to work, but I'd feel terrible taking advantage of my sister's generosity. Her husband, Tomas, has a good trade, but now I can assist with Mother's medical bills and pay old debts. The work I do helps my family. Besides, I feel good doing something for myself instead of relying on the kindness of others. It's not that I don't appreciate kindness, but working with my two hands gives me something to be proud of. Like I've told you, I've always been different."

"I know. That's what I like about you, Mila." His eyes were warm like the summer sun. He took my hand, rubbing his thumb over my knuckles. "I know that work is important to you. I didn't realize how important, and I don't want to take it away from you. Selfishly, I wanted more of your time."

"Well, you are my employer," I blurted out.

That knowledge hung there between us. What were we doing? If this happened in Solynn, it would be forbidden, but out here in the country, no one noticed or cared. A twist of something wicked and delightful simmered in my belly. Because what would happen to me if anyone found out? It was Ezra who owned the inn, and Ezra's final word was the only one that mattered. I was untouchable, for there were no politics, no rules, nothing that would drive us apart, and I basked in that satisfaction.

"I am." He sighed. "Which is what makes it harder. I must admit that I'm conflicted. It feels wrong to have you work for me even though you want to."

I squeezed his hand. "Ezra, I'm here because I choose to be here."

Tugging me to a stop, he spun me to face him. "Say it again."

Boldly, I grinned up at him. "I'm here because I choose to be here."

The slow kiss was sweet like sugar on my lips. His rough hand cupped my cheek, the other still holding my hand tight. My stomach fluttered as I closed my eyes, well aware we were in plain sight of anyone in the inn or meadow. But it felt real and right, and when he pulled away, my legs trembled with need. I wanted him to take me right then and there...preferably with no one watching.

Wordlessly we continued, and I basked in the miracle of what I had. I stole a glance at Ezra, tall and broad-shouldered with his muscled arms and warm fingers gripping mine. The breeze tousled his golden hair, and the set of his jawline and the profile of his long, straight nose were so beautiful and so perfect my heart melted. Was it possible that he wanted me? Mila? With plum-purple hair? A nobody from Solynn?

The knowledge that none of that mattered, that he actually liked me for exactly who I was, made a lump form in my throat. How was it possible that in the expanse of such a wide world that our paths had crossed? Was it fate? Luck? For this could be no coincidence. I made myself a promise not to ruin or lose what was between Ezra and me. I had the sense it was precious, beautiful, slowly growing stronger. We were only at the beginning, on the cusp, but I wanted to fall headlong, deeper.

It was cooler by the waters, and it left me refreshed as we walked down the soft bank. Ezra held my hand as if it was perfectly natural. It was quiet. A hush fell over the land. The bleating of the sheep and goats stilled, although soon the crickets chirped. Ezra led me to a grassy knoll, and we sat on the embankment, our backs against the rise of land.

"This is what you like to do?" I asked.

"I like the water and how calm the lake is. What do you see when you look out at it?"

"Water."

"Yes, water, but beneath the surface, there are hundreds of living creatures. You wouldn't know unless you went for a swim or dived below to see it teeming with life. Each animal is unique, the fish, the frogs, the serpents, and others that live below. Water creatures have always fascinated me, and the conditions that allow them to breathe underwater, unlike us with the air we breathe up here, pure, undiluted with liquid. Ah, but I am boring you."

"You're not boring me. I've never heard you speak like this."

"No, and nor should I. Wondering about creation leads me astray. It was one of my hobbies I put aside. Mila, I must admit, I haven't forgotten what you told me."

"Told you about what?"

I shifted as he moved closer, one hand on my thigh.

"You. Composing an original melody with your violin. I'd like to hear it."

I laughed then. "Ezra, it's not ready, and honestly something to amuse myself."

He gathered my skirt in his hand and inched it up, little by little. "I will pass no judgment on what you create. I enjoy your music, and I'd like to hear you play something of your own."

My dress was above my knees, and I drew in a sharp breath. "Let me practice more, and then I'll give you a private audition. Deal?"

"We have a deal," he said, his fingers skimming my inner thigh.

"Deal." My breath hitched as he moved my skirt still higher.

The last lights of the day were fading as he hovered over me. "Open your legs, Mila. I want to pleasure you."

I obeyed, wet even before he kissed me, his mouth warm, his tongue thrusting and demanding. I couldn't help the moan that escaped my lips as he pushed me back until I lay in the grass, legs spread, dress around my hips. He tossed my underwear away as if I wouldn't need them again and settled between my legs. When he blew over my bare skin, I jumped, my entire body tense.

Raising myself on one elbow, I peered down. His mouth was so near my wetness it made my entire body tingle with anticipation. "What are you doing?"

"I'm going to pleasure you. Lie back and feel."

My pussy clenched as he bent his head nearer, and when his tongue touched me, my breath hissed between my teeth. "Ezra..."

He did it again, lightly, gently, teasing.

My hips bucked up, rising to meet his mouth, and then his hands were on my hips, holding me down. I squirmed, but he drew out the moment, making me wait, making me want, letting desire pool within me as my breath came ragged and fast.

And then he dived in, his tongue exploring, tasting, unfolding.

I cried out, unable to keep my hips from bucking. This was heaven. A burning need consumed me, and mewling sounds burst out of my throat. My fingers curled through his hair as he thrust with his tongue, sucking, playing, breathing. When he found my nub, my entire body coiled, ready, waiting for that peak, that climax. He sucked hard, and I came with a cry of euphoria.

His mouth was gone only a moment, quickly replaced with his cock, and then he was in me, holding me, grinding against me. We moved in rhythm, a melody of hoarse breathing. I wrapped my arms around his shoulders and hung on tight as if he could keep my soul inside my body, keep me from taking flight, but it was already too late. I came again, an orgasm rocking through me so hard I thought I'd faint. But he held me, kissing my neck, my shoulders, my mouth. My heart thudded against his, and we were the drums pounding wildly in the night while the creatures of the wood danced in a blur and the stars twinkled in a midnight sky. And out there in the wild was the promise of everything.

MILA

"Ezra, where did the violin I play come from?" I asked one evening, standing on the balcony outside of his study.

Ezra uncorked a bottle of red wine and poured each of us a glass. "Does it matter, when it's available for you to play?"

"Yes and no." I tore my eyes from the leaves, which were slowly changing from green to orange and red. As September deepened, I imagined the colors would become bolder, brighter and the air cooler. "I've been thinking for some time that I want to improve my skills." Sitting across from him, I picked up a glass. "I came here to learn to play, to become better, and while I've done that, I've reached a plateau. I need guidance if I'm to become better."

Something dark flickered in Ezra's eyes, but he

disguised it by taking a sip. "What do you want? I am at your disposal."

Twisting my fingers in my lap, I reclined in the chair, his question taking me off guard. Now was my chance, my moment to bring up the violin I'd heard the other day, and yet for some reason, I held back. "I don't know. I hoped you might have some ideas. Is there anyone in these parts who might be willing to teach me?"

"No," Ezra said quickly. Placing the wine on the table, he towered in front of me. "Mila, let me speak plainly. Music is not something that can be taught here; it is innate. Solynn is where you must go for instruction. Is that what you want? To leave?"

Folding my arms around myself, I sat back, considering his words and what they might mean. "No, not now," I whispered. For there was still the mysterious violin and the potent lure of Ezra himself.

Relief shone in his eyes as he knelt in front of me. "If you change your mind, in the spring, I will send you back to the city, and I will pay your way. But for now, I want you here, with me."

Two words stuck with me, making my heart constrict: for now. "What happens in the spring?" I asked, for the idea of leaving him and our temporary arrangement sent flutters of panic through my body.

Ezra must have sensed the worry, for he turned

my chair and slid his arms around my waist, head in my lap. "In the spring, should all go well, we go to the city, and then I will bring you back here with me." His fingers were under my skirt, sliding up the material, but he pinned me with his heated gaze. "Mila. I love you. I'm not letting you go. Not now. Not ever. Where you go, I go."

I sucked in a deep breath, surprised at the passion in his words. My eyes went wet, and my fingers trembled as I curled them into his strands of fine hair. He truly was perfect, and his cheeks dimpled as he smiled at me. "What about the banishment?"

His smile disappeared like storm clouds crossing over sunshine. "That's why I can't go anywhere right now. I have one last task to finish before I'll be free to travel. Will you stay? I know the terms of your original contract were through summer and I asked you to stay through fall, but the cold comes in winter, and it is charming here. I'd be lonely without you." He smiled again, my sun god, gracing me with his splendor.

I nodded, unable to speak, for he had my dress around my knees and bent his head to kiss my exposed skin. Lips seared my flesh, and my entire body arched in anticipation of the pleasure he promised. Sliding my bottom to the edge of the chair, he spread my thighs further apart, one finger following the path upward to where my wet slit waited, hidden by clothes. I writhed, thrusting myself toward his mouth, but he paused, stroking me through my underwear. My eyes rolled back in my head as my breath came shallow. Lips parted, I struggled for the sweet air. Plans of finding that mysterious violin and learning to become a master of music drifted away, mere goals that lost their importance under Ezra's touch.

"Ezra," I groaned, my fingers digging into his shoulders.

"Tell me you want this," he said, a strangled note in his tone.

Rising, he bent over me, one hand still between my legs while the other twisted through my hair, lifting my mouth to his. The dark flavor of wine still hung on his lips, and he held me tight as his fingers roamed, stroking, spreading until one finger was inside me. I groaned into his mouth, my hips rocking, desperate for more. Ezra held me still, hindering my journey to the peak of pleasure. Opening my eyes, I met his gaze. Pools of liquid desire. The way he gazed at me only made me surer of myself. Tightening my grip on his wrist, I confirmed, "I'm yours."

After sliding his finger out of me, he took my head in both hands and kissed me. When he pulled back, his expression was raw, almost wet. Lifting both my hands, he kissed my palms, then my wrists. "This, this is enough. Thank you."

I had the slightest sensation he was speaking of more than the words we shared, and yet I was overcome by him and him alone. Nothing else mattered.

Standing, he pulled me to my feet, wine forgotten. "Come."

He led me into the study and to an adjoining door. Within was a small room with just a bed, nothing more. Ezra's chambers in the inn. Leaving me in the middle of the room, he lit candles, which cast a soft glow, banishing the shadows. Something quickened within me as he faced me again, holding my gaze as he discarded his clothes, slowly, piece by piece. A challenge.

I copied his behavior, undoing the buttons and ties that held me bound in my dress. I let it slip off my shoulders, tossing my underwear with it, but when Ezra led me to the bed, I pushed him down and climbed on top. His hand tightened around my buttocks as he hissed, and I rubbed myself over his hardness, unashamed of my need for him. He'd teased me on the balcony. It was only fair I teased him back.

Impatient, he yanked me forward with a growl, his broad hand palming my breast and bringing it to his lips. My nipples went hard as he lashed them with his tongue and bit gently, then not so gently at all, drawing a cry of pleasure from my lips. Thus far he hadn't played with my breasts, but now he took one, then the other, sucking, pulling, nipping. The blazing heat of desire filled my core. My hips bucked against him, and suddenly I needed to be filled, to be taken. I moved faster, my actions telling him what I needed. I arched my back, and he took both my breasts in his hands, rolling my nipples between his fingers until I gasped.

My chest tight, my muscles trembled as he rolled to his side, taking me with him. Hooking one leg over mine, he parted my legs. I waited for him to thrust inside, but he took his time, running his hand down my belly until slowly, tantalizingly, he ran his fingers over my wet mound. Once again, his fingers thrust inside my slick folds. He found my clit and played with it, making small circles. A lightness filled me, and my breath came hard and fast as he kissed me. This time, I couldn't stop the cries that left my lips. I arched into him, craving, demanding more while he held me tight.

When at last he took his hand away, a tightness coiled within, so intense that when he thrust inside, an orgasm ripped through me. I ascended to a new height of pleasure as he held me, thrusting back and forth, our moans and groans mixing, our bodies becoming one long shadow, the candlelight reflected on the walls. He took me, body and soul, and I clung to him, opening my mouth again and again to him, his love, his passion, and his embrace.

Ezra wooed me through the next two months as the inn grew quieter and the season changed slowly, beautifully. I heard the violin occasionally, a call, a summoning that grew sadder, shorter, and more distant each time I heard it. But Ezra was always present, and my desire for him was so deep and thorough and driving as if my very heart beat for him. It did not matter how long he kissed me or how long we made love; every moment away from him stretched. When I was with him, it was perfection.

He took me out to the lake, made love to me on the shore, found me in the garden, kissed me in the hall, whisked me away to his tower, and it was all incandescently perfect. My fears about falling in love melted away, for Ezra, my mysterious sun god, was true to his word. He would never hurt me or betray me. He wasn't like my mother's lovers, and it shook me that Aveline was correct. I had to write my own story. I composed a letter to Mother and Aveline, sharing my intentions to stay until spring. When a response came, it was full of love, and yet I read the silent reprimand behind the words. But I ignored it. I wasn't neglecting my family. I sent them money, and they paid the debts off. Originally, I'd come for them, and now I stayed for myself.

MILA

It was still dark, the air gray, maybe an hour before dawn, when I woke to the music of the violin. My dreams had been blissful, my mind still entrapped by memories of what Ezra had done to me last night, my heart beating fast with the anticipation of what he might do today. But the music, it poured out, a summoning, a beckoning, and this time, it wasn't sweet but low and slow, almost deadly. Each note was pulled out with agonizing slowness, and I knew this was my chance to find out who played the violin.

Throwing back the covers, I dressed quickly, pulling on trousers and boots. Careful not to wake Rachelle, I tiptoed out of the room, avoiding the creaks on the stairs as I made my way outside.

The October air was cool and made me shiver as I

stepped outside, hints of pumpkin, spice, and pine swirling. Closing my eyes, I listened to the sound to determine which direction it came from. In my heart, though, I already knew it came from the island.

I followed the rune stones up past Ezra's tower, feeling the slightest guilt as I turned downhill, following the path by the lake. The magnificent forest loomed before me, a blend of evergreen and aspen, shades of crimson, harvest orange, and blazing yellow creating a quilt of beauty to grace the land.

There I slowed to catch my breath, the air a mix of peppery herbs and tangy wood. Streaks of pink light bloomed in the sky. Soon the sun would rise, and my chance would be gone. Forcing away thoughts of shadows, I stepped into the dark wood. There was just enough light for me to see my steps, but otherwise, the trees towered high above me, hemming out the light. Twigs and stones littered the path, forcing me to slow down even more. The trail twisted away, and my heartbeat increased, from not only my quick pace but the fact I walked into a place unknown.

Silver light flickered, brightening the gloom of the trees. An enchantment hung in the air, and faintly came the rustling of woodland creatures. Occasionally a rich-toned leaf would drift in front of me, as if the trees welcomed me to their kingdom by tossing down leaves to brighten my path.

The island was old; that much I could tell from the thick tree trunks, flakes of white peeling off the aspen trees, and the impenetrable underbrush that appeared if one dared trod off the path. White mushrooms popped up at the bases of the trees, and eventually the scents of rot and mold and water wafted to my nose.

That was when I realized another sound was mixed with the violin, the same sound I'd heard on my first trip to the island. A waterfall. Except this time, it was much louder, like distant thunder. It would be a sight to behold.

I expected to come out of the wood at any moment, but the path wound deeper, twisting away from civilization. The woods thickened with vines and moss, gnarled branches overhanging like hands reaching out to snatch at me. The deeper I went, the more I wondered if I was being needlessly foolish. But music played on, and my imagination danced around the idea that it was nothing but a ghost meant to lure unsuspecting people into the forest, to their deaths. When a shadow crossed my path, I jumped, aware of the menace that lay over the forest.

Swallowing hard, I continued, promising myself that after one last turn, I'd go back. I took the turn and the next one too, and suddenly the forest ended, and the path opened up.

Relief swept through me, and I stilled, for the sound of the waterfall and the violin were loudest. I'd come to an open space where the blush of dawn covered the sky with hints of lavender, coaxing the radiant sun to appear. The path descended to the bank of a wide, shimmering pool where mist floated off the surface, waiting for the warmth of light to burn it away. A waterfall poured off a cliff that rose about twenty feet above me. Water cascaded into pearl-colored foam, churning under the falls before settling to find its place, and the sound of it was almost as lovely as the music of the violin.

Looming above the falls were other cliffs, each one rising higher than the last, some covered with greenery, others with golden trees, all leading to the heights of the blue mountains. My heart soared at the beauty of it, for this was no dark and dangerous place; nay, it was a picturesque isle of beauty, an ode to nature undisturbed by humans.

Along the bank was yellow-green grass, some almost as high as my waist. Slick gray boulders poked up, covered in furry moss. Two yew trees graced the pool, boughs hanging down like maidens washing their hair in a river. Near the waterfall was a gaping hollow, the black opening of a cave.

This was a secret place, a sacred place, and

suddenly I believed the old legends held truth. During the turn of the seasons, perhaps the gods appeared and played their music for all to hear. Perhaps they were demented beings, shadow creatures that dwelled in the cave, lured out to hunt for flesh and blood. It all was true and would continue to be true as long as this island was left in peace. A knowing gripped me so strongly I felt compelled to turn around and leave, but I hadn't seen what I'd come to see.

Heart in my throat, I took another step forward, careful not to make a sound. My eyes darted around the clearing to catch sight of the violinist. At last, I found him standing under a yew tree, facing the water and playing slowly, carefully.

My heart stilled as I stared at his profile, watching the way his golden hair caught in the low light. His muscular arms were bare and moved up and down, lovingly stroking the bow over the strings. The tune he played was heartbreaking, and tears sprung to my eyes. I'd know that golden hair anywhere, and the lines of his muscles. It was Ezra. My sun god. And he played the violin.

My heart sank to the bottom of my toes as emotions crashed and collided. The music Ezra played was beautiful, enchanting, a gift. He was the master of the violin, more skilled than any musician I'd ever heard. Yet he'd invited me to the Dawn to play music and told me no one could teach me how to improve my rudimentary skills. Why had he lied to me?

Silent tears streamed down my cheeks as I stared in disbelief, aware my lover had hidden an important piece of himself. Never had he hinted at this secret, and I wanted to step out, confront him, wail, and rage. Yet he played with such intensity I was afraid of disturbing him. Closing my eyes, I let my tears bleed over while the music bloomed. It filled every pore, making me ache and yearn and long to wield a powerful magic the way he wielded his song. Those rich tones were deep and heavy, the sounds emotions would make if only if they could be heard.

A splash made me open my eyes. Sniffing, I wiped salty tears off my cheeks and blinked until my vision cleared. The waters were bubbling. A lump swelled in my throat. Was the bubbling because of the music? Taking a step closer, I watched as the surface rippled, turning black, as if someone had poured poison into those beautiful waters. A violent spray of water shot up, and throughout it, Ezra continued to play, as if he did not see or care what was happening in the water. Something dome-shaped emerged out of the blackness, slowly but surely, as if drawn by the music, summoned by it. The notes of the violin became harsher, longer, if possible, and my stomach knotted with dread.

The thing in the water kept rising, and my heart kicked as the beast revealed itself. It was a being shrouded in a blackness so deep and intense it was hard to make out its features. Its back was to me, and as it turned, bile burned the back of my throat. The only thing human about it was its form, a body, two arms and legs. The rest was pure evil. Black horns poked out of its head, and its skin was stretched tight over rippled muscle. A scream welled in my throat as dead eyes, hollow, lifeless, and red as blood stared, not at me, but directly at Ezra. When the thing opened its mouth, wolfish teeth appeared, and two fangs jutted over its lip.

It held out clawed hands and then hunched, crawling out of the water toward Ezra. He kept playing, but now the song was different, faster, more urgent, intense. The air shuddered and pulsed. Flickers of violet light gathered, motes drifting together like pinpricks of starlight.

I stared at the demon, and Ezra playing, and horror upon horror consumed me. Knowledge slammed into my mind so hard I raised a hand to my cheek as if I'd been slapped, but the pain was much worse. Once again, I remembered the dark shape I'd seen, the hulking creature, the slurping sound, the red eyes, and now. This. Ezra hadn't told me about his gift because he was the one who summoned demons with his music.

I should have run. Instead, I screamed.

Ezra and the demon turned, notes jarred as Ezra's gaze met mine, his eyes blazes of horror and anger and fear.

I vomited, a slew of water and bile leaving my body. Bent over, I continued to heave. One thought screamed in my mind: Ezra had summoned a demon with his violin. Who was he? More importantly, *what* was he that he had such power? Such magic?

Ezra's playing had screeched to a halt, turning into a collection of sour notes, and the demon lunged at him.

"Ezra!" I shrieked.

He ducked from the blow of swiping claws and lashed out with the only thing he had, the bow of his violin. A sickening crack rang out as the wood connected with the demon's body, and it howled. Ezra struck again, this time with the violin itself. The magnificent instrument shattered under the onslaught of the assault, but Ezra did not stop. He brought it up again, using the broken bow as a weapon, and drove back the demon. It howled, a sound so inhuman my bones hurt. I was barely aware of the tears spilling down my face as I stood stock still, watching the fight. Ezra gave one last feral shove, and the demon fell into the water. Dropping his broken instrument, Ezra yanked a long knife from his belt, his face murderous. Before he struck, he cocked his head back at me, eyes flashing. "Mila. Run!"

The command was deep and guttural, as if it came from the core of his being. It sounded wrong, deathly, demonic. I didn't wait to see if he could kill the demon with the knife. I spun and ran.

Tears blinded me, so when my foot hit a rock, I wasn't ready. I stumbled, twisting my ankle and ripping my trousers. My ankle throbbed when I put weight on it, but behind me were rustlings in the wood and hoarse cries. If the demon escaped, it would come after me next. Pulse racing, I forced myself up, gritting my teeth against the pain, and ran on as a rumble of thunder shook the air.

A drop of rain stung my face. Rain. There hadn't been signs of a storm before, but now it descended in a torrent, wind whirling, rain lashing at the trees like the whip of a slave master beating its servants into submission.

Water mixed with my tears, and a numbness came over me as I ran on, slipping in mud, stumbling toward the trees. At one point, I fell again, my breath ragged. I cut my hand on a rock, and the pain seemed so real and raw, the only thing that felt true. Blood slithered down my palm, and tears shook my body as the truth sunk in. The man I'd fallen in love with was a monster.

MILA

I must have passed out, for the next thing I knew, I woke to warmth. My first hope was that it had been a bad dream, but my hand was bandaged and my ankle throbbed. Sitting up, I realized I was in his bed. A place once so familiar and cozy was now frightening. He'd dressed me in one of his robes, and I imagined my muddy clothes were elsewhere. I scanned the dark room, my breath catching as he opened the door. Snatching the covers around me, I scooted to the edge of the bed, a cry on my lips. "Don't come near me."

Every muscle in his body went rigid, but he came no further. When he spoke, a strange note quavered in his voice. "It's still me, Mila. I'm still the Ezra you know. What happened back there I can explain."

"Explain?" I cried, my fear getting the best of me.

Despite my attempt to be brave, tears threatened to rise again. “Ezra, first you lied to me about the violin, and then I saw you summon a demon. How can you explain that?”

He raised his hands, showing me they were empty, but he did not approach. The dimness in the room kept his face cast in shadows, allowing me to sense more than see his uncanny calmness. “Yes, that is what you saw. I don’t have a choice. My life is not my own, not yet, not until I give the sorceress what she wants.”

I opened my mouth to retort, but my tears choked me. “A sorceress? Why didn’t you tell me?”

The moment those words left my tongue, I remembered. He’d told me about a queen, a broken vow, and later, a banishment that came with stipulations. He’d hinted at things, darker, frightening, yet in all our vague conversations about his past, I’d never dreamed, never imagined…this.

“I told you part of the truth, to protect you.” His tone was hollow, with an edge to it that led me to believe he was on the verge of begging. “I never wanted you to find out, not this way, not until it was all over. Will you let me explain? Will you let me tell you the whole truth?”

Tears flowed, making me gasp between words. “Only if you promise to let me go when you finish, without harming me. You have to let me go…”

He was quiet for a long time. Slowly his hands came down, hanging slack at his sides like a man defeated. Except I was sure he was no man. "I promise."

Hiccuping, I nodded and willed the tears to stop. He would not hurt me. He was still the Ezra I knew, with a dark, terrible secret. Once more, I saw that soulless beast rise from the water and shivered. I thought I might throw up again, but I held myself still, taking deep breaths to allow the nausea to pass.

Ezra slid to the floor as if too weary to stand and rested his head on the doorframe. His words were measured and even as he spoke, hints of emotion banished, just like him.

"As I told you, I was raised as a serf. During my childhood I learned how to carve detailed, lifelike statues. What I didn't tell you is that I also played violin, an innate skill that came naturally to me. Whatever music I heard, I could replay, and when I did, odd things happened, but I was a child and could not explain it. When I became a squire, I forgot about those skills and advanced through the ranks, focusing on land and wealth and war. Eventually I became a well-known knight, sworn to serve a gracious queen, but it was not enough. I began to carve again and play the violin, and eventually I heard of a great and powerful sorceress."

Ezra paused and sighed. Running his hands

through his hair, he continued, his voice low and haunting, "The queen I served had several knights, but there were some who broke their vows. When they did so, she called upon a sorceress to punish them. The sorceress enjoyed inflicting misery on those who disobeyed. In fact she became legendary because of one of her own knights she banished, a man called Sir Rainer. When he stole from her, she exiled him to another land and sentenced him to a tower. Thus the fallen knights became known as the Tower Knights. There were others too, who murdered for sport, bribed and thieved for pleasure, but I did not think I would earn a sentence like theirs, because my desire was to create. When the queen released me from her service, I swore an oath to the sorceress, an unbreakable vow, because she had what I wanted. The power to create."

I waited while he stared off into the distance, as if summoning the courage to continue. I had no words for him, only a deep disquiet, a fear of what would happen next.

"The sorceress gave me land and a place in her court, and I gave her music. There were many musicians in the sorceress's court, and they used the magic of music to change things. I'd finally learned how to wield the magic of my violin, and in her court, I made indescribable things happen. But most importantly, I created portals to new worlds. They are beautiful, like purple starlight lighting up the world, and when the sorceress saw what I could do, she named me the Sorcerer of Portals, and I opened them into lands as she requested.

"But there were other things I could do too. I showed you the creatures I carved from wood because they remind me of what I did. When I wasn't playing in the sorceress's court, I made statues and endeavored to find a way to make them come alive. At first I thought the violin would help me because depending on the notes I played, I could summon spirits."

My mouth went dry at his admission, even though I'd seen it with my own eyes. It sounded even worse coming from his lips. A deadly truth all mixed with magic I did not, could not, understand.

"Mila, I'm a necromancer. It's what I've always been. When I play my violin, I summon death, and I can't teach for fear of passing my magic on to you. I should have been honest with you, but I was afraid you'd react like this, or worse, you wouldn't believe until it was too late. When you played in the symphony hall, your music was pure, untarnished, and I selfishly wanted it for myself. You make it easier to face the darkness when I have your light and beauty to return to."

Tears filled my eyes, and a sob welled in my throat. My shoulders trembled at his words as understanding swept through me. But not forgiveness, for he'd known all along who he was. He'd been responsible for death and shadows.

When I did not respond, he continued, "I thought I could achieve creation by putting souls into my statues, but that was not how it worked. Time and again I failed until I grew bold and stole the sorceress's staff. I used the power of its crystal to give my statues life, and I raised an army of monsters, who were wild and selfish and evil. They destroyed everything they laid hands on, and only the sorceress could stop them. When she saw the death and devastation I'd caused, she banished me and took a piece of my soul to force me to continue to work for her, even from afar. This year, though, marks the end of my servitude to her. If I complete one final task, she will return the piece of my soul and close the portal between this land and her land, once and for all."

I didn't realize I was holding my breath until I let it out, and all the pieces fit together. My fingers shook, and I clasped them in my lap so tightly they hurt. I knew what he was going to say even before he completed his story.

"She gave me one last year to live and demanded I summon a demon from the depths and deliver it to her. I wasn't going to do it. Death was preferable, and then..." His voice broke. "Then I met you, and I thought maybe all could be forgiven and forgotten.

Perhaps I didn't have to live under the weight of darkness and sway of the sorceress. I carved a new violin, and I waited, for my magic is often strongest during the seasons' change. I've played and played, but I didn't find the right notes to summon the beast until today. It was all so simple: summon the beast, open the portal, and then she would remove her claim on me and allow me a second chance to live and love. There's a purity to it, like being reborn, and everything…everything went wrong."

He broke off suddenly and sagged against the doorframe, as if he no longer had the strength to hold himself up. I considered the motes I'd seen, the gathering of a portal. Was it I who had ruined his second chance? Who had made him hope for redemption? But no, I was not responsible for him having summoned a demon, a deathly creature, to appease the sorceress, and that could not be overlooked. Warring sensations twisted through me as I replayed each conversation, each interaction we'd had. The past he was making amends for lay before me, all the pieces, and with one word, one look, I could forgive him or damn him.

"I love you," he whispered. "But I won't bother you anymore."

Standing tall, he twisted and walked away.

I waited, hands clasped, for what seemed like an eternity. But he did not return. The silence stretched, the rain slowed, and I sat there, weighing his words, turning over his story again and again. My mind was quick, for I knew what I should do: return to my room, pack my bag, and go into town. From there, I'd find a stagecoach and travel to Mother and Aveline. This would only be a memory, a nightmare —no, not a nightmare, a tragic love story, like the ones written in books. Instead of getting up, I curled into a ball, holding on to the sheets that smelled like him, and sobbed long and hard.

MILA

I hobbled back to the inn and snuck up to my room. Instead of packing, I lay in bed and cried some more until I was drained. When Rachelle came to check on me, I told her I was sick, and she returned with water and soup. I didn't have it in my heart to eat, but I knew I should keep up my strength. When I put a spoonful in my mouth, again I saw that demon, and my stomach heaved. I almost didn't make it to the chamber pot.

Curling in bed, I rocked back and forth, too numb to cry anymore. I needed to think, to decide, but I was tired of being strong, of being alone, of taking care of myself. I wanted to lie down and let someone else handle the situation for me. Even in my mind, I heard his voice break as the truth had spilled out, a truth so horrifying and damning. Still, this was the country, and as Giselle had said, old tales sprung from it. Giselle. My mind latched on her, wondering how much she knew of the truth. Before I left, I'd talk to her.

In the morning, I woke to a knock on my door. Startled, I rolled out of bed, realizing I still wore Ezra's robe. Pulling it tightly around me, I opened the door and stepped back, shocked to see Ginger on the other side.

She stood stiffly, eyes narrowed, jaw clenched. She studied me for a moment before pushing inside. "You and I are going to have a talk."

"Why?" I staggered back. "Did Ezra send you?"

Ginger snorted. "Why would he?"

I opened my mouth and closed it, perching on the edge of the bed. Ginger settled on the chair in front of the fireplace. It would have been helpful to have a fire to warm the room, but I'd been too morose in my disenchantment to make one.

"No, I am here of my own accord," Ginger went on. "The inn is closing."

I stiffened. "What? Why?"

"I'm sure you know why. After all, you witnessed it yesterday. There is a demon loose in the woods, and if anyone comes to harm…well…we can't let that happen. Again."

Again. Was she referencing what had happened with the lady? Had a demon been in the inn before?

"We are sending all the guests home and the staff away, at least those who will go. Moses and Marley are stubborn, and so are Dusty and Giselle. Rachelle, though, knows what is good for her and will leave. And you will go too, if you know what's good for you."

So she had made my choice for me, and suddenly I didn't like that at all.

"Is that what you told the others?"

"About the demon?" She rolled her eyes. "No, of course not, but I'm very persuasive."

I recalled how she'd handled the incident with the lady. "This isn't the first time it has happened, is it?"

She straightened up, shaking her short black hair. "No, it isn't. Nor will it be the last. It's not pretty business, summoning demons and adhering to the wishes of a sorceress. I just want to know one thing. Do you love him?"

My nostrils flared. "How dare you ask me that," I snapped. "Who is Ezra to you anyway? Why are you so loyal to him?"

"If you don't love him, then go, be like the others, run when it gets hard. He's doing this for you, you know, not that you should take responsibility for his actions. Just understand the weight of what is happening here. He decided to damn the world, to give the sorceress what she wanted, so he could give you what you desire most."

Tears pricked at my eyes, but I kept my jaw hard. "And what do I want most? What do you know about it?"

"Him. You want a chance to live a life with him, or at least you did until you saw him for who he really is. The side of him he's about to toss away for eternity. He was immortal, you know, powerful, godlike, until he fell from the sorceress's grace. This is all he needs to do to gain his freedom from her, once and for all. She is dangerous, devious, but she keeps her word. And so does Ezra. That's why I follow him. He saved my life, and I elected to serve him for the rest of mine. And I don't break my vows."

There. The truth of it was that she'd known him from before. I stared… Ginger didn't have a problem with who Ezra was. That was love, the power to see beyond the darkness to potential. Suddenly I felt scolded for my reaction, although it was only human.

"Why are you here?" I whispered. "Why are you telling me this?"

Ginger's mouth tightened. "Because he loves you. I disapproved and gave him my opinion, but he pressed on, cautiously, carefully, because he's in love with you. And what he needs from you is hope before he fights this fight. A man without hope is a dying man, and you can give him that before he goes to hunt the demon."

"What do you want me to say?" I squeaked.

"Say you'll come back, or that you aren't angry with him. Anything, however small it is, will help. It is up to you though, but if you change your mind before you go, he's in his office."

In the office where we'd had drinks on a blissful eve not so long ago. That had been my first glimpse into the man he was, and how appropriate for him to be there now. Ginger stood, frowning down at me. I sensed her displeasure even though she was trying to help Ezra, and an unfamiliar look crossed her eyes, a tired look.

Turning her back on me, she moved to the window. "I fell in love once, another time, another knight, when I was young, much too young to know what I had. He was pledged to another and promised to break that vow for me, said he didn't need land and status to gain happiness. I sent him away because he would have a better life with that woman than with me. At that time, I was poor. I thought possessions would keep me happy, and indeed they are a safe choice but not the wisest choice. He married and died in battle a year later, fighting to keep his lands safe. I've always thought back to that moment and wondered if...if I'd accepted him, would he still be alive today? Would our paths be different because I'd chosen love instead of running from it?"

I leaned back on the bed, pressing my fingers against the bridge of my nose. She was telling me this to speak to my inner fears. What if I left? Would I be able to live with myself and the possibilities I'd abandoned? What if I stayed?

Ginger let out a sigh, and for the first time, her tone was almost gentle. "I've lived a long time, and I've discovered the point of life isn't staying safe, or doing what's expected, or being complacent. Where's the fun in that? It's about being bold, leaning into adventure, and taking risks, even if you might fail or fall, because that is the only way to experience the height and depth and breadth of life. One can never experience the highs of passion, love, happiness, and sorrow if one sticks to the guidelines and expectations passed down by family or jurisdiction. Your choices have consequences and significance that carry from this life into the next, even across worlds. I was a coward when the greatest, truest love came my way, and I regret that every day of my life. I'd rather live without regrets than carry the weight of this one with me."

Clearing her throat, she spun around and strode to the door. "The carriage will be waiting this afternoon. Don't be late."

The door clicked shut behind her, and I stared,

her words humming within me. But even more so were words that Aveline had spoken that had only hinted at love and regret. She had chosen safety over love, and I was about to do the same thing. I didn't want to think about it, but the choice hemmed in on all sides.

Moving to the washroom, I ran water for a bath, undressing slowly. As I sank into the warm water, it was as if the imprints of his breath, his lips, his teeth were still on my skin. My legs were ready to open for him, my body already arching up to meet his warmth and hardness. As I sank beneath the waters of the bath, I knew what my body wanted, what my heart wanted. My head was the only part of me that disagreed.

MILA

I brushed my hair until it shone, staring at myself in the mirror, delaying the inevitable. My clothes were easy to pack for I wasn't taking the glamorous dresses Namen had made. There would not be a need for them in the countryside, and it felt wrong to take them when I hadn't paid for them. Leaving the packed bag by my bed, I took a trembling breath and made my way upstairs.

The inn was hollow and haunted by the lack of guests. Wood creaked under my footsteps as I climbed to the top floor and walked out into sunshine. The paintings still hung, breathtaking and magnificent, and the light from outside made it feel as if nothing was wrong at all. The doors to the library stood open, and I paused in the doorway, staring at the stacks of books, the plush chairs, and the velvet carpet. No one would disturb it for a long time. What a shame to close the doors on a wealth of knowledge.

My feet carried me to the end of the hall, where the door to Ezra's office loomed, tightly shut. One last obstacle between him and me. My heart raced as I knocked on the door. If he didn't answer or wasn't there, my decision would be made for me. I'd leave the Dawn and its blighted halls, cursing the day I'd agreed to work at such an illustrious place. I was a dreamer, and for all the pains I'd taken, my dreams had still turned to nightmares.

"Come in," Ezra called, sealing my doom.

Heart in my throat, I opened the door. He sat at the desk, head bent over a task, writing quickly. The doors to the balcony were open, letting in the fall air, although a fire crackled on the hearth. I stared at Ezra's golden hair, the slope of his shoulder, his firm jawline, and the sure and steady stroke of his hand as he wrote. When he finished, he lifted his head, and his eyes widened. He hadn't been expecting me.

"Mila," he gasped and stood up so quickly the pot of ink fell over, marring his work. He didn't so much as notice, only stared at me, a look of misery and expectation covering his face. "I thought you were gone."

All the words I'd wanted to say left my mind, and a lump swelled in my throat. Tears burned at my eyes as I shook my head, and then, as if under a spell, I ran to him. He moved in an instant and caught me, pressing me against him, his lips burning like a brand. Our embrace was desperate, our kisses filled with fire and passion. A tear slipped down my cheek as his mouth moved in sync with mine. I opened my lips, and his tongue thrust in, quick and demanding. I moaned, pressing myself against him, clutching at him to save me.

His fingers tangled in my hair, and his other hand squeezed my bottom. A strangled moan came from his throat as he steered me to the couch in front of the fire. He lay me down on it, gently, carefully, hovering over me, his lips never leaving mine. I kissed. I bit. Holding on to his shirt, I both needed him and was still furious that he'd obscured the truth to protect me. My fingers wrapped around his shirt, pulling him securely to me while I spread my legs, wanting him to take me, to claim me, again and again. I moved under him, squirming until we rolled and fell with a thump on the ground. Ezra was beneath me.

His grip on me loosened, and I straddled him, taking advantage of the moment to slip out of my dress. He sat up, tossing off his shirt, which almost landed in the fire. The breeze blew in from the balcony, but I didn't care. I just wanted him. I was wet and hot and broken, and he was the only one who could fix me, who could firm my decision. It took some maneuvering for him to wiggle out of his pants, and I helped, yanking them down his legs. He kicked them off as I bent and took the head of his cock in my mouth. I'd never done such a thing before. I wrapped my lips around it as best I could, moving my head up and down while he moaned, his hand tightening on my head, his voice lost, gone, strangled.

"Mila," he whispered.

I tasted him on my tongue, salty and tangy. Replacing my mouth with my hand, I gazed down at him. Placing his hands on my hips, he guided me over his length, rubbing back and forth against my wetness before he sank into me. Deep. My muscles clenched against his, and I cried out, leaning forward to ride him. My breasts grazed his chest as we moved in rhythm, and he guided me closer to him, lifting his head to take one of my erect nipples in his mouth. The sensations firing through me intensified, a mix of pleasure and pain, all building to the core of ecstasy. Throwing back my head, I closed my eyes and cried out as he tasted, sucked, lashed first one nipple, then the other. And then, as if him inside me were not enough, he reached between my legs, stroking gently until he found my hard nub and pinched.

I came hard, screaming, trembling, shaking. My vision went white as I held on to his shoulders, my fingers digging in, leaving marks, but it was the only purchase I had in a cascade of pleasure.

Ezra tilted, shifting me onto my back and kissing my legs, slowing the momentum as I caught my breath. My back was slick with sweat, my vision hazy, but he sealed my mouth with his. I reached the peak again, and he held me close as I bucked beneath him. A moment later he came too, gasping and shaking.

Afterward we lay panting on the rug in front of the fire, the fall breeze cooling our naked bodies. Ezra's arm curled around me, and I rested my head on his chest, my concern gone under the glow of his love. He caressed my cheek, then lifted my chin with his finger so that I could look up at him. His eyes were dark, his words hesitant. "What does this mean, Mila?"

"I love you. I'm not going to run. I'm going to stay."

"Oh. Mila." His voice broke, and he held me tight for a long time without saying another word.

When he let go, he kissed me, slowly, reverently, before rising.

"What happens now?" I asked, picking up my discarded dress and slipping it over my head.

"I'm going to find that monster and send it through the portal to the sorceress," Ezra explained. "First, I have to make a new violin. Dusty is finding the wood I need, and Ginger is putting up rune stones around the property. I sent all the guests away."

"She told me, and Rachelle too. The others won't leave you."

"No." He gave me his crooked smile. "They are stubborn even though leaving would be for their own good. I can only hope the wards hold. I don't know for sure."

"Wards to protect against demons?"

"Yes, evil spirits and all. It depends on how powerful they are, and the demon I summoned is powerful indeed. I took precautions. It can't get far, but regardless, it's not safe to go out after dark nor dwell in places with shadows."

I thought of the cellar and shivered. "Inside will be safe?"

"You'll be safe with me," he whispered, wrapping his arms around me. "Mila, it would be better to take the stagecoach to your sister's estate until this is all over. It's the selfish part inside me that wants you to stay."

"I made my choice. I'm staying."

Brushing a thumb over my lip, he scolded, "You're just as stubborn as the others."

Stubborn, perhaps, but I was also afraid for him, as if he was marching into doom and the only way I could keep him safe was with my love. Would it be enough?

MILA

Ezra did not let me out of his sight for the rest of the day, and when the stagecoach came and went, a cloud settled around me. My choice was final. With nothing to do but pace and wait, Ezra took me back to his tower to spend the night. I'd never stayed over before, and now I understood why. For in the middle of the night he'd slip out to walk the forest path and play the tunes that would summon that foul demon. I shivered at the thought, but after making love to me again, slowly, intently, holding my gaze the entire time, he held me tight all night long.

I woke in his arms, my back pressed against his chest, one arm around my waist while his fingers tenderly traced the swells of my breasts, making my nipples tighten with anticipation. Warm breath kissed my shoulders, and I turned in his arms while shades of light revealed his face to me. He watched me, patiently, and I wondered if at some point, he'd cried, for a wet sheen shone in his eyes.

"You haven't changed your mind?" he asked hesitantly.

"No, Ezra, I'm here." I waited a beat and then added, "But I have questions."

"You can ask me anything. I don't want to lie to you anymore." He stroked the inside of my wrist.

Tingling sensations shot up my arm, making me aware of how distracting he was, but I couldn't forget what had come to me last night. Not a dream but my mind trying to fix the problem presented to me. I said the words in a rush before I could lose my bravery. "Tell me the truth, Ezra. Was it my fault?"

His fingers stilled. "Nothing is your fault, Mila, but explain. What do you mean?"

"The other day, with the demon and the portal. I have to know, Ezra. Did I ruin it? I saw the motes of light, like violet starlight. You were about to open the portal and send the monster through it, weren't you?"

There, I'd said it and let the truth hang between us. This all could have ended, been over with, if I'd listened to him instead of exploring. But then I'd never have found out the truth or faced the horror of who he was and what he'd done. Turning to the curtained window, I took a deep breath and waited for him to confirm my suspicions.

Sliding one finger under my chin, Ezra guided my face back toward his, eyes dark and earnest as he spoke. "Mila, I need you to see the truth in my eyes. No. You ruined nothing. I've never come so close to doing what the sorceress asked, because it's impossible. By the time I summoned the…er…demon, I was too weak to open the portal. That's the caveat to magic: its physically draining, and I was already near the end when you appeared."

"Oh." Potent relief slid out of me, and I blinked hard as the weight of guilt I'd carried on my shoulders shattered. Still, my heart fluttered in my chest, and my slew of thoughts returned, rearranging themselves into an opportunity. "What if you had help?"

Ezra narrowed his eyes at me, his lips curling into a scowl. "In theory, it would be better if I had help. One violinist to open the portal, the other to control the demon, but I don't like what you're implying."

"I'm not implying anything," I protested.

Ezra slid his hand down my belly and parted my legs, stroking the soft skin of my upper thigh. "Yes, you are. I've known you long enough to spy the glint in your eye. You have a plan. You're thinking of something dangerous, and I won't let you."

His arm tightened around my waist. "It is true

that we both play the violin, but it takes magic to open portals, and the cost of using that magic is wearisome. Besides, a violin must be made from a specific wood to invoke the magic, wood that is rare and old and difficult to find. I don't have any of that wood here, which is why I sent Dusty and Giselle away to find some for me, and it served as an excuse to get them off the property for a while."

"What about the violin you gave me?" I asked. My breath hitched as his fingers moved higher.

"I would be foolish indeed if I gave you a magical violin. No, it is made from nonmagical wood. Pure. Uncorrupted."

I sighed as the idea of helping him drifted away. He would not wish it upon me, and yet a question still hung there. How close had I come to losing Ezra? If he'd attempted to open the portal and failed, would the demon have attacked him, overcome him in his weakened state?

"What happens now?"

"We wait until the wood is found, and then I will carve a violin and send that foul beast through the portal to her."

It was now or never. Lifting myself on an elbow, I trapped his hand between my legs, halting his trajectory. Keeping my tone low and serious, I spoke quickly. "Ezra, you brought me here because you wanted me to play violin, and then, in your hour of utmost need, you deny me what I came here for. To play, to make a difference, to use my passion for good. You are a master of the craft, and yet you decline to teach me anything. So I'm not asking; I'm telling you, you need me. I don't want to learn how to use magic to summon spirits, but surely the magic can be taught, shared. Teach me how to open the portal. At least teach me the notes. Give me something to do here, a way to help, because if you do it all alone, you will lose. And I don't want to lose you, just when I've found you and know the darkness that haunts you and your path to redemption. I see it all so clearly. Why can't you?"

Stunned, he opened his mouth and closed it. The tension in his body faded. Tilting his head, he lay flat on his back, eyes closed. I placed a hand on his chest, feeling his rapid heartbeat, the struggle within.

Emboldened by his silence, I went on. "You let others help you with this inn. This is vastly different. It's a choice between life and death. I've seen the darkness. I know the sorceress is dangerous, but I've met no one like you, and I love you. Don't force me to watch you ruin yourself. Let me help. That's why our paths crossed, for this reason."

Straddling him, I leaned over his chest, waiting. Watching.

When he opened his eyes, they were wet, and his smile was weak. His fingers threaded through my hair. “I don’t want you to help, because I was the one who got myself into this mess. It was my fault, my sins, my desire for power that belongs to the gods.”

“Yes, but we’ve been over this. You can’t go back. You can’t change the past, but you’ve done so much to gain your freedom. Doesn’t that count? Doesn’t what I want matter?”

He seized my hips. “You are the only thing that matters, and if you help me, if you assist, you will put yourself into the crosshairs of a very dangerous sorceress. Mila, you don’t understand. She holds a piece of my soul.”

“And so do I,” I breathed. “Because I love you. You said it yourself. This is your last task, all you have to do to be free of her, to seal the border between worlds once and for all. And if my reward is you, then I will put myself in danger. When we win at the end, it will be worth it.”

Yanking me to him, he kissed me hard, biting my lips, fingers lacing through my hair. I rolled with him, the push and pull of our conversation turning physical. Our hands were everywhere, our breathing changed to ragged pants, and when he entered me, I cried out not from pain but because the intensity of the moment was enough to bring me to the brink of climax. It was hard, hot, fast, and we both came quickly, gasping as we held on to each other. I straddled him, thighs locked around his hips. Resting my face in the crook of his neck, I closed my eyes and breathed in his scent, relishing that moment.

"I'm afraid," Ezra admitted. "But I see the wisdom in your words. I will teach you the notes, but you must not play unless you're in my presence."

I pulled back to study him, although I did not break our skin-to-skin contact. "I promise."

"And, Mila, you understand that these notes, these tunes, cannot be played anywhere else. They work because the island is a sacred place. There is magic there. But portals can open into worlds we don't know or understand, and dangerous creatures could come through."

"Like the creature in the cellar?"

"Yes, like that."

"Ezra?" I studied his face, the lines of his jaw, his slight dimples, the fall of his hair, disheveled from our lovemaking. "Are you human?"

He smiled. "Why? Do you think I'm not human?"

I shrugged. "You're from an unfamiliar land, you use magic, you sense others' feelings—none of that is very humanlike."

"Perhaps." He kissed my shoulder. "Perhaps I'm something else, something other, and if so, I don't know what that is. But you know what I think: once humans had more power, more authority in this world, they forgot the gods created them, and fell from grace. Those who remember who they are, what they are, can harness forgotten magic."

Flipping me onto my back, he spread my legs. "Now, no more questions. I want to make love to you."

MILA

Later that morning, I returned to my room. The inn was strangely quiet without the guests, and when I opened the door to the washroom, Rachelle's door lay wide open, her room empty. She must have already left with Rabon, dashing off with the horses, on an adventure. She'd gained all the things she'd desired: horses, love, and the opportunity to leave the Dawn. Would she ever return?

Drawing a bath, I took my time, washing and soaking as if I could wash away the very essence of Ezra. It kissed my skin, sending shivers up my spine. If this was what it meant to be blinded by love, I did not care. Wrapped in a towel, I brushed the knots out of my hair and braided it to the side. Opening the wardrobe, I stared at my dresses, realizing I hadn't bothered to unpack my bag. No matter; I'd take it with me to Ezra's tower. As I brushed my fingers over the dresses left hanging, a wooden box caught my eye. Parting the dresses, I stared at a box. No, not a box—a case.

My heart flipped, for I'd forgotten about my grandfather's old violin. I'd brought it with me on a whim, but now I opened it and stroked my fingers lovingly over the swells of the body. It was old, the strings broken. Blood rushed to my ears. What if it was made from the type of wood that Ezra needed? He didn't know I'd brought another violin, and my intent had been to restring it, to restore respect to the old instrument. After all, it was its broken strings that had brought me to the foothills of Lagoda. Heart pounding, I closed the case, aware I had only a slight chance, but it would be enough if I could help Ezra, if I could save him.

After dressing and setting the two violins by my bag, I sat to write a letter to Mother and Aveline. Each time I set the pen to paper, the words would not come. What was I trying to say? That I'd fallen in love with a man who wasn't from this world and I needed to help him send a demon through a portal? The more I thought about it, the more I sounded like a raving lunatic. They'd come at once to have me committed, and it was much too dangerous for them here. How ironic. A demon was on the loose and all I could think about was how it appeared I'd lost my mind.

With a sigh, I gave up and left the letter unwritten.

Ezra wasn't waiting for me when I returned to the tower, and it was odd to walk into the atrium and see all the statues frozen in place, as if one whisper, one word, was all they needed to speak again. A shiver went through me as I recalled Ezra's words. He'd summoned spirits and sent them into his statues, but the magic that had brought them to life had turned them into monsters. Why, then, did he have to keep them there?

"Ezra?" I called out, a thread of unease going up my spine. It was broad daylight. Why was I afraid? Nothing lurked in the shadows.

"Mila." He stepped out from behind the stairs, polishing a tool.

The way he smiled at me sent a surge of determination through me. I would do this. Leaving my grandfather's violin and bag by the door, I went to him. "I brought the violin. Shall we begin?"

A flicker of darkness crossed his face, his emotions still surging, warring within. But he nodded at me once. "Let's go upstairs. I have much to teach you."

Years of poor practice did not simply disappear, but Ezra was a patient teacher, showing me how to hold the bow. The tune was fast and complex, a melody long and intense to summon, to form, to create. By the time we finished, my arms ached and my fingers were sore from flying up and down the neck of the violin. Inside I felt alive, as if my playing was doing something, moving something.

"*El fin,*" Ezra proclaimed, clasping his hands together.

With a sigh, I rolled my neck back and forth. "I did more today than in the months I've been here."

Taking the violin from me, he wiped the strings before replacing it and the bow in a case. "I know, and this will not be easy, for either of us. But it was for good reason you were spared this."

EZRA

The threads of captivity tightened around my neck like a noose as precious freedom became so much nearer and dearer. If the sorceress could see me now, she'd laugh, her syrupy voice ripping through the shreds of sanity I had left to tell me it was all impossible, all part of her devious, devilish plan. I'd seen her punish others, and I knew better than to hope, because my hope gave Mila hope, and she didn't know that the sorceress disliked happy endings. She enjoyed others' pain, and the absence of pleasure made her strong. She thrived on blood and brokenness, and the darker the crime, the more power it gave her. When I stepped across the portal to deliver her dark messenger, I could not count on her to keep her word. After all, she'd changed her mind every time I'd been on the cusp of freedom, flinging my own words back in my face. I had no recourse, no way to ensure she'd keep her word, when I was the one who'd wronged her, subject to eternal damnation.

But Mila was pure and beautiful and strong. At first she struggled with the violin, but each day she improved, her fingers moving swiftly like a bird in flight, down the neck of the violin. The haunting tones to open the portal poured out, muted only by the lack of magic the violin carried. How could I let her do this? If the sorceress knew about Mila and my love for her, it would be the bait to seal my death. For I'd do anything, everything, to keep her out of the sorceress's reach. Portal magic was too dangerous, but I couldn't lie to her again.

My violin, though, was almost done, sculpted from the wood of an ancient hazel tree. With magic, the age of trees mattered. The older, the better. My fingers could sense the magic hidden within the wood, and I carved, breathing prayers the music would hold, that it would be enough to cast the demon back into her realm. It was a truth I'd never shared with Mila, for I'd never had the strength to summon a demon before. Spirits of the dead often floated to me, and when I was young, I'd used the music to lull them back to their eternal resting place.

It was a gift, the ability to give peace to souls, with music, a gift that could have been used for good. But I'd never been a selfless man. Born with nothing, I'd wanted everything, and now…I'd seen how hollow wealth and power and magic were. Now all I wanted was a second chance, a lifetime with her. If I was lucky, I'd get a few more days.

"Almost done?" Mila's sultry question floated to my ears, and I lifted my head, banishing my morose thoughts. A spot of sunlight graced her, and she looked like a queen, violet hair cascading around her shoulders, cream-colored dress clinging to her curves while her brown eyes danced over my work. My heart squeezed, and breathing turned painful, as if a sharp knife was caught between my ribs. If I could go back to the moment I saw her play in the hall, a place I had no business being, aside from my interest in music, would I still bring her here now I knew the outcome?

"Yes, it just needs strings." The words sounded ominous coming from my lips, because as soon as the strings were on the instrument, it would be time to walk out into the night and play one last song.

"Speaking of strings." Mila held up a case. "Will you restring this violin for me?"

"Your violin has strings…"

"No, this is my grandfather's violin. I brought it

with me because it's the one thing I've had since childhood. I didn't want to just leave it behind. But the strings are broken, and I haven't taken the time to repair them."

"Of course, I'll do so now." Mostly because I wanted to delay what would happen next and spend more time with her. Our final moments, and I could not be sure of what would happen next, nor could I prepare for the best outcome. That was the thing about the Tower Knights. We were all punished, but I did not know what happened to them after a punishment was carried out. Were any of them able to break the curse, to tear free from the clutches of the sorceress and find happiness? Did any of them deserve peace, with their magic, wild and untenable, calling out to the darkness within?

I cleared a space on my worktable, and Mila placed the case on top. While she opened it, I stood behind her, breathing in her scent, my cock pressed against the curves of her bottom. She shifted, and already I tasted her arousal and slid my hand around her waist, holding her still as I kissed her neck.

"Ezra," she whispered, her voice breathy, catching as her tongue stumbled over my name.

I could hear it again and again, and it would never be enough.

Releasing her, I moved to her side. "No matter what happens, never doubt my love for you."

"We are going to win," she said firmly.

Instead of contradicting her, I picked up the violin. The wood was a dark hue, immaculate under the sunlight, and the strings were a tangled mess. A whisper came to me as I stood there, holding the instrument, and then a pulse, a beat, a vibration. Closing my eyes, I leaned into the feel of the wood. It came alive under my fingers. The wind caressed my branches, and the leaves shivered in song. My roots dug down, deep into the ground, sucking up the moisture, feeding myself on sweet waters. Crisp, cold air danced around me, pure and fragrant but unable to penetrate my layers. I was the tree, still alive, still living, and full of deep magic.

Letting go, I spun to Mila, eyes wide. "Where? Where did your grandfather get this?"

Mila's eyes darted from the violin, back to me. "I don't know. Why?"

Twisting the nobs on the neck of the violin, I released the tension of the strings so I could remove them. "Sit," I instructed Mila. "I will tell you a story."

Tentatively, she took a seat at the workbench while I restrung the violin.

"Giselle told you the tales of the four seasons and the gods who brought them forth, playing on their instruments."

“Yes,” Mila said, caution and hidden concern in the undertone of her words.

Could it be true? “Old legends are full of myth for a reason, to obscure revelation from those who don’t believe or are unwilling to do the work to unveil the truth for themselves. It is said that when the gods discovered the humans were ungrateful for their gifts, they cursed the land and left, leaving the humans to toil and work and grind endlessly. But some tales say, in order to keep the world from falling into disgrace and to keep the seasons flowing seamlessly from one into the other, the gods left their instruments behind. When they did so, the music kept playing, but the instruments, without a player, could not remain the same. They rotted and moldered away, sinking into the ground, becoming one with the world, and then something magical happened. Something impossible. The instruments turned into seeds and grew into majestic trees, old trees, with roots that crisscrossed between the natural barrier of the known world and other worlds’. Blessed by the gods, the trees grew strong and tall and powerful, yet they were obscured, hidden, and only the few and faithful could find them. When they did, they took the gifts of the trees, offerings of branches and leaves, and brought them back. People developed many uses for them. Some put them over their doors as beacons of protection, and others used them as wards, but those who had tokens from the sacred trees gained blessings from the gods. They grew in wealth and health and wisdom, and they became the ones others looked up to, until they were persecuted for their knowledge. Where there is good, there is often evil, and they were hunted, tortured for knowledge of the trees, where they grew, and how to find them. But no matter how explicit the instructions, none could find the sacred trees. Some said the gods hid them from those who wanted to use the wood for corrupt purposes. But those who were blessed found other ways to share the wealth of the trees, and they passed the gifts from generation to generation, keeping them secret and safe."

Mila gasped, pressing a hand to her heart. "You think my violin is made from the wood of a sacred tree?"

"I don't think; I know it is." I gauged her reaction as her expression changed from awe to shock.

Drumming her fingers on the table, she asked, "What does it mean?"

"That you had magic all along." I wanted to deny the coincidence, but when I thought back, I recalled being drawn to the symphony hall for some unexplainable reason, as if the music had called me. Magic. "That night in the symphony hall, while you waited for your turn to audition, did you practice?"

Mila searched my face. "Of course. I had to warm up my fingers, and then I waited."

Unable to meet her searching eyes, I turned my attention back to the violin, tightening the last string. I badly wanted to play it, to hear what it would sound like under my fingers. But I was the one who cursed others with my song, who called the darkness forth with my music. I was not worthy to play. It belonged to her and only her. This was why I'd found her. This was why her music had called to me, because something deep inside me had recognized the magic.

"Ezra? What is it?" Her voice wobbled, edged with fear and uncertainty.

"I want to hide you away, lock you up so the sorceress will never catch a whiff of your presence. But perhaps this violin will be enough. I don't know the power of the gods, nor what magic is imbued here, but I feel it coursing like a river. I told you once about my sense, my ability to feel, and the power within this violin I've never felt before. We go tonight, and we will play the song of the dawn, summon the demon, and send it through the portal back to her. But Mila, the moment the demon is gone, the portal must be closed. I do not trust the sorceress. If anything, she'll find a way to change the terms, to keep me. You'll have to play, quick and accurate, like never before."

Her lips tightened into a firm line, and her eyes blazed with determination as she met my gaze. "Ezra, I'm ready."

I squared my shoulders. We were going to do this, but gods, her determination just made me want to kiss her one last time.

MILA

Ezra's story stayed with me as we awoke at midnight, dressing in warm woolen clothes and taking up our violins. I followed him down the twisting stairs while he held the lantern high. Even its small yellow flame could not dispel the terror in my heart as shadows flickered. Any one of them could be a horned, red-eyed devil rising from the depths to torment us. But we were so close. With the coming of the dawn, Ezra's punishment would end, the barrier would be sealed, and we'd be free to live and love. Together.

"We have to take the tunnel. It's not safe outside after dark," Ezra explained.

"What tunnel?" I asked as we stood on the first floor. My heart skipped, for the statues were menacing after dark, as though they might awaken and become an army of destructive monsters.

"There are underground tunnels that connect the inn and this tower." Kneeling on the floor, he removed a rug to reveal a trapdoor. With deft fingers, he unlocked it and pulled it open. "It is old and leads to a shrine in the forest, near to the waterfall and the cave. It's the quickest, safest passage."

Not trusting my voice, I nodded and followed Ezra into the musty, earthy tunnel. My skin crawled the moment my feet reached the floor, and I wanted to spin around, climb the ladder, and rush back upstairs where it was warm, it was cozy, and nothing would harm us. Gripping the case of my grandfather's violin tighter, I took shallow breaths to stay my panic.

"Hold on to me," Ezra encouraged. "And be careful of the roots. Sometimes they might graze your head, frightening if you don't know they are there."

"Okay," I whispered, squeezing a fistful of his shirt in my hands, grateful for his presence.

The gloom inside the tunnel was complete, and we moved, our feet brushing against loose dirt. Clinging to Ezra, I tried not to think about the rats and beetles that took up residence in such dark places, or what other supernatural beings might lurk nearby. Banishing thoughts of the cellar and the slurping creature within, I focused on taking one step at a time, keeping my eyes on the light Ezra held.

The path seemed to go on forever, up and down, curving into the forest, until Ezra came to a halt in front of a ladder. Passing the lantern to me, he went up, lifted the trapdoor, and returned. "Be on guard," he whispered.

One hand on the small of my back, he guided me up into a moldering hut. "Ginger?" he called, holding up the lantern.

It wasn't the only pool of light in the hut, for another was by a doorway, and slowly a shape formed, revealing Ginger. I gawked. She was dressed in black, blending in with the night, her short hair tucked behind her ears. Her outfit was formfitting, accenting her athletic body, but it was the weapons in her belt that gave me pause. A sword, a short knife, and another strapped to her leg. In one hand, she carried a bow, with a quiver on her back. I swallowed hard. Ginger looked as if she was going to battle.

"Ezra?" I asked.

Sensing my anxiety, he moved to my side, leaning so close his breath kissed my face, but none of it gave me relief. "I asked Ginger to meet us here because she's a slayer."

"I don't understand."

"She hunts demons, and with her weapons, she can slow them down should they try to attack. We'll be vulnerable out here in the middle of the night..."

He trailed off, the words he left unsaid resonating with me. He'd summoned a foul demon who might attack us while we played, and so Ginger came to protect us. It occurred to me as we left the hut, stepping out into the crisp night air, that I'd never considered Ginger's role in all this. After all, she was the one who'd gone to Lady Elodie's aid, and what had she done? Slayed the creature and disposed of the body?

Ezra led the way, with Ginger bringing up the rear. I was thankful for my woolen dress, for the night was cold, and even the beams of moonlight that peeked through the thick shade of the trees did nothing to dispel my anxiety. At night the trees appeared menacing, like shields meant to block the way, and every rustle of leaf and grass underfoot sent my eyes darting. Although, I was afraid to look too hard for fear I'd see red eyes watching, waiting to pounce. I was grateful Ginger was with us.

After leaving the hut, it did not take us long to reach the lake. Murky waters shimmered under silver moonbeams, and the enchanting glade was not as frightening as the rest of the forest. It was much easier to see, and Ezra led us under the yew tree, where he propped the lantern on the stone, something I was sure he'd done many times. When he bent to open his case, a sense of finality swirled. This was it. Placing my case in the grass, I pulled out my grandfather's violin, this time aware of the wild tale Ezra had told me and what he believed about the myth. Was it true? We'd find out now, but I desperately wanted it to be true. I murmured a prayer under my breath: "Please let this work."

A rhyme I'd learned when I was young came back to me, a prayer for protection and blessing. I whispered the words as Ezra tucked his violin under his chin and drew the bow across the strings. Music vibrated within my soul, and that dark cry, that call, soared. Notes blazed and scattered through the edges of the forest as though they had wings, and the water carried them further and faster, seeking, seeking the one they called.

I waited, for it was not my turn, and let the music fill me. That strange, haunting tone, the music he played to summon a powerful being and control it. I felt it deeply, as if I was the creature he summoned. Time slipped away, and a sharp cry came, and then a blur.

Ginger's voice came from somewhere above. "It's here!"

"Mila, now," cried Ezra.

With no time to warm up, I lifted my bow, adrenaline rushing through me, and played. The intricate web of notes unraveled as my fingers danced across the neck, pressing, wrenching each heavenly note out, delicately, sweetly coaxing it into being. I dared not look around for fear what I'd see would make me want to scream and run. Ginger was out there. She would protect us. All we had to do was play.

I played the song through, gaining my bearings as I did so. My fingers flew up and down the neck, but nothing happened. Ezra had instructed me once I reached the end to begin again and keep playing. He'd warned me the portal might not open at once, yet doubts crept through my mind. I started again, from the top, and realized that playing my grandfather's old violin differed greatly from playing the one Ezra had given me.

Memories formed, taking me back to a time when I was young, happy, innocent, and naive. The smallest things would bring me joy, like eating oranges with Aveline, laughing while Mother chased me around the house, and learning to create beauty with music. Grandfather's fingers had been old already and had shaken when he'd played, but his passion, his love for sound, had remained, and he'd given me that gift.

Taking a deep breath, I went back to those moments, pure and happy, then twisted them into what exactly I'd felt when I'd received the letter from the Dawn and the buoyant relief that had gripped me at the opportunity to play music. This was right; this was true. I'd come to the foothills of Lagoda for this moment and for Ezra. My sun god. He'd shown me his goodness, his kindness, and his burning passion. It was his love I wanted, and to see the weight of his past lifted from his shoulders. Kind. Generous. Considerate. Almost to a fault. And his kisses, his words, the way he teased me, making me laugh even though he had so many responsibilities. When he shone his radiance on me, I felt whole, complete, as if I'd been searching my whole life for something and now I had love, music, even wealth.

A surge of determination swelled through me, and I played through the song again. This time, tiny motes appeared and beyond them, a leering blurb of blackness. The demon neared, and Ezra's song was the only thing that held it at bay.

Focus. I had to focus. Closing my eyes, I played again, leaning into the music, putting my soul into it. Suddenly I was transported away, back to a field full of flowers, faces uplifted as I walked through them. Music flowed, and I danced, my fingers grazing the grass and flowers, and everything I touched bloomed.

A frigid wind made me open my eyes, my fingers almost stumbling on the strings as a bitter cold swept over me. Motes of violet light brightened the glade, swirls of purples and pinks so vivid and beautiful my eyes watered. I kept playing as the motes swirled together and a faint hum pulsed in the air. The water now reflected the night sky, a haze of silver starlight peppering the darkness, creating a blaze of light. Beyond that brightness, swelling, growing, I sensed another light far beyond it. Dawn. And it came to me that every night that Ezra played, he came out to welcome the dawn, to play through the darkness and bring the light. Because once, he'd been lost and now he was found. Once, he'd been in darkness, but now when I looked at him, all I saw was light.

The music we played blended together, the low and sorrowful, the high and sweet, a complex rhythm that invoked magic and sent tears streaming down my face. It was poignant, so beautiful, like nothing I'd ever seen or heard before. The water shimmered before us, the waterfall thundered, and we were part of nature in its glory, part of the magic of the dawn.

Light bloomed like a flower, and I began the rhythm again, my fingers moving faster, pain in my fingertips, but it did not matter. Nothing mattered at all, because we were part of it. The blur of blackness moved nearer, and the air turned cold and foul. But I would fear no evil, for the magic within us was stronger. As if clarifying, Ezra walked away from my side, still playing, his expression a mask as he strode toward the portal. A snowflake of coldness gathered around him as he stepped into that swirling mouth of light, and the quilt of violet starlight flickered.

The demon followed, hypnotized by the music, and when Ezra crossed over the threshold, he faced me. "End it, Mila."

My fingers faltered, for this hadn't been the deal. This was not what we'd discussed. He would lead the demon through and then return, and then, only then, would I play the final notes to close to portal.

Without waiting for my answer, he swung around and walked into that flickering light, that hideous darkness following him. But I kept playing, holding it open, even as my strength ebbed. A weariness washed over me as if I hadn't slept for days, and spots of blackness danced in front of my vision. Roaring filtered to my ears, but I ignored it, watching, waiting for my lover to walk out of the portal, to return to me.

A boom made my eardrums pop, and a rush of air, like a hand, threw me on my back. A scream burst out of my throat as I dropped my violin, and by the time I sat up, the portal was closed and Ezra and the demon were gone. "No!" I shouted, snatching up the violin. I shoved it against my shoulder, tears already beading in my eyes as I lifted the bow. My hand trembled badly, and my vision went black, sending me to my knees. My shoulders shook as I waited. Could he open the portal from the other side? Would he come back?

When I tried to play, a note went sour, and my fingers shook so hard I could not press the strings down. The price of magic, the energy it took, came rushing in, stripping away my vitality and replacing it with weariness. But Ezra was gone, and I needed him back. This wasn't the plan; this wasn't what was supposed to happen.

"Mila!" the shout came, and a moment later Ginger was in front of me. "We have to go."

"Why?" I gasped, unable to resist as she took my violin and placed it in its case. "We have to wait for Ezra."

Ginger slid one arm around my waist, supporting me as she picked up the violin. "Ezra is gone. He's not coming back."

MILA

"Gone? I don't understand." I told Ginger as she pressed a mug of warm tea into my hands. I was wrapped in a blanket in front of a roaring fire in the staff's lounge. Daylight streamed in, bright and unrelenting, but I couldn't stop shivering. Ginger had half dragged me back. Once I'd sat down, my limbs had stopped shaking, but more than anything, I was concerned about Ezra.

"Yes." Ginger poked the fire, then sat across from me and picked up her own mug of tea. "He knew the sorceress wouldn't simply let him go. She never has. It's always another task, another change. She's made threats against us, so he saw this as the moment to sacrifice himself and allow us to go on. Without him."

Eyes wide in shock and dismay, I stared at her,

then shook my head adamantly. "No. No! I refuse to believe you. Ezra wouldn't leave us, leave *me* like this. The sorceress has to keep her end of the bargain and send him back!"

Ginger's snort was bitter. "It doesn't work like that. Here, perhaps people keep their word and their promises, but the sorceress is all-powerful. She can do what she wants. She can bend the rules, summon demons, make our lives hell on earth. Ezra has atoned for his wickedness, but does he deserve to be forgiven? Not in her eyes. Not now. Not ever."

Pressing a hand against my mouth, I rocked back and forth. A knot of pain built in my belly, and my lips trembled. "So what will she do?"

"Do you have to ask? If he's outlived his usefulness, she will..." Ginger trailed off, but her not saying the words was even worse.

Anger and fury and sorrow rose within me. I leaped up, shedding the blankets. Why should I be so comfortable when Ezra might be fighting for his very life? I paced back and forth in front of the fire, stopping just short of gnawing on my knuckles. It was deeply unfair that I should be stuck, trapped on this side of the border when he'd gone through the portal to sacrifice himself.

"He didn't tell you because he loves you and he wanted you to live. You have an opportunity. Forget what happened here, go back to the city, start your life over. You have the gift of music, and you have a magical violin. Nothing can stop you."

My head pounded as I spun to face her, eyes blazing with fury and I didn't know what else. "I know he loves me!" I snapped. "But he doesn't get to make a choice for me. I get to choose, and I choose him. You said it yourself. Nothing can stop me. I have a magical violin, and we are going to get him back!"

I hadn't known what I was going to say until the words rushed out of my mouth, violent and angry, and I wheezed, sucking in air to help quench my panic. Why hadn't I considered it before? Of course I had the magic. I would simply open the portal, walk through it, and make a deal with the sorceress. I'd found love and happiness beyond my wildest dreams, and I wasn't about to let it go, not without a fight. Things had happened here at the Dawn, things I could not explain, the legends, the myths, the supernatural, all real. And a demon slayer sat in front of me, frowning as she sipped her tea.

Sitting down again, I took a drink, the burn of heat sliding through me. I was eager, desperate, now that I knew what I was going to do.

Ginger glared at me. "You can't simply waltz into the sorceress's domain and demand she give him back. She holds both dark and light magic. The deal you make with her will end your life."

Pressing my hands against my face, I burst out, "Well, I can't just sit here and do nothing. Can you?"

"Ezra told me to protect you."

Now it was my turn to laugh. How ironic. "But you don't even like me."

Ginger cocked her head. "What does that have to do with anything? My leader gave me a command, and I fulfill it, no matter how I feel about it."

Leaning back in the chair, I studied her. "But don't you want him back too?"

Ginger considered my words, and I wondered if behind all the tension and the hardness was softness. I'd only seen part of it, when she'd spoken about her former lover, but now I'd struck a nerve. "Yes, I admit it is easier with him here, and the inn was his idea. I'm a fighter, a warrior, and this life... well, it's been unusual."

I tightened my fingers into a fist. "Will you fight with me, then? Fight not simply for Ezra but for what is right and true? You know that land, you know their customs, and you've encountered the sorceress. I can't do this without you."

Ginger lifted her chin. "Fine, but you must listen to everything I say."

"Deal," I agreed. My heart was tight, but I struggled to calm the rising panic. We were going to get Ezra back, and everything would be okay. I hoped.

MILA

The glade was different in daylight, and yet I lifted my bow and played. Once again, the air was imbued with magic and ice, a sheer coldness that enveloped everything when the portal blasted open, humming and glowing. It remained open, even when I stopped playing and followed Ginger through it, my heart skipping as I walked. Was I ascending to another realm? Was Ezra beyond these starlit walls? My heart told me yes, but my mind screamed for sanity and reason when we walked out the other end of the portal. I thought we'd made a mistake.

We stood in a cave, dull light cascading around it, a dirty white glow offsetting the gloom. A massive throne took up one end of the room, a chair set into a white tree, with a pile of skulls beneath it. The woman who sat on it uncrossed her legs and stood, a crown like starlight gleaming on her head, points shooting up like wicked daggers to curse the day. I gulped, pushing away the words that rushed to my mind. Run. Hide. Don't look back.

If I'd thought the demon was haunting, frightening, evil, with the ability to suck out my soul, the sorceress was even more so. A mouth that looked like mischief, eyes blacker than night and nothing but round orbs of malice. She was both terrifying and beautiful, with a power that made me want to fall at her feet and worship yet run screaming to the ends of the earth. She had power over my beloved, and suddenly I understood oh so well she was not a person one should trick or disobey. Nor would she make a deal with a mere mortal.

The air in her court was stale as she rose, sheer garments moving as her gaze met mine. I dropped to my knees, holding on to the violin as if it was the only thing that could keep me upright. Revulsion stirred in my belly, and the desire to crawl away, back through the portal, was stronger than my desire to stay. This was who Ezra fought, obeyed. The vow he'd broken was to her, and I could see how she enjoyed making him pay.

"This must be that sweet violin I heard from the other side of the portal, the reason Ezra was so willing to sacrifice himself. I wondered why he closed the portal so quickly—to keep me from seeing you and your magic."

Boots rang out against stone as Ginger strode toward the sorceress, tall and proud, with her weapons by her side, head held high. It was what I should have done, but I wasn't ready, kneeling on the floor with my violin in hand.

"I've come to make a deal," Ginger announced, her voice ringing out. "Ezra in exchange for my soul, my services."

The sorceress picked up a skull and tossed it back and forth between her hands. "You're one of his loyalists. Ginger, is it? The she-knight. The slayer. And what would I do with your services? I have many knights who haven't broken their vows, and you, you've served one of the fallen."

"I've come to make a new vow, to serve you," Ginger said.

No. Not Ginger. She'd exchanged herself to give Ezra happiness. And I knew why. She'd told me about her lost love, her biggest regret, and perhaps she'd seen what Ezra and I had and had decided to let us have what she'd refused: a lifetime of pure and perfect love.

I'd already cried too much, and yet tears itched the backs of my eyes as I thought of what she was willing to sacrifice, more for Ezra than for me, and yet could I let her do this when I was the one who'd decided to come here to make a deal with the sorceress? I found my legs, ever so weak, and yet they held me upright. My body ached from the use of magic, and I found my voice.

"I have something better than an unbroken vow and better than service. I have a violin carved from a tree of the gods, with potent magic none can match. If I give it to you, will you give me Ezra?"

The sorceress cocked her head at me, her dead eyes considering. It was impossible to hold her gaze, so I stared down at the skulls, which weren't much better. Where was Ezra, and what had she done with him?

"Show me the magic," she instructed. "Play."

Play. My arms were weary from lack of sleep, and I'd already played twice today, invoking magic when I never had before, and my mind wanted nothing more than to sleep. Repressing the sob that built inside, I tucked the violin under my chin and forced my shaking fingers to play. The first note went wrong, a jarring sourness marring the air. The sorceress frowned, and my throat went dry. I took a deep breath. My song was within me, an original piece. It had always been. I just needed to let it out.

My fingertips hurt, the skin close to splitting as I played, moving my fingers up and down the neck. I'd never played the song for anyone before, not even Ezra when he'd asked. In secret I'd composed the melody, for this song was the cry of my heart. A song of hope, a song of love, a song of strength, calling out to the one who made my soul sing. Gritting my teeth, I forced myself to play through the pain, and as tears streamed down my face once more, I knew it would be worth it if the sorceress agreed to our deal.

Little by little, my strength ebbed, and I went from standing to kneeling. My limbs felt boneless, and yet I played until gold dust glittered above and the light across that dark cave became bright. Behind me the portal glowed, cold and purple, and the skin of my fingers burst open, crimson blood flowing down my arms. Still, I played. Because the pain did not matter—the sorrow was only a test—and if I gained my heart's desire, there would be euphoria.

I did not know how long I'd played, but my shoulders ached, my fingers bled, and my body was hollow when I stopped. The court was silent. Even the sorceress stood, poised with an unnameable expression crossing her face. The silence was like the lull between a lightning strike and thunder, and the bow slipped out of my fingers, clattering loudly on the floor.

Tiny creatures flittered above my head, and gold dust drifted like a soft spring drizzle. I faced the sorceress, too tired to open my mouth.

When she spoke, her voice was the clap of thunder, boiling and shaking the foundations of the earth. "Bring the prisoner."

Ezra did not look like my Ezra when he appeared, his hair damp and ruffled, blood darkening his tunic. He limped, a hand clasped to his chest, and my heart collapsed. They'd beaten him up, tortured him. What more would they have done had I not come?

"Ezra," the sorceress said. "My Sorcerer of Portals, it seems you've passed your magic on to another and captured it in a violin. This is your greatest achievement, and I count your servitude to me complete. On this day, you shall return beyond the portal, never to grace it with your presence again. Your soul is whole, yours, and you will never enter my lands again. As a token, I will keep your loyalist, Ginger the Slayer, and she shall serve me in your stead. Now go, before I change my mind."

Ezra's eyes were wide as his head swiveled to Ginger.

Lips tight, she nodded at him. "Go. This is what I want."

I felt his hesitation, his desire to fight for her too. But it was just a sliver, just a hint, before he turned and staggered toward me. His pain washed over me like a wave, and I went to him, delicately reaching out to support him. His arm was heavy on my shoulders, and when he murmured, "Mila," my name on his lips filled a book with words, with all the things he'd say to me, later, much later.

We stumbled to the portal, and behind me came a clap of thunder. An intense coldness filled me. All I saw was light as we stumbled across the barrier, and it hissed and closed behind us.

MILA

We landed in a tangled heap at the mouth of a cave. Ezra lay on his back, gasping, his breath shallow. I pressed a hand to his head but snatched it away as it burned. "Ezra," I sobbed, "don't leave me. Not now."

I had to get him back, back to the inn, back to bed, but we were so far away. I, too, still felt weak, but I pushed myself to keep going, rubbing my bloody fingers on my dress as I frantically sought for a way to get back to the Dawn.

A boat was tied up at the mouth of the cave, like a gift from the forest gods. Putting Ezra's hand over my shoulder, I dragged him upright as best I could. "Come on, we're going to make it."

It was with some maneuvering we got into the boat, and Ezra lay heavily on his back, drifting in and out of consciousness as I rowed. At first I'd thought the pool was self-contained, but as I nosed the boat across the water, I realized it was a stream. My hopes rose that it would lead back to the lake. Giselle and Dusty would be home, working the farm, and once they saw me return, they'd come to help.

I can do this, I told myself, steering the boat through the water. After all, I'd gone to the lair of the sorceress, I'd made a deal with my magical violin, and I'd gotten the love of my life back. And Ginger, had she truly wanted to stay? To work as a slayer for that dark queen? Regardless, that lifestyle fit her better. I only hoped she would not suffer because of her loyalty to Ezra.

The waters ended up being a maze, forking off to other lakes and streams, leaving me hopelessly lost and confused. The afternoon burned away, and evening shadows grew. My arms throbbed with exhaustion, and black spots danced before my eyes. Ezra's labored breathing had deepened into sleep, but if we were stuck out all night, lost in the streams, I did not know how we'd survive. He might take a turn for the worse. I needed to wake him to ask for help, but sleep was healing, and I needed him to live. I needed us both to live.

When a friendly light glowed in the darkness, I rowed faster. The streaks of sunset shot across the sky as I came out of the murky trees into the lake I knew well. Across the bay were the red barn and the homey lights from Giselle and Dusty's cottage. My limbs trembled as I rowed to the dock, and as I pulled, voices shouted at me, calling, "Mila! There you are! Are you all right?"

Voices I knew well. Voices I loved. Voices I'd known my entire life. As the dock neared, I saw them there. Giselle and Dusty, with a lantern, waving, and beside them was Mother. Aveline. And Tomas holding Luc.

All the bravery that had been inside of me, the rush to bring Ezra home, fizzled at the sight of them. Suddenly I was young again, and I just wanted to be held. I rowed the boat to the dock and stumbled into their arms, sobbing as I held tight. We were together. We were home. Everything would be all right.

Giselle and Dusty took the lead, creating a makeshift sling to carry Ezra. They herded us back to the inn, where Moses had a fresh meat and vegetable pie waiting. A roaring fire was set in the dining hall, and we gathered among tears and hugs. Together. It all passed in a blur, but it was Aveline who helped me out of my bloodstained dress and pushed me into a tub full of warm water. Later, with me exhausted and clean, she urged me into bed, and I fell into a dreamless sleep.

Ezra was my first thought the moment I woke alone in my bed, as if the last day had been nothing more than a nightmare. Heart in my throat, I dressed with haste and went downstairs. Breakfast was laid out in the staff's lounge, and Aveline and Mother were already there, sitting in front of the fire.

"Ezra," I breathed, my heart lurching. A tightness squeezed my chest.

"He's upstairs, still sleeping, according to Moses. Sit, eat before you go up and see him." Aveline pulled out a chair.

I hesitated, wavering between running to his side and sitting down with my family, but the scent of peppermint tea and the warmth of breakfast made my stomach growl. I sat, for there was nothing I could do for Ezra while I waited for him to wake up. "How are you here?"

"We got a letter," Mother said, reaching over to squeeze my hand. There were a few more wrinkles on her face, and a cane was by her side, but her foot was unbandaged, promising that she was healing.

"More like a telegram," Aveline interrupted.

Mother nodded. "Yes, from someone named Ginger. She said you were in trouble and would need our help."

I raised my eyebrows. Ginger? "When was this sent?"

"Almost two weeks ago," Aveline explained. "We wanted to set off right away, but there were some issues to be settled that took a few days.

Between Mother and Luc, we moved slowly and couldn't sit in a stagecoach all day for seven days. We arrived yesterday morning, but no one was here. It was the oddest thing, and then that woman, Giselle is her name? She came to welcome us. She's lovely."

"She is," I said, blinking back tears. I'd thought Ginger didn't like me, and yet the moment I'd decided to stay, she'd sent an urgent message to my family. How could she have known how everything would transpire?

"Mila, what happened?" Mother asked. "Giselle told us something was happening at the inn and they had to close until spring. Is that true?"

"Yes." I nodded. "It's true, but everything is okay. Everything is fine now. The inn can reopen. We're going to be okay. One day, maybe, I'll tell you the entire story." I thought of the letter I'd written, unsent in my bedroom. "How long can you stay?"

"Stay?" Aveline laughed. "As long as you want us to. We weren't sure if you needed to leave or if we should stay through the winter. We've winterized the estate, and we're here, as long as you need us. Besides, I'm pregnant again, and I'd like to stay put for a while."

Incredulous, I stared from Aveline to Mother. "Is that true?"

Mother beamed.

I hugged her, squeezing tight, then Aveline. "This, this is too good to be true."

"This all has to do with that man, doesn't it?" Aveline gave me a knowing look. "Ezra, the owner of the inn?"

My face warmed like a schoolgirl talking about her first crush. "Yes. I…we…I love him, and he was in trouble, and…I couldn't forsake him."

"You fought for love." Aveline's voice dropped in wonder. "I'm so proud."

"You told me to." I squeezed her hand.

"Go." Mother waved her hand. "See your man. We will be right here, making ourselves cozy. I'll have to speak to the cook. I've never tasted food so delicious."

"I'll be back," I promised.

Aveline shook her head, but she was smiling.

My heart was full as I made my way upstairs. Using the lift, Moses and Marley had moved Ezra up to his chambers in his office. Upstairs, nothing had changed, and yet everything was different. The paintings shone brighter, and the light was vivid, radiant, yet peaceful. The scent of parchment wafted out of the library, and someone had taken the time to build a fire, warming the floor. When I peeked in, I was surprised to see Tomas, reading out loud with Luc on his knee, staring at his father in fascination. That, I thought, was how legends were passed down, from parent to child, from one to another.

The door was closed, and I opened it. Moses padded out of the room, and it occurred to me I'd never seen him outside of the kitchen. He winked. "Still sleeping, but I brought up a tray, just in case he wakes up. I'll leave him in your hands, but ring the bell if you need anything."

"Thank you, and he…will he be okay?"

"Just bruises and mending bones. He'll be fine." Moses paused at the door before shutting it. "I've looked after him ever since he became a squire. Hard to believe you faced down the sorceress, but you did a good deed."

So Moses was from the other side too. Suddenly it was all too much, and a weariness came over me. I crept into the darkened room where Ezra slept, my sun god, oblivious to his allure. My heart ached just staring at him, and I sank into a chair that Moses must have dragged in. Pulling it closer, I ran my fingers over Ezra's arm, feeling his pulse. Tears came to my eyes, and this time, when I put my head down, I wept for joy.

MILA

At some point, I must have fallen asleep, and I wasn't sure what woke me. A slight movement or the stillness after so much chaos. When I opened my eyes, Ezra's forest-green ones, rimmed with exhaustion, peered back at me. There was a clarity in his gaze, a newness. His fingers curled around mine, and when he smiled, it was like the glimmer of dawn after a long, dark night. My lips trembled, and I blinked hard, determined not to cry again, not anymore.

"Mila," he said, his voice low and hoarse.

"Ezra?" Impatiently brushing at tears, I passed him a glass of water. "Here, you must be thirsty."

He drank deeply, closing his eyes briefly when he finished, as if the movement had zapped his energy.

"You did it. Your music came to me when I was in the dungeons, waiting for my sentence."

"Oh, Ezra, what did they do to you?"

Wincing, he placed a hand on his side. "I fought when she closed the portal, foolish, because she always wins. After they beat me, they locked me away, and I knew I had to bide my time. I never imagined you'd come for me. I admit I was angry at first, that Ginger had allowed you to use magic, that she hadn't spirited you away as I'd asked. When the guards came for me, I thought they'd make me watch your death, but the power of your music hypnotized them. Whatever song you played, its magic changed their minds, and perhaps even the mind of the sorceress. Mila, I underestimated you."

"I did it for you. For us. Although, I was so frightened. I thought we were going to die."

"Me too," he admitted. "But we didn't. Come here." He opened his arms.

"But you're weak and healing," I protested, half rising.

His smile widened. "As if that could keep us apart. Come, I want to hold you, love you. You've given me a second chance, and I will not squander it. I'm going to claim it, claim you, keep you, treasure this moment. I was dead, and now I'm alive. Don't deny me this pleasure."

I was in his arms in a heartbeat, my head

against his chest as he squeezed me tightly against his body. We were quiet for a long moment, enjoying it, until he began to play with my hair, then lifted my chin and kissed my mouth. That sweet sensation traveled through each limb, and I shuddered under his touch. "Ezra?"

"Yes, my love." He kissed me again, keeping me from speaking. His fingers wormed through my hair. Pulling back just a moment, he groaned. "Your lips are the sweetest elixir, all the life I need." He kissed me again, and I surrendered.

"I love you," I whispered.

"And I love you," he repeated over and over again as he kissed his way down my neck, skillfully parting my dress.

The tears started again even though I didn't want to cry.

"It's okay," he murmured, kissing my ear, wiping away my tears with his fingers.

"I'm just so relieved," I sobbed. "I thought I'd lost you forever, and I couldn't fathom going on without you. I know I'm supposed to be strong."

"But you don't have to be strong in everything. It's okay to let the tears fall."

"How are you so good? You always know exactly what to say."

"I've learned. A lifetime of mistakes has taught

me what's important. And now I can look forward to this one life. A mortal life with you."

I laughed through my tears, looking at him. "Mortal? Are you saying you are or were immortal?"

His cheeks dimpled into a smile. "Used to be, yes, but now eternal life is gone."

"You're not upset she took away your immortality?"

"How can I be? I abused both immortality and magic. It's best to let those vices go and simply live one beautiful life with you."

"And one life will be enough for you?"

Raising himself on one elbow, he hovered over me. "Mila, I don't think you understand my intentions."

"Oh? Then you'll have to enlighten me," I teased.

Taking my hand, he raised it to his lips. "I intend to take you as my bride, to marry you, to live each day with you by my side. We can do whatever you want, travel the world, reopen the inn, whatever your heart desires. As long as we do it together, we will be happy."

"You want me to marry you?" I gasped.

His smile faded. "Did I not ask properly? I must admit, I'm from another land and the customs here are unique."

"Of course I'll marry you. Ezra? Where are you going?"

For he tumbled out of bed, grunting and holding his ribs as he moved. “Stay there. I’ll be right back,” he said, limping into the office.

Sitting upright, I tucked my legs under me as he returned and sat on the bed. “Mila of Hadria, will you marry me?” he asked, taking my left hand in his.

“Ezra, I already said yes,” I laughed.

“Say it again,” he demanded, sliding something cool onto my finger.

I stared at a ring of diamonds, glistening in the light, and in the very middle was an amethyst of dark violet that matched the tones of my hair. My heart kicked and my mouth gaped open as I gazed from it to Ezra. “Yes, I’ll marry you. You know my heart; you didn’t have to ask.”

His expression changed as he climbed onto the bed, snatching me in his arms. “When I was in the dungeon, I realized, more than anything, I wanted to fight the sorceress, to live and not give in to her demands. I hoped I’d find a way back to you, and I did not know you’d come to me and use your magic to sway the sorceress’s mind.”

“I didn’t use magic,” I protested as his fingers inched up my dress. “I played the violin, and that was enough.”

“No.” His voice was husky as he kissed me. “The magic was within you.”

“It was the magic of the violin,” I objected

weakly, for his fingers were on my thigh, creeping higher.

"Sometimes a legend is only a legend. Wood is only wood, regardless of where it came from. The magic is always within us, within you and me. All we need to do is believe."

I did not dwell on the meaning of his words as he removed my dress, his clothes following the same path to the floor. Lying on our sides, we made love to each other, slow and sweet, pausing to plant heated kisses on each other's bodies. And as I lay in the nest of twisted sheets and potent love, I never could have dreamed of a happier moment.

Afterward, when we lay in bed, drowsy, happy, alive, together, I closed my eyes, and faintly, from far off, I could have sworn I heard the strings of a violin. But this tune was not sad and lonely. It was an enchanting litany played for one who'd gone through the depths of darkness and survived a tormented journey to come out the other side, changed, redeemed, forgiven.

Dear Reader,

I hope you enjoyed this fantasy romance and I'd love to hear your thoughts. Please leave a review on my website with a few words on what you thought about Ezra and Mila's romance.

Leave a review at angelajford.com/products/song-of-the-dawn

Ready for more? Order *Lured by the Dusk*.

EXCLUSIVE SHORT STORY

Don't miss this exclusive short story.

He's an immortal fae knight, she's a cursed warrior. To save their people from annihilation, they must go where the living have never gone before.

Every few years, the swarm comes, a terrifying pestilence that consumes the living. One sting from the deadly creatures brings not death but something much worse. . .

Every few years, Rainer, a fae knight sworn to protect the mountains, prepares his people to lose everything.

No one knows why the swarm comes, and no one can stop it.

Except for her.

Zelma is a warrior, sent to find the legendary firedrakes in the mountain. Instead, she's attacked by the swarm and left to die.

When she awakens in the hall of the fae knight, she's determined to continue her quest.

However, the sting has changed her, and new, frightening abilities awaken.

Afraid of becoming the target of the fae knight's wrath, she fights to control her magic as they travel into the heart of the mountains.

Will Rainer and Zelma save their people? Or will her magic kill them first?

Of Fae and Flame **is a complete, stand-alone short story set in the Nomadian universe.**

Only available at: https://angelajford.com/product/of-fae-and-flames/

ALSO BY ANGELA J. FORD

Join my email list for updates, previews, giveaways, and new release notifications. Join now: www.angelajford.com/signup

The Four Worlds Series (epic fantasy)

A complete four-book epic fantasy series spanning two hundred years, featuring an epic battle between mortals and immortals.

Legend of the Nameless One Series (epic fantasy)

A complete five-book epic fantasy adventure series featuring an enchantress, a wizard, and a sarcastic dragon.

Night of the Dark Fae Trilogy (romantic epic fantasy)

A complete epic fantasy trilogy featuring a strong heroine, dark fae, orcs, goblins, dragons, antiheroes, magic, and romance.

Tales of the Enchanted Wildwood (fairy tale romance)

Adult fairy tales blending fantasy action-adventure with steamy romance. Each short story can be read as a stand-alone and features a different couple.

Tower Knights (fantasy romance)

Gothic-inspired adult steamy fantasy romance. Each novel can be read as a stand-alone and features a different couple.

Gods & Goddesses of Labraid (epic fantasy)

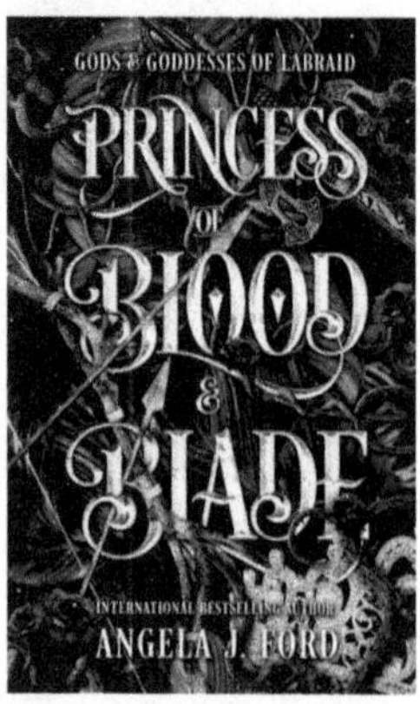

A warrior princess with a dire future embarks on a perilous quest to regain her fallen kingdom.

Lore of Nomadia Trilogy (epic fantasy romance)

The story of an alluring nymph, a curious librarian, a renowned

hunter, and a mad sorceress as they seek to save—or destroy—the empire of Nomadia.

Visit angelajford.com for autographed books, exclusive book swag and book boxes.

ABOUT THE AUTHOR

Angela J. Ford is a best-selling author who writes epic fantasy and steamy fantasy romance with vivid worlds, gray characters, and endings you just can't guess. She has written and published over twenty books.

She enjoys traveling, hiking, and playing World of Warcraft with her husband. First and foremost, Angela is a reader and can often be found with her nose in a book.

Aside from writing, she enjoys the challenge of working with marketing technology and builds websites for authors.

If you happen to be in Nashville, you'll most likely find her enjoying a white chocolate mocha and daydreaming about her next book.

facebook.com/angelajfordauthor
twitter.com/aford21
instagram.com/aford21
amazon.com/Angela-J-Ford/e/B0052U9PZO
bookbub.com/authors/angela-j-ford

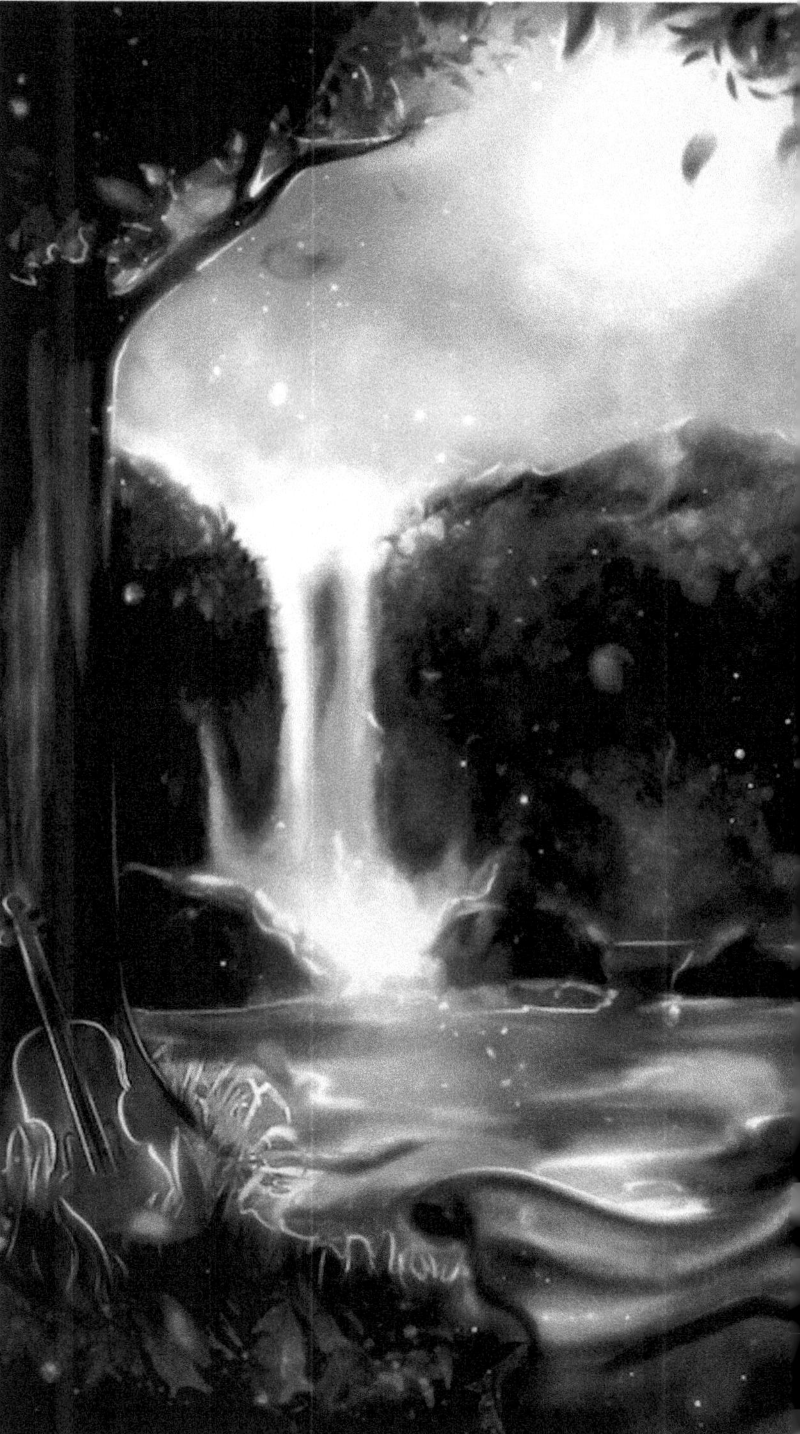

www.ingramcontent.com/pod-product-compliance
Lightning Source LLC
Chambersburg PA
CBHW070547310726
48982CB00011B/1485/J

9780578980607